LOUISIANA SAVES THE LIBRARY

Louisiana Saves the Library

EMILY BECK COGBURN

KENSINGTON BOOKS
www.kensingtonbooks.com

KENSINGTON BOOKS are published by

Kensington Publishing Corp.
119 West 40th Street
New York, NY 10018

All Kensington titles, imprints, and distributed lines are available at special quantity discounts for bulk purchases for sales promotion, premiums, fund-raising, educational, or institutional use.

Special book excerpts or customized printings can also be created to fit specific needs. For details, write or phone the office of the Kensington Sales Manager: Kensington Publishing Corp., 119 West 40th Street, New York, NY 10018. Attn. Sales Department. Phone: 1-800-221-2647.

eISBN-13: 978-1-61773-994-1
eISBN-10: 1-61773-994-4
First Kensington Electronic Edition: February 2016

ISBN-13: 978-1-61773-993-4
ISBN-10: 1-61773-993-6
First Kensington Trade Paperback Printing: February 2016

10 9 8 7 6 5 4 3 2 1

Printed in the United States of America

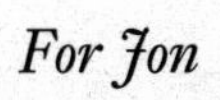
For Jon

CHAPTER 1

Louisiana Richardson was tempted to go back to her Cheerio-littered van and find a coffee shop to hide in. Cleaning the house, preparing for the babysitter, and tearing herself from her crying one-and-a-half-year-old daughter, Zoe, had been exhausting. Besides, she was sure that she'd just been invited to the shower so Trish's baby could be outfitted with the latest in high-tech infant gear. A fellow library science professor at Louisiana A&M, Trish had never graced her with more than a terse hello. The transplanted Texan sometimes gave her pitying glances when Louise opened her purse to find a discarded sippy cup or tried in vain to remove a juice spot that made her shirt look like a map of Europe. Trish's wrinkle-free clothes were always color coordinated, and she never accidentally wore one blue and one black shoe.

Louise shifted the gift to her other arm and rang the doorbell. One side of the package bulged with an excess of crumpled-up paper, and the box peeked out on the opposite end. With her children constantly interrupting, she'd barely managed to get the thing wrapped, let alone make it look pretty. The sight would have made Martha Stewart choke on her almond tea biscuit.

When a tall blond woman wearing a cream-colored pantsuit and gold high-heeled sandals answered the door, Louise nearly dropped the gift and ran. But it was too late.

"Hi, I'm Louise," she said, manufacturing an upbeat tone of voice. When she first arrived in Louisiana, she'd considered finally ditching the nickname, but quickly abandoned the idea. "Louisiana" had sounded exotic and interesting to her childhood friends in Minnesota. Here, judging from the incredulous looks she got the first few times she'd introduced herself, it was just too much. There were women in Georgia named Georgia and women in Virginia named Virginia, but apparently no one in the Pelican State shared its name. Except her. So "Louise" it was.

"Alicia. Pleased to meet you." The woman stepped back to let Louise in. Her toenails were not only painted but also professionally manicured. Alicia's hair and makeup were so impeccable that she looked like a living doll—the perfect embodiment of a Southern belle, if such an animal still existed. Once Louise was inside the house, the survival of the species was abundantly evident. Southern belles with blond-highlighted hair, wearing ironed, breezy blouses, sipped champagne by the fireplace. Southern belles in creased slacks balanced tiny plates of bite-size morsels as they admired the gifts piled next to Trish. Southern belles with charm-school posture and blemish-free skin trotted to the kitchen in their strappy, high-heeled sandals to refill drinks.

Louise was a mutt in a room full of purebreds. She hadn't realized that baby showers down South were so formal. In Minnesota, her jeans and plain black T-shirt would have been perfectly acceptable, but they were shabby next to the silk blouses and tailored pantsuits. As usual, her makeup was limited to an indifferent slash of cinnamon lipstick, and her straightish, shoulder-length brown hair wasn't tinted, fluffed, blow-dried, or permed. Louise couldn't afford a manicure or a dye job, and all her clothes were relics of the previous decade. When they were married, her ex-husband had enjoyed buying cute dresses and sexy little tops for her. Shopping for clothes with Brendan had made her feel like a princess. On her own Louise had no motivation to update her wardrobe. Her ex was gone, and chasing after children didn't require cocktail wear.

Louise tried to find a dark corner where she could become invisible, but Alicia's house was maddeningly bright and open. The combination of the ten-bulb chandelier in the living room/kitchen/dining area and the sunlight coming in through the windows lit up every inch of the space. The beige and white decor seemed unnatural—there wasn't a stain or smudge anywhere. It reminded Louise of the magazine-worthy perfection of her former in-laws' mini-mansion with its artfully placed vases of flowers, spotless floors and countertops, and beds piled high with decorative pillows. After the first visit, she'd understood Brendan's periodic comments about her lack of housekeeping skills. He didn't nag her; instead, he'd say something like, "Shouldn't we clean behind the refrigerator once in a while?" "We," of course, meant her. Just like his father, Brendan never did housework. When they were first married, that detail hadn't seemed important. Back then, their relationship was about long, passionate discussions over glasses of wine. The misery, betrayal, and pain came later.

Louise's own modest ranch home looked like a day care gone to seed. The toy-strewn living room was decorated with stickers and marker scribbles. That morning, Zoe had put a blanket on the coffee table and arranged a tea party for her stuffed animals, using every piece of play food she could find. Dinner dishes still in the kitchen sink gave off an odor of curdling milk and stale macaroni and cheese. Paper, crayons, and coloring books covered the kitchen table. Louise had done the dishes and swept the crumbs from under the kitchen table for the babysitter's sake. As she now endured Alicia's appraising gaze, she wished she'd skipped the party, left the housecleaning for later, and snuggled on the couch watching morning cartoons with her kids instead. Zoe was obsessed with Elmo, and her delight at seeing him on the screen was so infectious that it made the puppet's high-decibel voice bearable, even endearing.

Alicia half turned and glanced at the group of elegant women. It was clear that she wanted to join her friends but felt that she had to be polite. "So, do you go to Community?"

"No. What's that? A church?" Louise didn't recognize any of the guests. None of the other library science professors had apparently bothered to come, probably because they knew about the Community clique, whatever it was. Louise was out of the loop, as usual. She felt like a kid during her first day in a new school. She had the wrong clothes, the wrong name, even the wrong accent.

Alicia fluffed her blond mane. "Well, we like to say that life is inspiration." After an awkward pause, she glided back to the living room area, sitting next to another statuesque blonde and laughing about something, most likely Louise's nondescript jeans.

Louise didn't need an instruction manual on Southern manners to know that she'd been snubbed. All the assembled belles focused on Trish, who had draped her pregnant body in a pastel flowered dress and roller-curled her honey-blond hair for the occasion. No one looked at Louise.

She inched around behind the women, skirted the last love seat, and slid her present onto the edge of the pile, backing away slowly. From her perch on a straight-backed chair, Alicia glanced at her and then at the badly wrapped present. Her tight smile was the kind usually reserved for an errant child. Chastened, Louise took another step back.

Trish was busy tearing open a large, professionally wrapped gift. The woman sitting next to her—a sister, maybe—recorded the offerings in a notebook shaped like a baby's bottom. She gave Louise a genuinely friendly smile before her attention was drawn by the exclamations of the observing ladies. "I've seen those diaper pails!" someone squealed. "They use grocery bags so you don't have to buy expensive refills!"

All of the chairs were taken, so Louise stood next to the buffet table and searched for a kindred spirit in the group. But everyone focused on the gift-opening ritual with baffling intensity. The women appeared to be having fun, but maybe it was all pretense. How could anyone get excited about baby clothes, blankets, wipe warmers, pacifier holders, and other assorted infant accessories? When Louise was pregnant for the first time, she'd been new in town—Iowa at the time—and had no friends around to throw her a shower. Even though she could have used the gifts, she didn't miss the party. Big gatherings caused her inner shy child to reappear, making her awkward, bored, and miserable all at once. Feeling that unpleasant mix of feelings begin to churn around in her gut, she decided to leave while the belles were preoccupied.

She retrieved her worn black purse from behind the designer handbags and walked quickly toward the front door. Thankfully, her tennis shoes made no noise on the wood floors. They would be called "sneakers" in Southern speak. In Louisiana, sub sandwiches were po'boys, counties were parishes, minor wounds were bo-bos, lollipops were suckers, pop was . . . well, she hadn't yet figured out that one. Sometimes, she felt like she'd stepped through Alice's looking glass: everything was just a little bit off-kilter.

Opening the front door, she sighed with relief. Free at last. Except that a woman in a peach dress blocked her way. Louise let out a different kind of sigh.

"Lou-Lou! Where do you think you're going?" Sylvia set down a neatly wrapped present on the stoop, the better to adjust her underwear. Even though her pregnant belly strained the front of her dress, she was stunning with her wavy auburn hair, bright green eyes, and naturally pouty lips enhanced by glossy pink lipstick. Sylvia's makeup was always flawless, and she had a seemingly endless wardrobe of fashionable clothes. Despite being nearly six feet tall, she usually wore three-inch heels. The current pair were peach platform sandals that matched her dress exactly. She reminded Louise of a red-haired Barbie, but somehow they were friends anyway.

"I'm escaping the Museum of Southern Perfection," Louise said.

"Shut up! You are not. I just got here."

"Forget it. We aren't part of the Community community."

Sylvia checked her lipstick in a compact mirror. "The coffee shop?"

"No, I think it's a new-wave church. You know, the kind with electric guitars and preachers in headset microphones."

"So what? I'm hungry. Carry this present for me. Come on, I'm pregnant."

"I know, I know." Louise picked up the box. The pink wrapping paper was covered with winged cherubs. "What's with the girly stuff? Isn't she having a boy?"

"I don't know. Is she?" Sylvia stepped inside and speedwalked to the refreshment table, her heels clicking. All the other guests followed her with their eyes. Sylvia waved, taking the attention for granted. Unlike Louise, Sylvia was never ignored. "Hello, ladies. Trish."

"Hi, Sylvia. So glad you could make it." Trish set aside the onesie she'd just unwrapped and beamed, glancing briefly at Louise, almost certainly noticing her for the first time.

"Well, I'm sorry I'm late, but getting the hubs to watch Jimmy is always a challenge. Especially when there's a game on." Sylvia took a baby-blue plate and eyed the selection of refreshments.

Louise delivered the present, and Trish immediately tore off the paper. "Oh, Sylvia. This is lovely."

"Just a little something my friend made," Sylvia said, filling her plate with tiny shrimp quiches. "It's nothing."

Trish held up a baby-size quilt decorated with a boy fishing in a blue denim lake. The assembled ladies made admiring noises.

"Sneak. You knew it was a boy," Louise said, coming up behind Sylvia and also getting a plate.

Sylvia grinned, her mouth full of quiche. "No, I got lucky. My friend Bonnie from high school has a girlfriend who quilts."

"Everyone quilts around here, don't they?"

Sylvia pursed her lips, thinking. "Everyone knows someone who does. I'll say that, Minnesota girl. Do you have homemade quilts for your kids?"

"You can add that to the list of my parenting failures."

"Oh my God. I'll get you some, don't worry. Poor quiltless children."

Louise laughed as she selected some fruit and miniature cheesecakes, feeling at ease for the first time since she'd set foot in Southern-belle land. Even though Sylvia had long legs and a gorgeous smile, something about her was comforting. She could even make Louise stop worrying about the number of calories in each of the deceptively small desserts—at least temporarily.

Trish opened Louise's present next, a starter kit of baby bottles that she had picked from the registry. The gift seemed to sum up Louise's entire persona: safe, boring, forgettable. How had she ended up in bayou-and-alligator country with such a flamboyant best friend? It was one of the mysteries of the universe. Trish immediately set the gift aside and picked up a package wrapped in sparkly blue paper.

"Have you checked your e-mail today?" Sylvia asked.

Louise tried a bite of miniature quiche. "Are you off your meds? I just managed to dress myself and make the house minimally presentable before the babysitter came."

"We got a campus-wide e-mail. There are going to be big cuts at A&M."

"What do you mean?"

"Budget cuts. You know about that, right? Economic crisis? A&M's budget reduced by twenty percent?"

"Yes."

Sales tax revenues were down with the shrinking economy, and the governor had targeted the university for reduction. The previous week, all the faculty and staff had received an e-mail warning them that cuts were coming. No one knew exactly what would happen. There were rumors about killing programs, departments even. German seemed vulnerable, as did Classics and Latin. Everyone agreed that there would be layoffs, at least among the ranks of instructors and adjuncts.

"Well, the library science school is tier three. Which means we might—shoot, probably will—be eliminated," Sylvia said.

"Eliminated? The library school?" Louise nearly spit out a mouthful of quiche.

Sylvia snorted. “Never mind that our graduates run the public libraries, school libraries, and everything else around here. Yes, we are on the chopping block. And guess who still doesn’t have tenure.”

“Both of us.” Louise’s stomach sank. She’d just moved to this godforsaken place. For an apparently doomed job.

“Exactly. We are royally and completely screwed, sister.”

“But we don’t know for sure yet.”

“No, but they’ve already given pink slips to the German and Classics instructors. At the end of the semester, they’re out of a job.”

Louise set down her plate. She couldn’t eat anymore. This was almost worse than when Brendan told her about Julia. She was going to lose the position she’d worked so hard for, the one thing besides the kids that had kept her going after the divorce.

“Time for games!” Trish said, setting the bottles aside.

“Oh God.” Sylvia rolled her eyes and popped another mini cheesecake into her mouth.

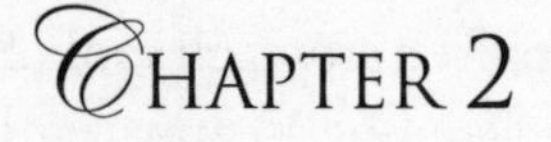

CHAPTER 2

Louise couldn't concentrate on the article she was trying to rewrite. She kept looking around her A&M office: the dull off-white walls, scratched metal desk cluttered with papers and pictures of her kids, creaky wooden chair circa 1975, ceiling-high green bookcases overflowing with textbooks and research volumes. It might be a crappy office, but it was *her* crappy office, and she might not have it—or her job—much longer. Now that she was going to lose it, the space seemed especially precious. The professorship was the only real tie she had to the state. Without her job, she'd be lost, not just financially but personally.

Becoming an academic was never her plan, though. Like so many of her life decisions, it had been Brendan's idea.

He didn't fit the profile of a deadbeat dad when Louise met him. They sat together in a German language class during their junior year at the University of Minnesota. He wasn't very good at German, but he had read practically every classic novel and remembered all the characters, plots, and themes. Louise didn't even have to read the assignments for her English class; she could just talk to him and take notes. Besides literature, they spent hours discussing life in general. He was genuinely interested in what she had to say and made her feel, for the first time in her life, that she might actually have worthwhile ideas. That was what she loved about him: the way he listened.

She followed Brendan to Indiana University, where he'd been accepted into graduate school in English literature. Louise landed a job in the university library. She spent sunny days checking in new issues of periodicals in the basement of the frigid building. The pay for the library tech job was so low that it seemed like a waste of time, so Louise decided to get a master's degree. Brendan talked her into the PhD program instead. When they completed their degrees, he was offered a position at the University of Iowa. Since she was already pregnant with Max, Louise stayed home to write articles on the history of public libraries. Two were accepted to journals.

Brendan changed after Max was born. He spent longer and longer hours holed up in his office, leaving Louise to take care of the baby by herself. Max never slept through the night, waking up three or four times for feedings. Louise was too tired to clean, cook, write, or even think. She fell asleep holding the baby in the glider chair and woke up terrified that he would roll out of her arms onto the floor. Brendan justified his disappearing act with a flip "How do you think we're paying for all those diapers?" As Max got older, Brendan showed interest in the toddler for a few days or even weeks, but always fell back into his old ways.

It was obvious that Brendan was having an affair. Louise saw the way he looked at a perky graduate student at one of the few English department parties she managed to attend and she planned to confront him about it. But before she worked up the courage, she realized that her period was late.

The pregnancy test showed a plus. Brendan was out that night, supposedly with his English department colleagues. Louise collapsed on the bed and cried herself to sleep alone. She wanted another baby, but not with Brendan. Those days were over.

Three months after Zoe was born, Brendan told her that he wanted a divorce. Louise lacked the energy to throw his books and clothes out the window. She didn't say anything, just watched him walk out the door, suitcase in hand. At that moment, she vowed not to be dependent on anyone again.

She wrote two more articles, applied for jobs, and received an offer from Louisiana A&M. Even though it was spring and the job didn't begin until school started, she left Max with Brendan and brought Zoe to Saint Jude to house hunt. A few months later, she and the kids moved into their new home and endured their first stiflingly hot and humid Louisiana summer together.

That was a year ago, but Louise still hadn't realized her dream of independence. She needed Brendan's child support check, and to make things worse, he was a slow pay. Living in Louisiana was cheaper than somewhere like Chicago, but library science professor salaries were even cheaper. Add student loans and diapers, and the result was hand-to-mouth living.

Just thinking about it all—the physically and mentally taxing relocation halfway across the country, the late nights working on articles and the book that was supposed to get her tenure, Brendan and his young girlfriend—made Louise's pulse race with barely contained rage. She fished her cell phone out of her purse and dialed his number. Voice mail, of course.

"Brendan, can you please send the check? I really need it. I know you have my work address. Thanks." She tossed the phone back in her bag and looked up to see Russ Adwell standing in the doorway. The aging professor wore his usual button-up shirt and slightly crooked bow tie.

"Sorry," he said. "I was going to knock."

Louise resisted the urge to put her head down on the desk and maybe even bang it a few times. She didn't need Adwell to hear her angry voice mails. Still, she was glad to see her eccentric colleague. "That's okay. I was just verbally abusing my ex-husband's voice mail."

Adwell had a tendency to corner unsuspecting students and give long discourses on everything from the history of Masonic persecution in Nazi France to chemical differences between different kinds of fruit. Cataloging was his main area of interest, and he would sometimes launch into a speech about why the Dewey Decimal System was manifestly superior to Library of Congress. Louise had already heard it at least seventeen times. Regardless, he was one of her closest friends. She understood him much better than Trish and her crowd of former debutantes. Adwell said exactly what he was thinking, something Louise found reassuring. With him, what you saw was what you got.

"Two weeks," he said now, an ironic smile appearing under his pockmarked nose.

"Until what?" Louise was muddle-headed, half inside the article she was reading and half thinking about what to feed the kids for dinner.

"That's when they're going to tell us if we're done." He made a slashing motion across his throat. "They might not kill the whole program, of course. By which I mean, they might not fire everyone. They could dump some of us into the education school. That is to say, the old farts like me who have tenure."

Whenever he deviated from one of his canned lectures, Adwell's speech slowed down like a clock that needed winding. Louise patiently waited until he was finished. He wasn't telling her anything she didn't know, but it was worse coming from him. "Or maybe they will find some money somewhere and leave us alone," she said.

"Don't count on it, sister. I assume you are on the market." Adwell sounded less like a clock now and more like a robotic synthesizer.

Louise was surprised to see that he was truly upset. She'd never known him to be bothered by anything. Obnoxious students, pushy administrators, and even the creepy brown American cockroaches that sometimes grew to mouse size in Louisiana had no power to move him. But now his world—and hers—was crumbling. His discomfiture made it all horrifyingly real. "I haven't looked for jobs yet," she admitted.

"You haven't? Goodness' sakes. I'll write you a letter of recommendation this afternoon. You've already missed the deadline to apply for some of the jobs. The American Library Association conference is on December twenty-seventh."

"I know. I just can't stand the thought of moving again." Dread collected in the pit of Louise's stomach. Coming to Louisiana with two little kids was one of the hardest things she'd ever done. The thousand-mile drive alone had been torture. Zoe spent half the trip crying because she wanted out of her car seat. When they stopped at a hotel each night, neither child fell asleep until after midnight. Louise had been so worried about passing out on the road that she drank coffee until her hands shook. She'd arrived in Saint Jude feeling strung out and exhausted. The idea of doing it all again terrified her.

"Well, you need to think about it. Unless you want to end up scanning bar codes in some public library." Adwell spat out the last words as though they were poisonous. Apparently, he didn't go in for the idea of librarians as fighters for free access and education on behalf of the downtrodden. But his concern for her welfare was touching.

"It might not be that bad," she said.

"Don't kid yourself. I've been there. You want to stay in academia. Trust me."

"Well, academia might not want me anymore. I think it's considering a divorce. I know the signs."

"I mean it. I'm writing you a letter right now." Adwell left, slamming the door behind him.

Louise closed the word processing program and opened her Internet browser. As she checked the ads on the ALA Web site, her worst fear was confirmed. There were no jobs in universities. At least not in her field. She had indeed missed the deadlines for a few, but it didn't really matter because they were all in children's services, cataloging, disability services. She was, as Sylvia had put it, screwed. Defeated, she closed her laptop and slid it into its case.

Louise wiped the dust from her favorite picture of Max and Zoe. Taken by a professional photographer at the school, it showed them smiling with their arms around each other in front of a painted forest. She had to be strong. Failure was not an option with two vulnerable and precious children depending on her. She decided to work on her book about the history of public libraries in Louisiana. She'd already visited the State Library many times and done all the digging she could within Saint Jude. Now she had to travel around the state to complete her research, beginning with the closer counties—parishes in the local parlance.

Finding time to work on the book was a challenge. While the children were in school, she was usually teaching or dealing with students. After she was done with her obligations, there was never time to drive to a library outside the city and get back to pick up the kids by three o'clock. Maybe they could stay late just one time. She got out her phone again and dialed the school. The secretary answered.

"Ms. Susan, this is Louise Richardson. Do you think Max and Zoe could stay until five o'clock today?"

There was a pause at the other end of the line. Louise felt the little strength and hope that she'd managed to gather fade away. She knew what was coming.

"Ms. Louise, you're ten days late on your tuition payment."

"I know. I'm trying to get the child support check from their father." Louise hated the pleading in her own voice. Being reduced to begging favors from the day care workers was too humiliating.

"Sorry. I mean, really, with your payment being that late, we shouldn't have let Max and Zoe come to school today at all."

"Yes, ma'am. I'm sorry. I'll be there at three."

"I hope you'll have the money soon." Susan's voice softened a little. "If you just paid some of it now, then you could give us the rest when you get the child support."

"I'll do that." Louise thanked her and hung up. The day had just gone from worse to unbearable. She had one hundred dollars and fifty-five cents in her checking account, and soon she might not have a job. Reaching into her shoulder bag, she took out her lunch: leftovers of a homemade pizza that the kids had refused to eat, a chewed-on apple, and a yogurt drink that Zoe had picked out at the store and then decided she didn't like. Sushi or a fresh salad from the A&M cafeteria would have made her feel a little better, but buying lunch wasn't in her budget. She took a bite of cold pizza and got out her laptop again. If she couldn't work on the book, at least she'd finish her article "The Effects of Computerized Card Catalogs on Public Library Circulation."

* * *

By two thirty, Louise was completely sick of the article. She'd cleaned up the writing, added a few citations, and formatted it in the style of the journal she wanted to submit it to. Hitting "send" to e-mail the article to the editor gave her a small sense of accomplishment. In that moment of optimism, she rashly decided to bring the children with her to visit one of the libraries for the book project.

She retrieved Max and Zoe from school and strapped them into their car seats. "We're going on an exciting adventure into the uncharted Louisiana frontier," she announced, handing them drink boxes and identical snack holders full of Cheerios.

She programmed the library's address into the GPS that her mother had sent as soon as Louise told her that she was moving to Louisiana. The present had been symbolic, an acknowledgment that she was going to need help navigating in this new and different place. Louise would have preferred a visit, but her mother was declining in health. She had to settle for the electronic device with its cold female voice.

"Let's go," Max said from the backseat.

Louise pushed the "navigate" button. According to the system, Alligator Bayou was a thirty-minute drive.

Thirty minutes and thirty years back in time.

As a child, Louise had loved to accompany her grandmother on errands. Long after everyone else had moved on to big-box stores and the mall, Gram continued to do her shopping in dying downtown North St. Paul. The pharmacist marked down the toothpaste and aspirin prices for her before ringing everything up. The barbershop had a striped pole out front and a Zenith inside tuned to one of the two network stations that came in without too much fuzz. Afterward, they went to Anderson's bakery for donuts. Everything Gram needed was contained in those few blocks. It was wonderfully simple.

Alligator Bayou was a little like that Minnesota town. A salon called the Cut and Dye replaced the barbershop, and the Mark's drugstore was larger and more brightly lit than old Mr. Rupert's. The Piggly Wiggly looked a lot like the old Kendall's Louise remembered, though. It even had a screen door rather than a modern sliding-glass one. Instead of a bakery, next door was a Dairy Queen knockoff with a red roof and a walk-up window. A few feet away from the Icy Cone, a gas station with a rooster mascot advertised "crispy fried chicken." Selling fossil fuel and breaded bird together was unprecedented in Minnesota. But the main difference between Alligator Bayou and North St. Paul was the configuration of downtown. All of the businesses occupied one side of the street, and there was nothing but swamp and railroad tracks in the other direction.

Louise parked in front of the library. When she had first moved to Louisiana, the tinted windows on commercial buildings led her to believe that everything was closed. She'd become used to perpetually dark windows after a few months, but the slate-gray glass on the Alligator Bayou Parish Library shone like two menacing eyes.

The library brought back less comforting memories than the rest of Alligator Bayou. Louise had difficulty fitting in long before her move to Louisiana. As soon as she started kindergarten, the kids in school singled her out like tigers attacking the weakest gazelle. She took refuge in books, hiding from the world in a library much like this one. She was safe there among all the fictional characters she loved. Wandering the dark, cool stacks, she could be someone else, at least for a little while. It was a lonely existence, though. The library was a reminder of her conflicting desires—to find a place in the world and to escape from it.

She opened Zoe's door, and her snack container fell out of the van. Cheerios covered the car seat, and Zoe's top was stained red with Cherry Yummy juice. Louise unbuckled her and pulled off the shirt, replacing it with one from the emergency bag. The backup had a spot of something resembling chocolate on the front, and its bright orange color clashed with Zoe's pink pants. Louise briefly considered changing the pants and decided it was too much work. Exhaustion enveloped her like a fog and desperation wasn't far behind. *Please let them behave for once.*

Max was in better shape than his sister. He had eaten all his cereal but tossed his drink box on the floor, where it had created a sticky puddle on the carpet. His clothing was relatively clean, at least.

"Guys, this is a library, so let's try to remember to keep it to a dull roar," Louise said, setting Zoe on the sidewalk.

Max jumped out of the van and ran toward the library. Zoe raced away in the opposite direction. Louise scooped her up and she wailed in protest.

Inside the building, she released Zoe, who immediately plopped down on the floor and stuck her lower lip out in a comically exaggerated pout. Max terminated his hyperactivity at the circulation desk and became surprisingly still, staring around as though he'd landed on a deserted alien planet.

That time of afternoon, the library should have been filled with moms and young children, shift workers, retired men reading the newspaper, kids on their way home from school. But the place was so quiet that the ticking of the clock above the circulation desk sounded like something out of an Edgar Allan Poe story.

Rows of gray bookshelves dominated the room. The dust covers had been removed from the books, leaving the dull grays and faded reds of the exposed cloth spines. A few uncomfortable-looking plastic chairs were arranged around the periodical display. The children's area was marked by a crude handmade sign and decorated with faded cartoon pilgrims and turkeys that must have been from the Reagan era.

Louise wasn't surprised that the library was empty. No one would want to use the obsolete computers, dusty books, and magazines that looked like they had seen double duty in a crowded dental office. Something was wrong here, and it wasn't just the creepy clock. Adwell's comment about scanning bar codes took on new meaning. If Louise didn't publish and apply for jobs, she could end up in a depressing, neglected place exactly like this. She swallowed hard.

One benefit of the lack of patrons was that no one was around for Max and Zoe to disturb. Already, Max had snapped out of his contemplative state and headed to the periodical rack, probably to tear up the magazines. "Let's see if they have any kids' books published in this century," Louise said, leading the way.

In the children's area, she chose a few of the coverless picture books and tossed them onto the plain brown children's table. Max sat in a chair and opened *Curious George Rides a Bike*. Zoe followed his lead, taking *Blueberries for Sal* from the bottom shelf. Louise fantasized that they would remain well behaved for the entire visit. More likely, she'd soon be apologizing for a misdeed such as a torn book or a smashed knickknack like the ceramic turkey perched at the edge of the circulation desk. Her neck muscles tightened.

She walked up to the circulation desk. The high counter was dominated by two computers with fat old-style monitors for checking out books, should the library ever have any patrons. The lower desk faced the children's area. There was only room for one employee to sit, and a woman in her sixties with indifferently dyed brown hair occupied the spot. She set down the newsletter she was reading when Louise approached.

"Hi, I'm Louise Richardson from Louisiana A&M. I called about the library documents."

"Oh, yes." The woman stood. She wore ironed khaki pants with a tie-front blouse. "My name is Lily. I'm sort of the local history expert. Genealogy mostly. We have microfilm of all the census documents here, some old family Bibles, letters, things like that."

Louise nodded politely. She wasn't the least bit interested in genealogy, and local history as practiced by people like Lily was mostly folklore. A few well-worn stories told by the oldsters, written down by their grandchildren, and self-published in thin, slick paperbacks.

"I might could take a break." Lily turned around. "Hope, can you watch the desk for me?"

Louise was momentarily distracted by Lily's choice of words. She'd very clearly said "might could," an odd phrase that Louise had never heard during her time in Louisiana. She mentally added it to the list of unique local vernacular she'd been collecting. Perhaps someday she could work it into an article.

A squeak of sneakers on tiled floor announced Hope's entrance. She was nothing like the delicate waif her name suggested. A pair of sturdy polyester pants and a polo shirt encased her blocky body, and her dirty-blond hair was cut into a bob that made her face look square. Heavy, Southern-style makeup emphasized her penetrating blue-gray eyes. At a glance, Louise pegged her as a force to be reckoned with.

"Those your kids?" she asked.

Louise turned around, guiltily realizing that she'd momentarily forgotten about them. Max was ripping the last page from the Curious George book. Zoe had already denuded an entire row in the young adult section and was deep into a novel about vampires. Louise bit her lip to keep from screaming. It was not too late to cram the kids back into their car seats, drive home, and pour herself a glass of wine.

"Max! We do not tear the pages out of books." Louise did her best stern teacher impression, which usually had no effect. "Pick up those pages right now and tell Ms. Hope you're sorry."

Max closed the book and grabbed *Blueberries for Sal*.

Hope came out from behind the desk. "Max, you are not to do that. Ripping up books is a bad thing to do."

Max stared at her, his eyes wide with awe. "Yes, ma'am."

"Come here and give me that book."

Hanging his head in an uncharacteristic show of remorse, Max carried the book to Hope.

"It's ruined now," Louise said. "Don't ever do that again."

"Yes, ma'am." Max went back and sat on his chair.

"I'm sorry about that." Lately, the children were determined to destroy the world. Their last trip to the grocery store had resembled a mini twister, ending with two broken eggs and one smashed jar of pickles. Sometimes, she couldn't wait for them to grow up—or at least get through this phase of utter carelessness.

Hope followed her to the young adult section, taking long strides with her stocky legs. "No harm done. That there book was so old, the pages been taped a hundred times already. Got an excuse to throw it out now."

When they reached Zoe, Hope pulled a worn white rabbit puppet with a pink nose out of her back pocket. Zoe dropped the vampire novel.

"Fred the bunny will play with you," Hope said, pulling the puppet back. "But you have to come back to the children's area, okay?"

Zoe nodded.

"I'll take care of these two. Y'all go about your business." Hope took Zoe's hand, led her to the children's area, and brought out Fred the bunny again. The kids watched the puppet with an absorption they usually reserved for TV.

Lily put aside the newsletter she'd begun reading again and pushed through the circulation half-door. "I'll show you our history room."

Louise gave her strangely well-behaved children one last glance before following the librarian past two gray cubicles shoved against the wall. One was empty except for a computer like the ones on the circulation desk. In the other, a tall, gray-haired man hunched over a telephone. His limbs seemed to take up every inch of space in the tiny enclosure.

Louise trotted to catch up with Lily as she opened a door in the back of the library. Once they were inside, the librarian flipped the light switch and a fluorescent bulb buzzed on overhead. "Microfilm of census data is in this cabinet. This one has a copy of the city charter and some old maps. I don't even know what all's in there. You can look at whatever you want as long as you put it back."

"Is there anything about the first Alligator Bayou library?" Louise asked.

"The State Library set up a demonstration around 1946. The first branch was in the courthouse. Then the voters passed a property tax to keep funding it. I think there's a picture of the bookmobile in there. They started that after the tax passed. It ran until the 1980s. I guess they figure everyone around here has a car anyway." She opened the file cabinet and handed Louise a folder. "I'll go get Hope. Sometimes she knows more about the recent stuff than I do."

Louise sat down with the file and sifted through old flyers for county fairs, historical society newsletters, photographs of the town from the early 1900s, a few papers in a language she didn't recognize. Inside a stained brown envelope, she found a photo of the bookmobile, a modified truck with "State Library" painted on the side. Another photograph showed five girls in short dresses standing next to a brick building. Someone had written on the back, "May 10th, 1947. First story hour at Alligator Bayou Library."

She turned the photo over again and studied the girls. They were all white, five or six years old, with faces scrunched in little-kid hilarity. Three wore Mary Janes with white socks, and the other two were barefoot. Louise's grandmother had been a proper lady with a once-a-week hairstyle-and-wash appointment and a closet full of pastel polyester suits. She never would have allowed her children to go anywhere without shoes. But Louise's father had been the type of kid to take his off as soon as he left the house. By his own account, he and his brother had driven their straitlaced mother crazy. Louise had grown up hearing stories of his antics—dyeing their white cat pink, cooking up bogus science fair projects. When she was a child, the tales had made her wish she were a boy. They had all the fun, it seemed.

"You got a question?" Hope's voice was too loud in the enclosed space. Louise hadn't heard her enter and she jumped up from her seat. The librarian smiled.

"What language is this?" Louise held up one of the flyers.

Hope came closer, her black sneakers squeaking again. "Hungarian. Town was settled by them, mostly. Not sure why. They were farmers, of course, except for the ones in the timber industry. Guess one family came and brought the rest. No one was really interested in settling this part here until the railroad came through. Lots of trees to cut down, but you needed a way to move them. A few years ago a train crashed into a truck right out there." She pointed to the far wall, where a window was obscured by miniblinds. "Derailed and spilled some kind of toxic waste all over. That's how we got this land for the library. It was part of a settlement from the railroad company. Which reminds me, don't drink the water. Now, seems like nobody wants to pay for the library anymore. Last tax vote failed. Guess people think everything's on the Internet now. That or they're too lazy to read."

Louise absorbed this information. Colorful, but she had to get back on topic. Without Hope to entertain them, the children might well be tearing pages out of books and breaking Thanksgiving statuettes. "Lily thought you might know about the early libraries around here."

Hope sat down in front of the microfilm reader. She straddled the chair backward, like a man. "All's I know is, I used to work in the old library, before they built this one in 1987. It was in the courthouse building. You seen it?"

"I don't think so."

"Dumpy brick thing from the fifties. Anyway, they used to walk the prisoners right through the library to get them to court. Handcuffed and everything. Kinda disturbed the atmosphere."

"Was that the first library?"

"Officially. Seems like Glenda's mom used to talk about one before that. I think it was run out of the schoolhouse on Route One. That count?"

"Maybe."

"Glenda comes in sometimes for the children's programs. I can ask her. She runs the Oak Lake branch. You could ride over there, but it'd take you thirty minutes. Oh, wait. Glenda's still in the hospital over to Saint Jude, I think. Pelvic floor collapsed. Poor woman, just sitting there on the toilet, doing her business, when she felt something hanging down. Was her guts coming right out. Can you imagine?"

Louise shivered and resisted the urge to clutch her own stomach. "What about her mother?"

"Can't hardly talk to her now. She has the Alzheimer's. Glenda's got her in that home over to Saint Jude. Nothing much out here like that, except that dump on Route One. I wouldn't put my husband's cat there and it'd bite you as soon as look at you."

Louise held up the photo. "Who are these kids?"

"Dunno. That one looks like a Krasky, I'd say." She pointed a blunt finger at the girl on the end. "There are a million of them around here. They all have that hooked nose. Hungarian. No Cajuns in this area. 'Round here, you got more Germans, Hungarians. And blacks, of course. They used to call them Jerry Brindels. The blacks that mixed with the white Hungarians and Germans. Not sure why."

"Anything else I should look at here?"

Hope shook her head, her hair-sprayed blond bob barely moving. "Don't think so. State Library has a lot of historical stuff."

"Yeah, I've been through most of it. They don't have much about Alligator Bayou or any other towns besides Saint Jude and New Orleans, though."

"You could try the local history center. I gotta warn you, though, they don't have much there except moldy old baby bonnets and wedding dresses."

Louise hadn't even filled one page in her notebook. She'd found out basically nothing that she didn't already know. Alligator Bayou might be a very short chapter in her history of Louisiana libraries. She'd dragged the kids all the way out here for nothing. It was the perfect end to a perfectly lousy day. "Mind if I copy some of this stuff?"

Hope pushed the chair aside and stood. “Bring it out and we’ll set you up.”

Louise took a folder, stuffed in a few flyers and newsletters, and followed Hope into the patron area. Before they stepped around the cubicles, Louise heard the combination of noises that meant big trouble: a crash and then crying.

“Darn it, Lily was supposed to be watching those kids,” Hope said.

An angry-sounding man called out from the back area. “What’s going on out there?”

“Now, y’all done woke up the dragon.” Hope pumped her arms as she speed-walked across the library.

Louise started running when she saw Zoe trapped under a wire rack of romance novels. Hope was faster. She dropped to one knee, freed Zoe from the mess, and hugged her. “It’s okay, honey.”

Even though she wanted to comfort Zoe herself, Louise looked for Max first. He was playing with cotton balls in the children’s area. The floor looked like snowstorm aftermath.

“Who’s letting those kids destroy my library?” A red-faced bald man wearing wire-rimmed glasses and a tangerine-orange polo shirt walked up behind the counter.

“I done told Mr. Foley to get rid of this rack. Some kid pushes it over once a week. That’s him there, the library director. He’s three kinds of useless,” Hope said quietly. She hooked a thumb in the direction of the man, who was watching them with his arms folded across his chest. “She’s okay. Just scared.”

Zoe got up from Hope’s lap and ran toward Louise. She clutched her mother as though they’d been separated for days instead of a few minutes. Zoe could be frustrating, but she was endlessly affectionate. Louise kissed her soft, wet cheek and stroked her hair. “It’s okay, honey. It was scary, I know, but you’re not hurt, are you?”

The girl shook her head and hugged Louise harder.

"If those children can't behave, they'll have to leave," the director said.

Hope stood up and fixed him with a hard gaze. "Mr. Foley, we got this covered."

"You could have fooled me."

"I ain't fooling at all. They're just children."

Mr. Foley grunted and went back into the work area. A door slammed. Lily strolled out from behind a stack of books.

"Ms. Lily, I thought you were watching these here children!" Hope put her hands on her meaty hips. "Now we done got Mr. Foley all worked up again."

"I was just shelving a couple of books. I thought they'd be okay."

"Why didn't you come out when that rack fell on the girl?"

Lily dropped her eyes, hunched her thin shoulders, and returned to her place behind the desk. "I heard you, so I figured I couldn't do anything that you weren't already doing."

"You wanted to leave me to handle the boss man," Hope said.

"Come on, Hope. You know how he gets on to me."

" 'Cause you got no guts. You let him walk all over you." Hope took Zoe's hand and led her to the children's area. "At least show Ms. Louisiana here how to use the copier."

Louise stared at Hope's back. How did she know her full name? The librarian looked at her as if she could somehow see all of Louise's secrets. She opened her mouth to explain—about the name, Brendan, the kids, everything. But instead she just brought the folder to the photocopier.

"Now, Max, you need to clean up this here mess," Hope said, selecting a book from the pile.

"Yes, ma'am." Max dropped to the floor and began gathering up cotton balls, moving with an unprecedented level of focus and determination.

Louise hurried through her photocopying, half listening to Hope entertaining the children with a story about a cat playing in the rain. She wished that she could leave them for a while—just long enough for a nap or a cup of coffee in a cafe somewhere. A little sanity break before the long drive home and the always vexing question of what to make for dinner. She stuffed the copies into her oversize handbag.

"I'll refile the originals," Lily said.

"How much do I owe you?"

"Don't worry about it."

"Thanks." Reluctantly, Louise turned toward the children's area. Hope was using an astonishing variety of cartoon voices as she read. Louise waited until she was done before telling the children that it was time to leave.

"I don't want to," Max said.

"I don't want to either," Louise whispered, too softly for anyone to hear.

CHAPTER 3

Sal Fortuno brought his books up to the counter and placed his library card on top. The woman and her kids were leaving. She wasn't wearing makeup, which somehow made her chocolate eyes even more striking. He had the crazy urge to run after her, but what would he say? "Hey, let's go get a shake at the Icy Cone"? That would be creepy.

Lily smiled as she scanned his card. She'd seen him looking at the woman. "Her name is Louise," she said. "She's a professor at A&M. I didn't see a ring. She does have two rather spirited children, though."

"I saw that." Sal had wanted to help when the rack fell on the girl. But he'd been way in the back by the history books, and by the time he'd gotten out of the stacks, his cousin Hope had already freed her. Afterward, he returned to the high shelves. He'd told himself that he wanted to find the Stephen Ambrose book he'd been searching for, but he was really just nervous.

Lily finished scanning the books and pushed them toward him. "She wouldn't be hard to find. Check out A&M's Web site. She's in the library science department."

Hope came up to the counter carrying her bunny puppet

and a bag of cotton balls. "Hey, Sal. Didn't know you were here. Were you hiding or something?"

Sal gathered his books. Nothing got past his cousin. When they were growing up, she'd had an annoying habit of somehow knowing which girls he had crushes on and telling anyone and everyone. The result was always a lot of eye rolling and giggling. With his skinny legs and unruly black hair, Sal hadn't been an object of female desire. He'd filled out some in college, though, and no longer resembled a scarecrow. Even Hope had stopped calling him Skinny Sal.

"Why would I hide from you?" he said, winking at her.

"Beats me. I ain't got you figured out yet. Still can't understand why you're back here and not up north lawyering," Hope said, planting her hands on her hips.

"I didn't like it. I like it here. Or maybe I just missed you."

Hope stuffed the rabbit in her back pocket. "Wasn't the same around here without you, that's for sure. I, for one, got sick of the lost-puppy look your sister had on all the time."

Sal had felt guilty abandoning Betta. Their parents had passed away while he was in Chicago, and after that, she'd sounded distant on the phone. Even telling Sal the bits of gossip she picked up from the hair salon didn't animate her anymore.

Leaving Chicago hadn't been difficult. He'd lived in a studio apartment with furniture that he was happy to leave for the landlord. Back home, he'd put a trailer on his parents' land—less than a mile from his sister's place—and taught himself to grow strawberries. The first three years, he'd depended on the money he'd saved from his lawyer job, but by the fourth he managed to turn a small profit. That money meant more to him than the thousands he'd made working at Robb and Anderson.

"Well, now Betta has me to take care of again," he said.

"Good thing too. I was gonna have to find me another stylist. She was cutting my hair all uneven while you were gone," Hope said.

Sal laughed. His cousin's hair was always the same: a dishwater-blond bob. She'd also worn the same shade of too-red lipstick for as long as he could remember. One of the things he liked about Alligator Bayou was that things didn't change quickly. In fact, his return was the most exciting thing that had happened in a while, which was why his cousin still felt the need to bring it up four years later.

"Guess you'd better get back to your cows or whatever," Hope said.

"How many times I gotta tell you I don't have any cows?" Sal shifted the heavy books under his arm.

"Till you get you some. I'm waiting on fresh milk."

"You're gonna be waiting a long time. I got cabbage and potatoes, though, if you want some."

"I reckon I could make my Irish stew."

"Come on by after work." Sal waved to Lily and left. As he got into his truck, he considered searching for Louise on his now outdated computer. But he couldn't show up at her office on campus with his muddy boots and John Deere cap. He got in the truck and started the engine. Betta had set him up with every single woman in town, and he had suffered through exactly one date with each one. She said he was too picky. All the while she sat home and made him red beans and rice and mended his jeans. Sal didn't know what his sister wanted from life. But he knew what he wanted, even though he wasn't sure he'd ever get it.

CHAPTER 4

"We are screwed." Sylvia put down her decaf mocha latte on the coffee shop table. In her black dress with matching sash and black platform sandals, she looked more like a model wearing a strap-on belly than a truly pregnant woman. Louise's own pregnancies had been fashion shows of baggy T-shirts and sweats. She'd even borrowed Brendan's dress shirts until she got too big for them. It didn't take long since her ex stayed slim no matter what he ate.

The coffee shop was part of the campus bookstore. Tucked into a corner behind a tall magazine rack, it was constantly crowded with students hunched over laptops. Louise had spent enough time there to know which tables had wonky legs and what barista insisted on seeing her faculty ID before giving her the ten-cent discount on her small coffee.

Today, all of the tables were occupied by students studying for midterm exams. Most wore earbuds and studiously ignored everyone around them. But across the aisle, a pigtailed young woman raised her head from her textbook and stared at Louise and Sylvia in alarm. As usual, Sylvia was too loud and too dramatic. The student appeared to be on the verge of whipping out her cell and dialing 911 in case the crazy woman was going into labor.

Louise put on her most reassuring face, more for the benefit of the girl than Sylvia. "You're freaking out our impressionable young scholars. Dial it down a notch before the barista cuts you off from those decaf chocolate things you drink. It's not that bad."

"*Hello*, have you seen the ALA newsletter? There are no jobs. None. Even if I could relocate. Which I can't. At least I hope I can't."

Sylvia hadn't been upset about the possibility of losing her job a week ago. It stood to reason since the stakes were lower for her. Unlike Louise, she could live on her husband's salary, but she loved being a professor. Her security didn't stop her from publishing her articles about special libraries—information centers located in private companies—in the top journals in the field. Sylvia didn't coast, even though she could. So Louise couldn't begrudge Sylvia her good fortune, even though she had fed her own kids beans and rice for the last two days while waiting for Brendan's stupid child support check. Being dependent on him made her furious, but she couldn't dig herself out of the financial hole she was in. It was partly Brendan's fault for talking her into taking out loans for graduate school when she could have just sold her car. He'd always pushed to dine out too when they both knew they couldn't afford it. He'd seemed to believe that they'd be able to pay off their debts sometime—whenever he landed the prestigious job he was convinced he deserved.

Louise sipped her coffee and looked at Sylvia. Her mascara had smudged, making black semicircles under her eyes. "What do you mean you hope you can't move?"

"Bayou Oil. Haven't you heard?" Sylvia said.

"I'm not exactly an expert on the oil-and-gas industry."

"You are supposed to be an information specialist. This is important information."

Louise rolled her eyes. She could do without the drama. Sylvia might have problems, but she had plenty of her own. "Just tell me. Please."

Sylvia leaned back and tried to cross her legs but failed. She settled for sticking them out to the side, providing an obstacle for the students walking by with their frozen coffee concoctions. "Bayou Oil is laying people off."

"But Jake has been there for years. He's safe, isn't he?"

"He makes enough money to be a good layoff candidate, but isn't quite high up enough to be immune. I'm supposed to have this baby in a week. I'm freaking out. We could lose our house."

"Yeah, me too," Louise said. She didn't want to beg for more money from Brendan or her aging mother. Asking for a loan was admitting defeat, and Louise was not ready to do that. She'd take a job at Walmart first.

"I could go on maternity leave and never come back. Damn it, Louise, we worked really hard for this. Being a professor is my dream job. I don't want to do anything else. Shoot, I might just stay home with the kids and bake cookies all day."

"You don't even know how to make cookies. You use those dough rolls from the supermarket." The thought of Sylvia trying to cook almost made Louise smile.

"Maybe I'll learn how to sew."

"This isn't happening tomorrow, Sylvia. A&M has to give us a semester's notice. It's in our contracts."

"No, it isn't." Sylvia pulled herself up straighter in her chair. "Those are guidelines from the American Library Association. If the university declares exigency, they can do whatever they want. Even fire tenured professors. That's the law of the land."

"State law?"

"State law. And the administration can't wait to get rid of us."

Pigtail Girl was watching them again. She clearly thought Sylvia was crazy now. Of course the administration would fire a huge pregnant woman who sat in coffee shops complaining about the university all day. Louise shrugged. So much for the public relations campaign.

Sylvia shifted in her chair. "Crap, my water just broke."

"Don't mess with me. I am seriously not in the mood."

"Nope, the exact same thing happened with Jimmy. Let me get to the bathroom and you pull the car around."

"My van is on the other side of campus." Louise silently cursed the inflated faculty parking prices. She'd opted for a free student lot pass rather than paying fifty dollars per month to use the faculty garage.

"We'll take mine." Sylvia tossed Louise her keys. "It's right in front of the Magnolia building."

Before leaving, Louise glanced at the pigtailed student's table. Her icy drink had left a wet ring.

Bringing the kids to the hospital made about as much sense as driving a monster truck into a department store. But Sylvia insisted that she was going nuts lying in bed all day with no one to talk to. She needed her best friend. Louise missed Sylvia too. Her A&M office was lonely without Sylvia dropping by to complain about a demanding student or yet another rejected article. Adwell had wandered in a few times, but his robotic presence hadn't made her feel any better.

So she walked down the Lysol-scented hallway with the kids following, sort of.

"Zoe, come on!" Max was constantly frustrated with his

little sister lately. In his eyes, she never did what she was supposed to.

Zoe had stopped to peer into one of the rooms. She stepped toward the open door.

Max turned to face her, on the verge of tears, and called out, "Zoe, this way! Zoe!"

Rather than following her brother's instructions, Zoe collapsed on the floor, sobbing. Max grabbed her hand. "Zoe, you're supposed to go this way."

Louise backtracked and picked up her daughter, trying to comfort her by stroking her hair.

"No!" The girl turned herself into a limp, slippery noodle.

Louise was afraid she would drop Zoe, so she gave up and put her back down. Maybe she would follow. She did sometimes, at least more often than Max had at her age. But after a few steps, Zoe stopped to examine something on the floor. Exasperated, Louise took her hand.

"No!" Zoe threw herself down again.

Max ran back and stood next to his sister. He was sobbing now too. "Zoe, stand up."

How hard was it to walk down a hallway without stopping, fighting, freaking out about nothing? Louise began walking again. Max started to follow, but stopped when he realized that Zoe was still sprawled out on the floor. "Mommy, pick Zoe up!"

Max didn't understand that she'd already tried that. In fact, she'd tried everything she could think of and she was ready to give up. She wished she had someone standing next to her. Someone who would say, "Let me do it." When she tried to picture who that person could be, her mind was blank. Brendan wouldn't have helped. He'd either expect her to handle it or yell at the kids or her. He had no idea how to deal with little children. Worse, he didn't want to learn.

Jimmy's slightly maniacal laugh drifted out of one of the rooms.

"Jimmy!" Max dashed toward the sound, leaving his sister behind.

For some reason, that got Zoe moving. She ran down the hall after her brother, laughing. Tragedy had turned to elation in the course of a minute. Louise hoped none of the nurses were around. Everyone connected with Sylvia would be making way too much noise. Thinking about seeing her best friend made a tiny crack in her bad mood.

In the room, Zoe was transfixed by a bouquet of balloons above the bed.

"Ba-oon!" she said. "Ba-oon, Mommy!"

The baby was asleep in her hospital bassinet, somehow undisturbed by Max and Jimmy's excited shouting and Zoe's high-decibel voice. The cozy hospital room brought back memories of Max's birth. Brendan had slept on a foldout bed and changed the baby's diaper with an awestruck expression. During those two days in the maternity ward, Louise had believed that the three of them would be a happy family. The room was a warm, comfortable cocoon sheltering the little family from the world and providing them with everything they needed. The tiredness and arguing didn't start until they were back home. Louise spent the rest of their marriage trying to re-create the contentment and unity of those days. Zoe's birth was completely different. That time, she was alone for most of the hospital stay, enduring the pitying glances of the nurses. When it was over, Brendan had returned to pick her up from the hospital and driven her home in silence.

Sylvia reclined on a pile of powder blue pillows. She wore smoky eye makeup and a lacy nightgown. The slippers next to the bed had kitten heels and pompons. Zoe plopped down on the floor to try them on. "Shoe!"

"How's little Madeleine doing?" Louise asked.

"Great. She sleeps through everything," Sylvia said. "I wish they would let us out of here."

"Did you expect to pop the baby out, jump out of bed, and go home? You just had her last night." Louise handed her a ten-piece box of Godiva chocolates.

"Thanks, girl. The food here is okay, but way too healthy." Sylvia tore the cellophane from the box and examined the selection. She handed the caramel to Louise.

"Are you sure?"

"I know they're your favorite."

Louise accepted the caramel and looked automatically for Zoe. The girl was already a chocolate fiend, but she was too busy knocking Sylvia's cards and stuffed animals onto the floor to notice the candy.

The boys were trying to pop the balloons and laughing. Jimmy was taller than Max, with lanky limbs and a thin face. He had his mother's red hair, but Jimmy's hair was more carrot than auburn. Louise never bothered to comb Max's hair because it tended to fall neatly into place. In contrast, Sylvia was constantly smoothing down Jimmy's unruly mop. She threatened to give him a buzz cut at least once a day.

"Maybe Jimmy will get us kicked out. He's driving the nurses crazy. One of them has told me three times that he needs to be quieter." Sylvia shrugged.

"Where's Jake?"

"He ran down to the cafeteria for my fake latte. I'm thinking I should go ahead and wean Madeleine so I can have caffeine again."

"How's his job looking?"

Sylvia ate a chocolate heart. "We haven't heard anything yet."

Jake walked in, and Sylvia put a finger to her lips.

"What are you two gossiping about?" he asked, handing her a tall paper cup.

Sylvia accepted the coffee, tore off the top, and took a long swallow. "How we can find Louise a man as wonderful as you."

"I don't come cheap." Jake ruffled Jimmy's hair. "I'm going to get this boy out of here before he gets eighty-sixed. Come on, Godzilla."

Jake gathered up Jimmy's toys and stuffed them into a tote bag. Sylvia's husband was amiable and nice-looking. He liked sports, which didn't interest Louise in the least. But he smiled a lot and put up with Sylvia's drama queen routine. Sylvia loved Jake in part because he was water to her fire. Calm to her storm. Louise preferred a man with more personality, more ideas. She sighed. There was no use daydreaming about what kind of man she would like to date. She didn't have the energy, and by the time she was ready, it would be too late.

"Jimmy!" Max cried.

"What a tragedy. You won't see him for twelve whole hours, until school tomorrow," Louise said. "We should go too, before these kids wake all the poor sleeping sick people two floors up."

All of the cards and stuffed animals were scattered on the floor. Zoe stood on top of a fat pink teddy bear and reached for a glass vase of roses on the end table. When Louise picked her up, the girl wailed and stretched her arms back toward the flowers.

Louise wanted to stay and talk to Sylvia, but Zoe was still shrieking, so she let Max follow Jimmy out the door.

"Bye, girl," Sylvia said. "Call me later."

"Do you want to walk?" Louise asked Zoe.

"No." Zoe said no to everything these days, but Louise

asked her anyway. She held out hope that someday the girl would say yes. About something, anything.

She set Zoe down on the floor and took her hand. Amazingly, her daughter walked placidly by her side. Jake was holding Jimmy's hand and Max trailed behind them. The sight made Louise sad. Max didn't have a dad, not really, and maybe he never would. At the moment, though, Max was happy to be with his friend. He didn't know what it meant to have a father. But he would start asking soon. What would she tell him?

CHAPTER 5

Trish was sobbing next to the library science department copier when Louise walked in. There was no reason for Trish to even be in the office. She and Sylvia had given birth only two weeks apart, and Sylvia hadn't set foot on campus since. Louise checked her friend's mailbox every day and threw out the junk—flyers from presses, desperate letters from the writers of self-published books, glossy brochures from pseudo-academic institutions promising online degrees.

Louise briefly considered sneaking away and pretending she hadn't seen Trish, but she couldn't do it. Even though her colleague might be a fussy snob who hadn't talked to her since the miserable baby shower, Louise felt a surge of pity. Trish's blond hair was uncharacteristically greasy with dark roots, and her sweat suit had a variety of different colored stains.

"Louise! What am I going to do?" Trish held out her arms.

"What happened?"

"The university declared exigency. We might get shut down!"

"I know," Louise said. Sylvia, who checked her e-mail at all hours, had called that morning while Louise was trying to convince Max to open his mouth so that she could brush his teeth. She'd been too distracted for the news to really sink in. Even though no layoffs in the library school had been announced yet, the possibility was real. They might lose their jobs. Trish's breakdown made Louise's head ache with the weight of the truth.

"We'll be unemployed, Louise. I just had a baby. I'm still on maternity leave."

"I know."

"It's horrible."

Louise touched Trish's shoulder lightly, trying to project a calm that she didn't feel. "Why don't you go home and get some rest? You don't need to worry about this right now. You have a baby to take care of. Anyway, we won't know anything for a few weeks."

Trish covered her face with her hands. "I had to come and get my mail. Look, I brought little Aubrey."

Aubrey? She'd actually named the poor boy Aubrey? He'd be doomed to a life of junk mail perfume samples and gender misidentification. "He's beautiful."

"Thank you. He stays up all night, though. I'm so exhausted. I mean, Frank tries to help, but he still wears me out."

"It'll get better," Louise said. "Go home and get some rest."

"I know I shouldn't be here, but I was so worried about the department."

Adwell strolled into the office. Either he didn't notice Trish's puffy eyes and smeared makeup or he decided to ignore it. In the face of strong emotions, Adwell generally made jokes or simply walked away, sometimes both. "Hello, ladies. I see you have the little one."

"Yes," Trish said. "Aubrey."

"Oh, that was my grandmother's name. Lovely woman. She drank like a fish and smoked like a chimney. Lived to be ninety-two." Adwell's voice was its normal mechanical drone, but he recited the speech without any awkward pauses, a sure sign he'd given it before.

Trish's smile looked pained.

"Come on," Louise said. "You really should go home and take it easy."

"Yes," Adwell said. "You sure don't want to be around here. Everyone is overreacting to the university president's ill-conceived comment."

"What did he say?" Louise asked.

Adwell snorted, reached into his mailbox, and tossed the contents into the recycling bin. "Something about how the university will be just as deep but not as wide after the cuts. Everyone takes that to mean that they are going to close programs."

"Oh, no," Trish said.

"Well, we don't really know anything," Adwell said.

"We know we're one of the departments that might be eliminated," Louise said, mentally giving herself a forehead slap. Why was she antagonizing the freaked-out new mom?

Adwell studied the ceiling tiles. "We might."

Trish's face crumpled again. "I'll see you all later. I need to go home." She pushed the stroller out of the office, head bowed.

Louise checked her box. Brendan had finally sent the previous month's child support check. Two weeks late. She waited until Adwell left before opening the envelope. It was fifty dollars short. Brendan had enclosed a note in his disgustingly neat handwriting. "This amount is what was left over after I paid off the joint credit card. I closed the account."

Louise clenched her teeth, crumpled the note, and tossed it in the trash. She wanted to do the same with the check, but she couldn't afford to. She tucked it into her purse instead.

CHAPTER 6

The Bouncing Crawfish Party Center was filled with inflatables of all kinds—castles, slides, miniature jungles. Zoe refused to go in any of them. She played with a Hula-Hoop instead while Louise sat on the metal bleachers with Sylvia and baby Madeleine. Louise didn't know where the boys were, but she'd seen Max climbing up one of the big slides a few minutes earlier, so she wasn't worried. She dreaded the upcoming gift ritual most of all. The modest Play-Doh set she'd sloppily wrapped would pale in comparison to the expensive Legos, remote-controlled helicopters, and Teenage Mutant Ninja Turtle action figures.

"Come on, these are the kids from Max and Jimmy's class, you know that," Sylvia said. "There's Ethan and his dad, Toby. Mahalia is at the top of the slide there, and her mom, June, is sitting at the table. Josie, Lindsey, and Martin are jumping in the ball pit."

"How do you keep all these characters straight? It's like reading a Russian novel, except that all the dialogue is about whose kid is already reading and which one is still sleeping with a pacifier."

"I like Tolstoy. Besides, I pay attention." Sylvia adjusted Madeleine's swaddling.

At one month old, the baby spent most of her time sleeping. She was incredibly calm compared to Max and Zoe, who had done nothing but cry and nurse at that age. Though, to be fair, the worst part of their babyhoods was Brendan and his disappearing act. Seeing Madeleine and smelling her sweet baby scent brought back the good memories of cradling the children and staring at their tiny faces in rapture. Sometimes, Louise wished she could go back and rewrite that period of her life, replacing her ex-husband with a more likable character.

"Even without a newborn I don't have the mental energy to keep up with what day of the week it is," she said. "Saturday, right?"

"Shut up," Sylvia said. "I'm starving. When do you think they're going to do the cake?"

"They don't pass out the sugar bombs until the end. We only got here fifteen minutes ago."

"Yeah, but we were half an hour late."

"True."

Zoe dropped the hoop and climbed on a rubber horse. She bounced up and down. "Horsey!"

The other parents congregated in groups, laughing and talking. They were way too upbeat. Clearly none had been up half the night with kids who took turns having nightmares and demanding snacks and drinks. Louise yawned. Starbucks needed to open a store inside Bouncing Crawfish. Right away. "Kids' birthday parties are worse than junior high dances," she said.

"Hey, I had fun at those things. Girl, you are such a grump." Sylvia gave Zoe a finger wave.

"Please. At least in junior high, there was always some

cute boy with a skater haircut to make it exciting. Here we don't have anything but a bunch of moms and a cardboard pizza. Speaking of which, I'm tired of kid food. I want a mocha latte with extra caffeine, a nice sandwich, and a piece of pie."

"Let's make friends." Sylvia shifted Madeleine to her shoulder and grabbed Louise's arm.

"Hey, wait!"

Under Sylvia's strong grip, Louise felt like a kid being dragged to the principal's office. But she gave in to the inevitable and allowed herself to be guided off the bleachers.

Sylvia approached a group of women standing near one of the inflatables. They were all wearing skinny jeans, baggy A&M sweatshirts, and high heels. They looked impossibly young, rested, and beautiful. Louise glanced back at Zoe, still bouncing happily.

"Howdy, y'all." Sylvia unleashed her best "Hey, gals" smile.

"Is that your child?" a woman wearing fake-fur-trimmed heels asked, pointing at the top of the slide.

Max was trying to push the birthday boy out of his way. Luckily, Josh was nearly a year older than Max and outweighed him by ten pounds. He shrugged it off and continued down the slide.

Louise put on her authoritative voice. "Max, you do not push. If you push anyone again, we're leaving, do you hear me?"

Max looked in his mother's direction, but said nothing. He went down the slide, crashing into Josh at the bottom. They both laughed crazily.

"They're just being boys," Sylvia said.

None of the other women answered. They affected identical expressions of disapproval. The woman with the fur heels ran to the end of the slide and caught Josh by the arm.

"Don't let him do that to you. If he pushes you, push him back."

Sylvia raised her eyebrows, but Louise ignored her. Her stomach hurt, and it wasn't the smell of overspiced pepperoni coming from the party room. Max had been better about playing rough lately. She was terrified that he was relapsing and they would have to avoid all birthday parties and playgrounds for the foreseeable future. She'd been bullied herself as a child, so her child couldn't torment other kids. It was unthinkable.

The group of women resumed their discussion about the relative merits of different birthday party places. Louise had been planning to have Max's party at home, apparently only an acceptable option if you rented a bouncy house or hired a clown. She watched Max out of the corner of her eye. He clambered up one of the slides, following a girl in a pink dress. Louise prepared to intervene, but he didn't touch the girl, just slid down after her, laughing.

Sylvia's phone binged. She handed Madeleine to Louise and fished it out of her purse. The baby stirred for a moment before falling back asleep. Louise kissed her head lightly.

Sylvia stared at her phone as though it had bitten her. "I just got fired. Over e-mail."

After checking that Max was still behaving, Louise carried Madeleine back to the bleachers and sat down with Sylvia. They traded phone for baby, and Louise skimmed the e-mail. None of it made sense except for the line "termination effective January 15." Her whole body went numb. The worst had happened.

Zoe left her bouncy horse and perched next to Sylvia. As usual, she seemed to sense that something was wrong.

"Do you want to check your e-mail?" Sylvia said. "See if you got the same message?"

"Not really. I can't imagine why I wouldn't have." Louise hugged Zoe and brushed back the hair from her sweet face. She pulled away and returned to the horse.

An hour later, Louise was sitting at Sylvia's kitchen table. Her house was a scaled-down plantation home with five bedrooms, three bathrooms, and a parlor area that no one ever used. It was seventy years old, and remodeled in such a way as to retain what real estate agents like to call "character." One of the bedrooms was a permanent guest room, and another had been designated as Jake's office, where he could hide out from the kids. The house was luxurious, a giant step up from Louise's little ranch house. Sylvia said that it sometimes seemed too small.

Louise sipped her wine and admired the living room/kitchen area. Floor-to-ceiling windows looked out onto the landscaped backyard complete with pool and playscape. Built-in bookshelves and a flat-screen TV filled the other wall. Two couches with soft, inviting cushions were positioned around a coffee table crowded with books and toys.

Sylvia bounced Madeleine in the crook of her arm as she watched the boys playing with action figures. "Right now, deciding not to breast-feed doesn't seem like such a good idea."

"I don't blame you. I don't understand the women who love nursing so much. All your clothes smell like sour milk, and you're stuck in a chair while the older kid asks embarrassing questions and searches the house for matches." Louise wouldn't have shared her ambivalence to one of the most cherished aspects of motherhood with just anyone. But Sylvia wasn't just anyone. Louise had known that the first time they'd met. That day, Louise had been sitting at her new desk in her disappointingly run-down office, feeling more tired and lost than she ever had. She was doubting her ability to handle two small children on her own and publish enough to earn tenure while also teaching two large classes of undergraduates. Sylvia had come in bearing a bottle of wine and a plate of cheese and crackers. By the time the bottle was empty, they were both laughing so hard that their sides hurt.

"I might have tried to put up with the breast-feeding a little longer if I knew we were going on the breadline. Formula costs a hundred dollars a month," Sylvia said, switching the baby to her other arm.

"We have jobs until after Christmas. What about Jake?"

"They gave him two months." Sylvia drank the rest of her wine and refilled her glass. "He'll get unemployment, but we won't."

"Of course we will. Why wouldn't we?"

"State of Louisiana doesn't pay into it for their employees. We have no social security. No unemployment. Girl, I've been here my whole life and it never ceases to amaze me just how effed up this state is."

Zoe climbed up on the chair next to Louise and looked at Madeleine. "Baby."

"That's right. That's a baby. You used to be a baby, did you know that? My life was actually easier then," Louise said.

"Baby." Zoe climbed back down and found a truck that one of the boys had abandoned under the table. She made sputtering sounds as she drove it along the rug. "Truck."

Louise poured a little more wine into her glass. No job, no unemployment. Her fragile facade of independence was crumbling. She would have to ask someone for help. She couldn't get a loan from her mother. Her older sister was in the process of trying to find a nursing home she could afford. Louise had been the late-life surprise, not necessarily unwanted but a stretch to her parents' budget. Even as a child, she had worried about money, ordering the cheapest item on the menu on the rare occasions when her family ate in restaurants. She'd felt guilty for every penny she cost them. Her father's salary as a schoolteacher wasn't enough to support four children. For some reason, her mother never worked. She'd filled her time volunteering, cooking, and cleaning. Louise had sworn she'd never be like her. Now, she was in a worse situation, dependent on a man who wasn't even her husband anymore. She would have to ask him, no matter how much it hurt her pride.

Across the room, a battle erupted.

"Mine! That's mine!" Jimmy screamed, pointing at a car that Max was driving along the coffee table.

Max stopped and looked at his friend like he'd turned into something unrecognizable but not very interesting. Jimmy grabbed the car, and Max wrestled it back. Jimmy gave up and picked a dump truck from the mound of toys. He smashed his vehicle into Max's. "Crash!"

"What was with Josh's mom?" Sylvia said. "Telling her kid to fight Max? Is she nuts?"

"She has lousy taste in footwear," Louise said. She didn't want to think about the incident again. During Max's period of hitting other kids, she'd felt like she was holding a live grenade. She was terrified that he would hurt Zoe or some other child. If his sister grabbed one of his toys, he would push or hit her. She couldn't leave them alone together, even for a moment. Playgrounds were even worse because the potential victims were other people's children. After he pushed another boy in the sandbox, she stopped taking him altogether. Either her constant punishments, lectures, and rewards for good behavior were finally working or he'd grown out of the stage because lately his behavior had been better. Until today. Louise felt like a black hole had opened in front of her. Max the bad kid again. Her job gone.

"I mean, geez, the kid is four. What is wrong with her? I'll tell you what, I'm not inviting him to Jimmy's birthday party. Not that I'll be able to afford one anyway." Sylvia put Madeleine in her baby swing. "So, what's your plan?"

Louise drank some wine, hoping that it would stop the frantic thoughts taking over her mind. "I don't have one. I don't want to move across the country again just to get a job in a public library."

"We're staying. Jake and I talked about it in case this happened. Our families are here. Besides, it's not worth moving for a library position, even if I can get one. He'll apply for jobs. If he gets something really good, maybe we'll move then."

"That makes sense." Louise finished her wine and pushed the glass away. She wished she had such an easy solution to her problems or even just a husband to talk them over with. She shook her head. She'd had a husband and he'd been no good at discussing anything. Arguing was more his style. She didn't need a man. She needed a job.

"So here's my idea. My sister-in-law told me about two openings in the same library. We could work together. At least for a while. If we hate it, we can always quit. But it'd be something. A little money coming in. They're so desperate, they practically hired me when I called to ask about the job. And they'd let us start after Christmas break."

"What is it?"

"Alligator Bayou Parish Library."

"He hit me. Max hit me!" Jimmy yelled.

Max was calmly playing with the toy car. He didn't even seem to realize that Jimmy was upset.

Louise squatted down in front of him. "Did you hit Jimmy?"

He nodded.

Louise closed her eyes for a moment. This couldn't be happening. She couldn't deal with losing her job and Max hitting again all at the same time. She took a deep breath. "We don't hit people. Tell Jimmy you're sorry."

"I'm sorry, Jimmy."

Jimmy grabbed a Mr. Potato Head and ripped off its arms.

Louise walked back to the kitchen area. She couldn't decide which was worse—that Max had relapsed or that Sylvia had just suggested that they work at the pathetic rural library. "Did you eat too many of the special jelly beans? Alligator Bayou?"

"They need two librarians at their main branch. It wouldn't be that bad. It's twenty-five miles, but we'd be going against traffic. Most people live out there and work in Saint Jude."

"I'm not worried about the traffic. I've been to the library—if you can call it that." Louise sat back down at the table and rested her head in her hands.

"That's right. Your library project. How's that going?"

"It's not. But I can tell you that Alligator Bayou is three trees away from nowhere."

"Do you have any better ideas?" Sylvia drained her wineglass.

"No. I don't. But the library building looks like the Department of Motor Vehicles with a few extra bookshelves, the librarians are glorified file clerks, and the director has short-man complex."

"I don't care," Sylvia said. "I want to keep this house. We don't have much savings. Dumb, I know. But we kept thinking we'd start socking some away and then we had kids and bought this house and . . . you know. If I don't get a job, we lose it."

Louise exhaled, but the tension in her body remained. "Yeah, I'd probably lose mine too."

"If we hate the place, we can find something else. It won't be forever."

"Okay, fine."

"Good. Do you want to make dinner? There's a premade pizza crust in there. Jake should be home in a few minutes."

Louise waved this off. Even though Sylvia didn't do much more than heat chicken nuggets and frozen pizza, she had a professional stove, a massive refrigerator, and a large kitchen island with a wooden top that was basically a huge cutting board. Louise always welcomed the opportunity to cook there.

She stuck her head in the stainless steel fridge and checked out the selection of produce. Ten minutes later, she had a pot of pasta on the stove and the beginnings of a salad.

"That doesn't smell like pizza." Sylvia had moved to one of the couches and turned on the afternoon cartoons. All three children stopped playing to stare up at the TV.

"Nope." Louise cut up some salami and mozzarella to mix in with the pasta. Cooking never failed to make her feel better. She felt almost optimistic about Alligator Bayou. Maybe they could give the library a makeover. It sure needed one.

Jake arrived just as Louise was mixing together the pasta ingredients. He turned off the TV, convinced the boys to come to the table, and strapped Zoe into a booster seat. As they all sat down together, Louise wished for the hundredth time that she could switch places with her best friend. She would like to be tall and beautiful with a nice husband. Even with their current problems, Sylvia led a charmed life. Jake would find another job and it would all work out. Louise wasn't so sure about herself. Her life seemed like a complete disaster.

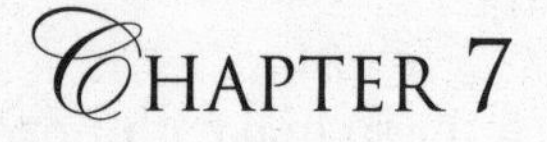

CHAPTER 7

Two days after New Year's, Louise drove Sylvia into Alligator Bayou for their first day of work. As the strip malls and big-box stores of Saint Jude gradually disappeared, nothing was left except trees, grass, cloudless blue sky, and occasional roadkill.

The closer they got to the library, the more Louise worried. They were going to work in an institution that had ground to a halt sometime around 1987. No one used it; no one cared about it. She and Sylvia would either have to resurrect the library or go crazy with boredom. She also dreaded Brendan's inevitable caustic remark: "Geez, Louise. You can't do any better than *that?*"

"You know, I've lived here all my life and I never came to Alligator Bayou Parish until we had our job interviews," Sylvia said.

"Really? I thought you majored in Louisiana studies." Louise was surprised. Sylvia acted as Louise's guide to everything Southern. She'd explained to her Yankee friend that ordering a sandwich "dressed" meant with lettuce, tomato, and mayonnaise; stressed the importance of a termite contract on her house; and talked her through her first experience with a hurricane threat.

"Ha-ha. Little-known fact: my undergraduate major was biology. But seriously, I never had any reason to come to Alligator Bayou. I mean, look at this. We're only ten miles outside of Saint Jude and there's nothing here."

"So far, I've counted two dead opossums, one raccoon, and a shredded tire."

Sylvia pulled down the sunshade mirror and refreshed her lipstick. "To be honest, I really don't know much about rural Louisiana at all. I'm a New Orleans girl. I wouldn't even be in Saint Jude except for Jake's job." She flipped the shade back up and sighed. "Former job."

"I guess we'll have to learn fast," Louise said. She got off at the Alligator Bayou exit, passing a junkyard and a service station with two gas pumps. After that, they drove by a succession of dilapidated houses and mobile homes set back from the road. Yards were decorated with broken-down cars and lawn ornaments varying from fake wells to nonfunctioning toilets. Instead of trash cans out front, the houses had metal cages designed to keep wildlife from pawing through the garbage.

Louise turned onto the main drag of downtown Alligator Bayou—the Icy Cone, the Stop 'N' Gas, the Cut and Dye. For nine hours on weekdays, this would be their street, their town.

Sylvia shook her head as they came to the Piggly Wiggly. "There really is nothing out here."

"There are a courthouse and city hall somewhere. I think maybe on Main Street. Do you want to look? We have time." Louise wasn't in a hurry to get to the library. As long as they were in the van, she could pretend that they were just visiting.

"No." Sylvia leaned back in her seat. "We'll see it eventually, I guess. God, I am so tired. I need coffee. Is there anywhere to get a latte around here? A Starbucks, maybe?"

"Yeah, right next to the gourmet sandwich shop and the twenty-four-hour spa."

"Right." Sylvia sighed again.

"You got us into this, remember?"

"It seemed like a good idea at the time."

"The story of my life." Louise pulled into the library lot and parked next to a white van. She wanted to turn around, drive back to Saint Jude, and forget about Alligator Bayou. Except that there was nothing there for her anymore. She didn't belong at A&M, and it was only a matter of time before she'd have to sell the house. There was no way she could afford it on a public librarian's salary.

"You look miserable," Sylvia said, taking off her oversize movie-star sunglasses. "Come on, we can do this."

"I miss my kids."

"Oh, please. They are having a great time. They love school. It's good for them. Stop feeling guilty. You are doing what you have to do."

"I guess so." Louise got out of the car. She was wearing a navy-blue suit with nylons and black pumps. It wasn't even eight o'clock yet, and the panty hose already itched. She wanted her jeans and T-shirt back.

Sylvia wore a billowy white shirt, black pants, and three-inch heels. She looked like a slumming model. "It's go time," she said, stepping out of the van and tossing back her long, thick hair.

Louise shouldered her bag and regarded the low brick building with trepidation. The surrounding weedy grass was tawny brown, and the live oaks from the vacant lot next door stretched their branches toward the library, as if protesting its presence. She imagined that the forest wanted the library back, but the truth was just the opposite. More and more land was being cleared nearby for clapboard housing developments and fast-food restaurants. She even heard construction equipment rumbling in the distance, like the threat of rain.

Louise speculated that there were no other buildings around the library because of the train accident. Thinking about the unidentified chemicals dumped on the land made her skin itch even more. She sniffed the air, but all she smelled was Sylvia's perfume.

Sylvia was already on her way through the glass doors. Louise adjusted the strap of her bag on her shoulder and followed.

"Here we are. Our library," Sylvia said.

Louise didn't answer. If Sylvia hadn't been standing next to her, she might have started crying. She didn't want to be in this crappy nontown in the middle of nowhere scanning bar codes, as Adwell had put it. Thinking of the professor, she tried to summon the will to prove him wrong. There were people in town who deserved library services, and this completely inadequate facility was all they were getting. She and Sylvia were going to change that. She needed to focus on the challenge. Otherwise, she'd spiral into depression.

Lily came out from behind the counter. Her dull brown hair had been roller-curled and hair-sprayed into submission. She wore the same blouse and slacks that Louise remembered from her research visit. "Ms. Louise. Nice to see you again."

"You too," Louise said. "This is Sylvia Jones."

"Yes, I know." Lily took Sylvia's hand in both of hers. "How are you?"

"Fine." Sylvia flashed her biggest smile. "Are you going to show us around?"

"Yes. Mr. Foley and Mr. Henry should be here soon. But first you all have to clock in."

Sylvia raised her perfectly plucked eyebrows as they went into the back work area. The last time Louise had clocked in for a job was when she was in college, working in the dorm cafeteria. Sylvia had probably never used a time clock in her life.

Someone, maybe Lily herself, had used an actual typewriter to put Sylvia's and Louise's names on beige time cards. Lily showed them how to insert the cards into the old-fashioned time clock. It made a *ca-chunk* that indeed brought back college memories. Louise had hated that tedious, mind-numbing cafeteria job. After quitting, she'd used her uniform shirt to polish her black Doc Martens.

"Y'all have any coffee?" Sylvia asked.

"I just made a pot," Lily said. "This mug here is Hope's, and this one is Mr. Foley's. You can use any of the others."

Sylvia chose a cup decorated with flowers and poured some coffee. "Whoa, mama. This is strong."

"We have creamer and sugar."

While Sylvia doctored her latte substitute, Louise looked around their new work environment. Four cubicles smaller than bathroom stalls lined the back wall, and carts of books were parked at odd angles around the room. The main branch of the Alligator Bayou library system would have to employ enough people to order new books, take care of payroll and accounting, and manage the other three branches. Someone also had to coordinate children and young adult programming. The numbers didn't add up. Either most of the employees had more than one job description or a lot of work wasn't getting done.

Next to the kitchenette was a glassed-in office with its miniblinds tightly closed.

"That's Mr. Foley's office. He's the director," Lily said.

"I saw him the first time I was here. For the research project," Louise said, trying to make her voice sound neutral. Mr. Foley had been strangely absent during Louise's and Sylvia's job interviews. Mr. Henry had made an excuse for the director that he didn't even seem to believe himself.

"That's right. You surely did." Lily poured herself some of the midnight-black coffee and added a generous amount of sugar. She concentrated on her cup, stirring.

She had to be embarrassed about hiding when Zoe knocked over the romance-novel rack. Was Mr. Foley really enough of a monster to justify that kind of fear? If so, taking this job was a huge mistake.

Sylvia drank some coffee and set the cup down on the counter. She was so tall, especially in her high-heeled boots, that she seemed too big for the kitchen, too big for the small-town library. Still, she leaned against the counter with the ease of an actress playing the role of her life. Louise wished she had her friend's poise. But her panty hose were cutting into her belly fat, and her feet already hurt in the stiff shoes. She was uncomfortable in every possible way.

When a loud crack sounded from the patron area, even Sylvia jumped. Louise had visions of rednecks wielding guns, but it was just the circulation desk's half-door slamming. Mr. Foley shuffled in wearing slipper-like, backless shoes. Up close, he didn't look like someone who ran a library system. His polo shirt had a frayed collar, and the cuffs of his khaki pants had been stapled, not sewn.

Louise had been dreading this moment. Would he recall her children wreaking havoc in the library? If he did, he probably thought she was an incompetent mother and he'd conclude that she wouldn't be any better as an employee. Not a good way to start her career as a public librarian.

"Lily, I've told you before, haven't I? We don't unlock the doors until eight o'clock. We don't need the public wandering in before we're open." The library director put his hands on his hips in a surprisingly ladylike gesture.

"Yes, sir," Lily said, hanging her head.

Mr. Foley turned his frown into an unconvincing smile. "You two must be our new librarians. Welcome."

Louise searched his bland face. If the director remembered her, he gave no sign. She shook his pudgy hand. It felt like sandpaper.

Sylvia had to bend down to greet her boss. She gave him the full force of her white teeth.

Mr. Foley's smile faltered, just for a moment. Louise almost thought she'd imagined it. Everyone liked Sylvia. Even if they didn't want to.

"Well, I'll leave Lily to show you around," he said, ducking into his office.

"What a lovely man," Sylvia said, her voice sweet and sarcastic at the same time.

Lily turned on a computer with a label machine attached, bending down lower than she really needed to in order to accomplish the task. Louise detected the hint of a smile at the corners of her mouth.

"Direct us to our digs, would you?" Sylvia said.

Lily straightened up. "Of course. There are two empty cubicles. This first one belongs to Matt—he handles the computer system and payroll—and the last one is Hope's, but y'all can decide who gets the other two."

Each cubicle had a window facing the parking lot. Louise was grateful for the view of the outside world, even though there was nothing to see but asphalt, railroad tracks, and the trees beyond.

"I'll take the one near Hope," Sylvia said. "I hear she's very entertaining."

"Am I?" The librarian appeared behind Lily, demonstrating her eerie sneaking yet again.

Sylvia extended an elegantly manicured hand to Hope's rough one. "Sylvia Jones."

"So I've heard." Hope pumped Sylvia's hand. "I'm supposed to teach y'all our computer system. You got a lot of book learning, but you ain't ever worked in a public library, am I right?"

"No," Louise said. "We haven't. But I'm sure we can learn."

"I need to get up front in case we have any patrons," Lily said, backing away. "Good luck, y'all."

"Set up your stuff and then we'll go see Mr. Henry," Hope said.

Louise went into her carpeted stall and tested her desk chair. Unlike the museum relic in her A&M office, her new chair was less than ten years old and featured black cloth and an adjustable seat. The computer wasn't much newer than the furniture, though, and it made an ominous cranking noise when she pushed the power button.

As she sat down on the chair, her foot hit something under the desk. She got down on her knees and pushed the chair out of the way. Stacked up underneath her desk was a trove of outdated equipment: two rotary-dial telephones, a roll-paper fax machine, and a dot matrix printer. Louise put the machines on the desk, one at a time.

"Where'd you get all that stuff?" Hope asked.

Louise hefted the fax onto the chair and rolled it toward her. "A time machine from the 1990s."

"Good Lord." Hope picked up the machine and examined it. "Let me get a box."

Sylvia came out of her cubicle. "Hey, how come she got all the cool stuff?"

Hope loaded the fax into an empty paper box, stepped into Louise's cubicle, and piled in the rest of the equipment. "This here's embarrassing. Mr. Foley done said he got rid of this junk."

The back door opened, and the assistant director walked

in. "Good morning, ladies." Though almost six feet tall, Mr. Henry hunched over in a way that made him appear shorter. He seemed to be only in his sixties, but he moved slowly, like a fragile old man.

"I'm just gonna toss this junk in the trash," Hope said.

"Where did all that come from?" Mr. Henry asked.

"Under Ms. Louisiana's desk."

"Goodness. Well, it's parish property. We can't just throw it away. We have to send it to surplus. I thought Mr. Foley had done that already."

Hope lifted the box in her sturdy arms. "He shoved it in a corner instead. Typical."

"Put it back there near the door. I'll make some calls and find out what we are supposed to do with it. Let's sit and talk for a bit."

Hope rolled her eyes and deposited the box by the back exit. They moved into the kitchen area, where Mr. Henry poured a cup of coffee for himself and added a generous amount of nondairy creamer.

Louise, Hope, and Sylvia took chairs around the folding table. Mr. Henry lowered himself into the last seat like someone in pain. "I have arthritis, back problems—all the old-man afflictions," he explained. "Not to mention the stomach. Can't drink coffee without all this whitener."

Sylvia arched an eyebrow. Louise nodded in agreement with her friend's unspoken message. Everything in the place was breaking down, even the employees.

Mr. Henry sipped his coffee. "I'm really happy you all are on board. Mr. Foley and I are getting old. We need some fresh blood in here. No offense, Hope."

"None taken, Mr. Henry. I ain't no spring chicken." Hope scraped back her chair and poured herself a cup of black coffee. "I just hope these city girls stick around for a while. Last new person we had up in here skedaddled after a few months. Guess small towns ain't for everyone."

Mr. Henry ignored Hope's comment. "There's a few things that need doing. A newsletter, like this one." He produced a Saint Jude Parish Library flyer from the pocket of his tweed sport coat. "Someone needs to do programs for the young adults—the teenagers, you know. Hope here is in charge of the younger children, but we've never done anything for the teenagers. Then, there's interlibrary loan, cataloging, and adult programming. I know the Saint Jude Parish Libraries do book clubs and computer classes. I think our patrons would really like those."

"Well, Mr. Henry, I would love to do your young adult stuff, if that's okay with Louise here," Sylvia said.

"Great," Louise said. Dealing with teenagers brought back too many memories of her own awkward, miserable high school experiences. Let Sylvia organize vampire games and read the *Divergent* books. "I can do computer classes, book clubs, and interlibrary loans."

"This is going to work great. I know it." Mr. Henry glanced up as Mr. Foley's office door opened. "I take it that y'all have met our director."

Mr. Foley stopped at the head of the table. "Mr. Henry, don't you and these young ladies need to get to work?"

"We were just getting acquainted." Mr. Henry got up, taking even more time than he'd needed to sit down, and washed out his coffee cup in the sink. Still moving like a man in pain, he walked out to the patron area.

Hope glared at Mr. Foley. He stared back at her for a moment before retreating to his office. When the door was closed behind him, Hope said, "I known that man all my life, but that don't mean I like his fat butt." She dragged two chairs over to the computer near the worktable. "Well, the party's over. Now I got to teach y'all the ropes."

* * *

An hour later, Louise's neck hurt from craning to see the computer screen around Sylvia's mass of red hair. Hope had taught them her cataloging method, which consisted of searching the Library of Congress Web site and copying their record. If the librarians at the nation's book depository hadn't yet classified the title, she tossed it back on the truck. It took willpower for Louise to resist pushing her out of the way and taking over. But she and Sylvia settled for shooting each other incredulous glances as Hope copied the records after giving them no more than a cursory glance.

Hope hit a button and a miniature dot matrix printer churned out the labels. She pulled the dust cover from the first book and stuck the label on the spine. Then, she rubbed the end of a heat gun over it, fixing the label in place.

"Did you ever think about leaving the dust covers on? Most public libraries do that now," Louise said.

Hope shrugged. "We always take 'em off. Reckon they'd just get messed up anyhow."

"You can cover them in plastic," Sylvia said.

"Why?"

"Because it looks nice."

Hope snorted and tossed the book onto the cart. "Y'all do the rest. I got paper flowers to make for the story time tomorrow." She went back to her cubicle.

Sylvia picked up one of the books that Hope had discarded and moved into her chair in front of the computer. She'd just started typing in the title when there was a loud crash from inside Mr. Foley's office. It sounded like someone breaking a hundred glass bottles all at the same time. Sylvia dropped the book and it fell to the floor. "What the hell was that?"

"Bikers having a bar fight?" Louise said.

The miniblinds on the director's office windows were completely closed. Now, judging from the noises, someone was throwing the furniture against the wall. Mr. Foley had apparently gone crazy and decided to trash his own office.

A moment later, the director ran out, slamming the door behind him. He'd lost his glasses, and his forehead was red and slick with sweat. He collapsed on the floor, clutching his chest. Louise's own heart began to race. She had put her life in peril. Who would take care of the kids? Their father? Doubtful. Sylvia would have been her first choice, but now they were both going to die. After the rush of panic subsided, she realized that her boss wasn't bleeding. In fact, he seemed terrified but unhurt.

"Deer," he said, his breath coming out in an old-man wheeze. "A deer in my office."

Louise felt a wave of relief. An animal in the library wasn't good, but it was better than crazy people with firearms. "What do we do?"

"I'll take care of it." Hope left through the back door.

Mr. Foley heaved himself up off the floor and lumbered into the employee bathroom.

Louise walked over to Mr. Foley's office. The miniblinds on the door had fallen down, probably when he slammed it shut. The window facing the street was shattered, and pieces of glass were scattered among the books and papers that littered the floor. After breaking through the window, the buck must have gotten confused, and now it couldn't figure out how to get out again. In the small, cluttered space, it ran in circles, tripping over its own legs, blood dripping from its side. The panic in the buck's eyes was haunting. As it whipped its head around frantically, its antlers caught the painting of flying ducks above the desk. The deer shook its head back and forth until the painting crashed down onto the desk.

"Poor thing," Lily said. "I'll call Wildlife and Fisheries."

"Hope told us she'd take care of it." Sylvia's voice sounded unsteady, as though she was trying not to cry.

"I'm just going to see if there's anyone in the patron area." Lily hurried through the door to circulation.

Hope returned with a rifle and a pair of orange plastic ear protectors. "All y'all get outside. That thing is dangerous. Is there anyone else in the library?"

"Mr. Foley's in the restroom," Louise said. "Lily went out to the patron area to see if there was anyone around."

Hope rolled her eyes and banged on the bathroom door. "Mr. Foley, you got to get out. I'm going to unleash some firepower here."

Mr. Foley emerged, water dripping from the tufts of hair around his ears. At the sight of Hope with the gun, his eyes widened. "You can't shoot it."

"You got a better idea?" Hope inclined her head toward the office, where the deer was butting its bloody head against the wall.

Mr. Foley waved his hands and disappeared out the back door. A moment later, a vehicle started and left the lot with a squeal of tires on asphalt.

Inside the office, the deer was still turning around and around with frantic energy. Hope watched with a frown, her eyes soft and sad.

Lily returned and tapped Hope on the shoulder. "All clear. I locked the front door."

"All y'all get out," Hope said, still focused on the deer. "I gotta open this office up and do this thing."

Sylvia, Louise, and Lily left through the back exit. A moment after the door swung shut, Louise heard the shot. She sat down hard on the curb.

CHAPTER 8

Sal stuffed the phone back in his pocket and surveyed the row of cabbages he'd been weeding. He wasn't surprised to get a call from his cousin. Hope always had some little job for him. Her own husband wasn't capable of hard labor anymore. Lewis had collected disability ever since a stint in the army left him with various health complaints. Sal suspected that some of the problems were mental. Lewis had hinted once that he'd seen things he wished he could forget during his tour in Afghanistan. His injuries were probably the reason that Lewis and Hope didn't have any children. Sal had never asked.

A herd of pint-size dogs followed Sal to his truck, and he gently shooed them away with his foot. He supposed he should make them go inside the trailer, but his parents had left him twenty acres and they wouldn't stray that far. Besides, the dogs were good at keeping rabbits and deer away from his crops. Not that Sal considered the Chihuahuas working dogs. Betta called them his furry children, and he had to admit that she was right. He was nearly forty and not yet married. He'd accepted that he wouldn't ever have any actual offspring. The thought made him feel even more alone than he'd been in Chicago. Returning to his hometown was his way of trying to ease the aching emptiness that seemed to grow every year. Being around Hope and Betta helped some, at least for a while. But lately, it wasn't enough.

He even found himself thinking about Chloe sometimes. She'd wanted a life he couldn't give her, though—charity balls, rich friends, and a mini-mansion by the golf course. By the time her parents finished planning the wedding, he'd already decided that he couldn't be a corporate lawyer anymore. Sure, he probably should have told her before he put in his letter of resignation. That wasn't fair; he saw that now. But the lines of communication were already breaking down at that point, and maybe he was scared or maybe just angry. He finally told her the night before the wedding, the absolute wrong time to break the news. So he wasn't completely surprised when she refused to walk down the aisle. Her parents were devastated. He felt terrible—but relieved at the same time.

As he leaned forward to start the pickup, his sweaty T-shirt clung to his back. He could have changed, but Hope would want him to bring the deer home and dress it. After a job like that, he'd need a shower anyway. He adjusted his John Deere cap, turned the truck around, and drove down the gravel driveway to the street. He knew who lived in most of the houses he passed on the way to the library. The town was changing, though. Sometimes the growth made him sad; land that used to be filled with trees was now broken up and mowed down for housing developments. The old school that he and Betta attended had served the whole parish—grades K through twelve. It had been replaced by three separate schools—elementary, middle, and high.

Sal turned onto Route 1 and headed toward the old downtown. At least that hadn't changed much. The Pig and the drugstore were the same, though both buildings had been expanded during a short-lived boom in the 1990s. When they were kids, he and Betta had ridden their bikes to the Icy Cone on sweltering summer days, peddling across asphalt hot enough to burn bare feet. She'd always ordered a cone covered in that weird hard chocolate that cracked when you bit into it. Sal preferred the plain vanilla.

The library had been built right at the time he'd discovered the pleasures of reading. Sal had loved the cold of the air-conditioning in summer and the Hardy Boys and Encyclopedia Brown books he checked out by the backpackful. Pulling into the parking lot, he realized that the place needed an update. He felt the same way about the whole town; he hated to see it change, but he understood that it was necessary. Towns grow or die. He didn't want Alligator Bayou to die. On the other hand, he didn't like the idea of it becoming a strip mall–infested suburb of Saint Jude.

Sal got out of the truck and walked up to the building. For some reason, the library had a picture window on the director's office. The glass had been shattered from the outside. He wasn't surprised that a deer could break through, but he wondered what had caused it to panic and crash through the glass. He'd seen frantic deer caught in fences and scared by headlights, but a buck breaking through a window was a new one on him. Through the hole, he thought he saw the animal lying in the mess of glass and books, but the darkness inside and the tint on the remaining window glass made it hard to tell.

He went in the front door of the library. Ms. Trudy was sitting on her usual chair by the periodical racks.

"Hey, Sal. I missed all the excitement because of my hair appointment. You heard about the deer?" The old lady set aside the celebrity magazine she'd been reading. Ms. Trudy's hair looked the same as it had as long as Sal could remember. She'd grayed early—a genetic condition and not the result of her job as a high school teacher—and it was always styled in wavy curls piled on top of her head. She wore pastel suits even after her retirement, along with nylons and thick-soled shoes.

"Yup. I'm here to pick it up. Hope called me."

Ms. Trudy had taught Hope, Betta, and Sal. She knew more about them than their own parents did. She never told about how they'd smoked together behind the school building and skipped classes to swim in the little bayou behind the old courthouse. But Sal knew she knew. Nothing got past Ms. Trudy.

"They got a couple of new girls back there," she said.

"Huh?" Sal took off his hat and attached it to his belt loop.

"Can't remember their names right now, but they just started today. Imagine that. City girls too."

Sal wasn't sure what Ms. Trudy was talking about. He hoped she wasn't beginning to lose her faculties. She'd always been sharp as a tack, to use an expression his late father had favored. "Okay, well, I'm gonna go see about that deer."

"I think the pretty redheaded one is married," Ms. Trudy said, picking up her magazine again.

Still confused, Sal pushed through the circulation half-door and walked into the back room. Hope occasionally asked him to fix a leaky faucet or a refrigerator coil, so he'd been in the employee area of the library before. Every time, the director's office had been closed, miniblinds covering every inch of the windows. But today, the door hung open and the sight made him uncomfortable.

"Took you long enough to get here." Hope walked up to him, hands on hips.

Beneath her bluster, his cousin was upset. She must have

shot the deer herself. Naturally, Hope would have a gun in her pickup truck.

"Let's get that deer out of here," Sal said.

She nodded and gestured to the open office door. The mess was as bad as Sal had imagined. The deer had knocked down the cheesy painting above Foley Hatfield's desk and leaked blood all over the books and papers on the floor. Glass crunched under Sal's work boots as he approached the carcass. Hope had done the job with one shot to the buck's head. Amazing, considering that the animal had clearly been flailing around frantically. It had to weigh at least two hundred pounds. Seeing the magnificent buck lifelessly lying among the junk of the office, Sal felt lonely emptiness again, like a hole in his gut.

Hope came up behind him, uncharacteristically silent. She grasped the back legs of the deer and Sal lifted the front. It was awkward, but he thought they'd make it to the truck. His cousin was the strongest woman he knew. She'd competed in shot put at the state level during high school. The sport suited Hope—slow and methodical. The grim line of her mouth as she held the deer reminded him of her father's funeral. She'd helped him carry the casket. Though her brother and cousins also served as pallbearers, Sal and Hope could have done the job alone. Sal's uncle had weighed less than half as much as the deer, his body eaten away by the cancer. He'd spent his last year of life on a fold-out bed in Hope's living room, quietly deteriorating into a living skeleton.

Sal backed out of the office. It was hard to keep the deer's antlers high enough off the ground not to snag on the carpet. He kept his eyes on the buck as they negotiated the cubicle area and headed for the back door.

Hope paused at one of the cubicles. "Hold the door, would you?"

Someone ran around them to the exit. Sal glanced up from the deer just long enough to see that it was a woman wearing a navy suit. Maybe she was one of the "girls" Ms. Trudy had mentioned. He backed toward the exit. The buck was like a huge sack of lead. Sal adjusted his grip on the furry legs and stepped out into the sunlight. By unspoken agreement, he and Hope turned so that he could walk forward, and they both quickened their pace to the truck. Lifting the deer, they slid it into the pickup bed. Sal shoved the legs farther in so he could close the back. Only then did he turn around and look at the librarian standing against the brick wall of the library.

"Hey, Louise," Hope said, dusting her hands on her pants legs. "This here's my cousin Sal."

Sal was too shocked to do anything but nod. He'd occasionally thought about Louise after seeing her in the library, but he'd never looked her up as Lily suggested. No reason to think a professor at A&M would be interested in dating a strawberry farmer. He started to run his hands through his hair, then remembered that they were filthy.

"This here's Louisiana Richardson, one of our new librarians," Hope said. "Reckon the cat got her tongue."

"I'd shake hands, but I better wash 'em first," Sal said. He gave Louise a half-smile. She smiled back and his heart gave a little jump.

The back door opened, and a tall, red-haired woman appeared. "Hey, y'all. Got the deer taken care of?"

"Yup. Sylvia. Our other city girl," Hope said.

The married one. So Ms. Trudy wasn't losing it. He disagreed with her judgment, though. Clearly, Louise was the prettier of the two. "Pleased to meet you both," Sal said. "I wouldn't say no to a cup of coffee if you've got some."

"Oh, absolutely," Sylvia said, nudging Louise as they went back inside.

"One cup," Hope said. "But then you best get back and dress that deer for me."

"I thought you were gonna do that," Sal said, ribbing his cousin reflexively. He headed straight to the kitchenette and squirted soap on his hands. He wanted to look at Louise, but he forced himself to focus on his hands instead.

Hope stomped in after him and leaned against the counter next to the coffeepot. "I got work to do here."

"Yeah, well, I got work to do on the farm." Sal grabbed a paper towel. "I'll just make me a cup of coffee and get out of your hair."

"No, you let me do that," Hope said, washing her own hands before filling the coffeepot with water and scooping a generous amount of grounds into the machine. "I ain't that busy. You dress that deer, I'll give you some sausage."

"All right, but only because you're my sweet little cousin." Sal sat at the table and stuck his legs out in front of him. "So what's a deer doing in the library? Checking out the new Stephen King?"

Sylvia sat down and gestured for Louise to take the chair nearest to Sal. She was close enough for him to touch. He deliberately folded his hands.

Hope switched on the Mr. Coffee. "Now, you know deer can't read. It was lookin' at the picture books."

"My cousin ought to do stand-up," Sal said. "So, the boss is gone."

"Took off," Hope said. "Didn't know the man could run that fast."

"Mr. Foley shook his chunky little butt, that's for sure," Sylvia said.

Louise laughed. Her shiny milk-chocolate-colored hair obscured her face, and he wanted to reach out and push it back behind her ear. She turned slightly, and her gaze met his for a moment.

Hope got up and fetched her cousin a cup of coffee. "Y'all want some?" Without waiting for a response, she poured two more mugs and put them in front of Louise and Sylvia.

"So, where y'all from?" Sal asked.

"I grew up in New Orleans. Went to St. Francis of Assisi. Louisiana's from Minnesota," Sylvia said. "Sorry, I always wanted to say that."

"How'd you end up named after our wonderful state?"

"My dad was from Lafayette and he always wanted to move back, but he had a job in Minnesota," Louise said, drinking some of her black coffee.

"Well, now he can visit you here."

"He's deceased. Anyway, my parents hated to fly. That's why we never came down here when I was a kid."

"I'm sorry about your father. Both my parents are gone now too." Sal gulped half his coffee. It was still hot and burned going down his throat. "So you are named after Louisiana, but you've never been here?"

"Not until I got the job at A&M."

"My cousin here pretends he's just a country boy, but he done worked as a lawyer in the frozen north," Hope said.

"Chicago," Sal said. "But I didn't like it much, so I came back here."

"Are you kidding? I love Chicago," Louise said. "If I could get a job there, I'd never leave."

"Reckon you might if you were a country boy working in corporate law," Sal said. "I never wanted to do that. It was all my dad's dream, God bless him. I wanted to be a strawberry farmer. Wish I'd gotten a horticultural degree 'cause all that JD's gonna do is collect dust."

"Education is never wasted," Sylvia said. "If nothing else, you might have always wondered what it was like. Now you know."

"Still wish I'd got that plant studies degree. Oh, well, at least I know how to dress Hope's deer. Thanks for the coffee." Sal took the cap from his belt loop and put it on. "Very nice meeting y'all."

Sal got in his truck and rested his hand on the gearshift. He should have asked why Louise was working at the library. Was it some kind of research for the university? Hope would tell him, of course, but he'd have to be careful. If she and Betta had any clue how interested he was in Louise, they'd make his life miserable. He turned the radio up loud. He felt nowhere near miserable now.

Chapter 9

Brendan leaned back in his leather armchair and scrolled on his smartphone until he found Louise's number. He'd made himself a scotch before calling her, and it rested in the convenient cup holder built into the arm of the chair. Julia had bought him the fancy recliner for his fortieth birthday. Her father was a retired CEO. Brendan wasn't sure what the company did, but the family had enough money to own a house in Rhode Island as well as a vacation condo in Seaside, Florida. Once he'd found out how wealthy they were—after he'd started dating Julia—he'd gently advised her against marrying him. Her money meant that Louise could argue for larger child support payments. Julia was a traditionalist, though, and she insisted on tying the knot anyway. She didn't seem to mind contributing to his children's welfare. Brendan guessed that was what it was like to always have had money. He wouldn't know. His own father was a history professor, and his mother picked up adjunct classes in the department whenever she could. She'd followed her husband to the University of Nebraska before finishing her PhD, leaving her doomed to a life of academic second-class citizenship. They hadn't been destitute, but his childhood was nothing like Julia's. She'd grown up with a nanny and a maid.

Brendan stared at Louise's number for a moment. She still had an Iowa area code, but it hardly mattered in these days of cell phones. New technology made Brendan feel old and obsolete. He hadn't even wanted the stupid phone, but Julia had talked him into it. She seemed to do everything with hers. He just used his as a phone. He put his finger on Louise's number.

"What do you want?" She sounded irritated, as usual. Another reason to hate cell phones. Louise knew he was on the other end, and she felt no obligation to be polite, even for a moment.

"Nice to talk to you too." Brendan sipped his scotch. "I got a job at Louisiana A&M."

"What?" There was a crash on Louise's end. It sounded like she'd dropped the phone.

Brendan felt a tiny prick of satisfaction. This was her fault for moving the kids halfway across the country. When he'd seen the job advertisement, he couldn't believe his luck. The chances that A&M would be hiring in his field were slim. After some nudging, they'd even agreed to pay him more than his current salary. During his on-campus visit, he'd restrained himself from calling Louise. He hadn't wanted to tell her anything until he had the job. "Julia and I are going to get married, and she wants to do it in New Orleans. Her family has never been there and they're excited about a big Southern extravaganza. They already booked some fancy hotel for the reception. I'm not arguing since they're paying for it. And we can look for houses in Saint Jude while we're there," he said.

"How did you get a job? There's a hiring freeze."

"The administration made an exception for designated flagship departments. English is hiring eight more lines."

Brendan wasn't surprised that Louise had been laid off from the library science school, something he'd found out only when she'd given him a new address to send the child support checks to. Library science was a useless field in his opinion. Certainly not an area that would qualify as a top priority for the university. He'd tried to talk her into a legitimate area of study—history or even English maybe. But she'd thought she was being practical. Big laugh on that.

"I can't believe it," Louise said.

"We'd like you to bring Max and Zoe to the wedding," Brendan said.

"They're too young. No."

"Louise, I'm their father and I'm getting married."

"So what? They don't understand that. They barely remember you."

"I know. That's why I applied for the job." As he got older, Brendan was beginning to regret not spending time with his children. You couldn't just waltz into a kid's life when he turned ten and expect him to want to go to model train shows with you. Little kids bored him, though. Thus far, he was a complete failure as a father. At least he could admit that.

"In case you didn't know, I lost my job. Besides, do you realize what it's like to travel with two little children by yourself? No, of course you don't. You've never done anything with them by yourself," Louise said.

"Why didn't you tell me you needed more money?"

"Because you hardly can be bothered to send the child support we already agreed on."

"I get paid once a month. I have to wait for the direct deposit to go through every time. I can send more if you need it." Brendan rattled the ice in his glass. Was he supposed to be thrilled about sending money to his ex-wife? Writing the check was like an admission of defeat. The marriage had failed, and now he had to interact with his children through dollars only. Well, that was about to change. For better or worse.

"That doesn't explain it being three weeks late."

Brendan sighed and got up to pour more scotch. "I'll send you some money for the tux and the dress. Do you think two hundred will cover it?"

"I have no idea. I've never rented a tux for a three-year-old."

"I'll make out the check for four hundred. Get yourself something nice to wear," he said. "Look, do me a favor, though. Don't apply for academic jobs. I don't want you moving out of state again."

"I'll do whatever I want. You can't push me around anymore, Brendan."

Brendan poked the button on the fridge, and ice cubes clattered into his glass. "I didn't mean it that way. I just want to be around the kids. Is that too much to ask? We'll support you. Julia's family has money."

Louise snorted. "Good for her."

Brendan gave up. The job market was terrible anyway, and only a few universities had library science programs anymore. He didn't need to worry. He measured some more scotch into the glass and went back to his leather chair. "When the wedding details are worked out, I'll send you an e-mail. And keep your eye out for houses near campus with swimming pools."

"Whatever." Louise disconnected.

CHAPTER 10

When Louise and Sylvia arrived at work the next morning, a Ford station wagon was parked at a crooked angle directly in front of the library. A white-haired woman wearing a polyester pantsuit stood by the door, a bag of books on the ground by her feet. "Good morning, ladies!"

"Hi, Ms. Trudy. Are you early, or are we late again?" Sylvia picked up the bag and unlocked the library door.

"Oh, no, honey, you're not late. I don't sleep so well anymore, you know. I wake up at five and nothing's open 'cept that Walmart off Fifty-one. I will go there and sit, but I have to tell you, their coffee's not very good."

"Come on, we'll fix you a cup," Sylvia said.

Inside, Louise headed straight for her desk while Sylvia started a pot of coffee. They had fallen into the habit of arriving at work before everyone else. Sylvia said she didn't like to deal with anyone except Louise before her second dose of caffeine. She made an exception for Ms. Trudy. Louise liked the old lady too. She knew everyone in the parish and was full of stories about who was having babies, getting married, dying, or moving into a nursing home. Louise's own mother was shy, staying in her own little world of housework and low-key volunteering. In contrast, Ms. Trudy never seemed to be at home. She told Louise that her husband had passed away a few years previously and since then she had tried to stay busy all the time. When she wasn't in the library, she served as a volunteer "grandmother" at the elementary school, took art classes, and worked at the food bank.

Ms. Trudy sat in her usual chair near the periodical rack and perused *People* magazine. When the coffee was ready, Louise brought her a mug. "Don't let Mr. Foley see you with that. He'll be coming in any minute."

"Honey, I taught your Mr. Foley in high school. Never gave me any trouble."

"Really? Well, he hasn't changed much, I guess," Louise deadpanned.

Ms. Trudy sipped her coffee. "Once he realizes who's boss, he's as nice as pie. You just remember that, honey."

"I'll try." Louise had a hard time imagining Mr. Foley being nice. During her first month of working at the library, he'd only left his office to complain about the noise the employees—especially Sylvia and Louise—were making or to go to Anthony's for lunch. Louise's nerves stayed on edge whenever he was in the building. Luckily, he came in late and left early.

"Come on, now. That kind of attitude isn't going to help you one bit. I've been living in this town a long time and I can tell you, the old guard here's going to swear up and down that nothing can change. Claim they don't have the money or the support of the community. Don't you believe it. Mrs. Gunderson and her cronies been threatening to shut down this library for years. You stay here, you'll be fighting Mr. Foley's inertia and her antagonism, but there's plenty who will support you."

"Who's Mrs. Gunderson?"

"You don't know? You'll find out soon enough, honey. She's just a police jury member, but she's angling for to be the next mayor. She hates the library because Hope's cousin Beatrice ran against her in the last election. Nearly won too. Mr. Henry and his family supported Beatrice and she'll never forgive them. She aims to shut down the whole system. She did manage to stop the last library tax from passing."

"What's a police jury?"

"It's like a city council, but for the parish. You do know what a parish is?" Ms. Trudy gazed at Louise over her coffee cup.

"The Louisiana version of a county. I know that much."

"Well, the police jury are basically your bosses. Mr. Foley's too."

"Wow, small-town politics."

"You got that right. But I'm telling you, don't let them intimidate you. Stand up to them."

"I will." When they were first married, Louise had always let Brendan have his way—sitting through movies she didn't want to see, eating food she didn't really like just to please him. Until she had Max. The children made her stronger because she had to be, for them. No one else was going to ask the cashier at the fast-food restaurant to swap out the toy they didn't like or tell the nursery worker that they wanted to watch Elmo rather than Thomas the Tank Engine. Louise's shyness had been put away by necessity. She would have to summon some of that courage to deal with her boss and the political forces in Alligator Bayou.

Louise left Ms. Trudy to her celebrity magazines and went back to her cubicle. A few minutes later, the back door of the library banged against the wall. Louise got up to see who was already in such a bad mood. Nobody's morning could have been worse than her own. Max had refused to put on his shoes, throwing them across the room and nearly hitting Zoe. Then, he'd grabbed Louise's shirt repeatedly while she was trying to dress the girl. Finally, the shirt ripped and she pushed him out the door barefoot. In the car, he'd turned into a sweet boy again, allowing her to put his shoes on and promising to be good. Just another exhausting day with a three-year-old.

The door slammer was Hope. She stomped into her cubicle and tossed her purse on the desk. "That darn Hilda. I swear I'm gonna beat her behind from now till Sunday."

Sylvia stood, stretched, and went to get her third cup of coffee. "What now, girl?"

"She done put more of them tires in my yard. Where one woman gets so many bald old tires, I'll never know."

"This is your neighbor?" Louise thought she'd heard about Hilda before, but Hope talked about everyone in the parish and sometimes it was hard to keep track. Louise looked forward to her stories like the latest installments of a soap opera.

"Next door. Crazy witch parks her truck close as she can get to my property. Darn thing blocks the sun to my kidney bean patch. Now, she's taken to dumping tires in my yard."

"What are you going to do?" Sylvia asked, returning to her cubicle with her Santa Claus coffee mug.

"I done rolled them right over to the bank parking lot on the other side, like I always do. They'll toss 'em somewhere. No sense putting them back in the old bat's yard. She'll just stick them in my flowers tomorrow."

Louise smiled as she applied a label to another book. The week before, Hope had told them about her third cousin who climbed through the parish jail window to visit a friend. "You gotta be one dumb nut to get arrested for breaking *into* jail," Hope had observed, shaking her head.

Louise got up for another cup of coffee. As she was

returning to her cubicle, Mr. Foley shuffled in, grunting a greeting before disappearing into his office and pulling the miniblinds closed. Sylvia had taken to calling his office "the Man Cave."

"Do you think he looks at porn in there?" Sylvia said, poking her head above her cubicle to grin at Louise.

"I don't want to know."

"Nah, he stays mostly on breeding and gambling sites." Matt slouched up to Louise's cubicle, wearing a rare smile. The skinny computer tech spent most of his time huddled over his keyboard or troubleshooting at the other branches. Hope said he had two young children, which was hard to believe since he looked like he wasn't old enough to drink. Despite the braided belt he wore, his pants always seemed like they might slide down his narrow hips.

"Come on," Sylvia said. "You can't just dangle that out there and then let it drop. You mean he trolls for prostitutes or something?"

"No!" Matt waved his hands in a warding-off gesture. "Goat breeding. He raises goats and dogs. Shows them too."

"What is a goat breeder doing running a library system?" Sylvia came out of her cube and stood, hand on hip, waiting for a response.

Matt looked away. Sometimes, Louise wanted to remind Sylvia that she was gorgeous. Not that it would do any good. Even if she stopped putting on makeup and started wearing sack dresses, men would still stare.

Matt focused on the corner of Sylvia's cubicle. "I don't know. I think he was a school librarian for a while. Anyway, he posts pictures of his goats and chats with other breeders. I showed him how to reset his cookies and history, though. I really don't want to know what he looks at."

"So no weird secret hobbies?" Sylvia leaned against Louise's cubicle, crossing one long leg in front of the other.

"I hope not." Matt met her eyes for a moment before dropping his gaze again.

The back door opened, letting in a beam of sunlight that illuminated the dust hanging in the air. Mr. Henry came in, holding a travel mug. Matt mumbled a greeting to the assistant director before retreating into his cube.

"Good morning, ladies," Mr. Henry said, stopping in front of Sylvia's cubicle.

"Mr. Henry, I wanted to ask you something," Sylvia said. "Why doesn't the library system have any DVDs, CDs, or e-books?"

The assistant director took a sip from his mug before answering. "Mr. Foley thinks that libraries should be about books. It took a lot of doing to get him to order books on tape even."

"This is the only library I've been to that doesn't have any multimedia stuff at all. I think it would increase our circulation," Louise said.

Mr. Henry lifted his mug to his lips again. "You can ask him if he'd be willing to order some. He does all the buying, you know."

"We will definitely bring it up." Sylvia sat down and began typing, bracelets clanking against the keyboard.

Mr. Henry walked slowly to his cubicle in the patron area. Louise wondered what exactly he did out there. He'd mentioned coordinating the other three branches, each of which had two or three employees. Like Matt, he often traveled between the locations. It was hard to imagine him standing up to the nasty-sounding Mrs. Gunderson, but maybe he'd had more fire in his younger days. He'd visibly declined even during the short time Louise had known him.

In contrast to Ms. Trudy, he seemed to be giving up on himself. Ms. Trudy was probably twenty years older than him, but she wouldn't stop until her body forced her to.

Louise took another pulpy thriller from her book cart and typed in the title. During her library science classes, she had learned all the codes and fields that needed to be included for each item. But most libraries simply copied the records that the Library of Congress generated or, barring that, some other authoritative library. She searched through the extant records on the book. As far as she could tell, it was about an attack on Fort Knox by a group of greedy terrorists. The Library of Congress hadn't processed the book yet, but in the meantime, they could use the one from the Saint Jude Parish Library system. As she read the record, she heard Sylvia walking by in her stiletto heels.

The Saint Jude Parish librarian had done a decent enough job with the thriller, so Louise copied the record. She was examining the book again to make sure that everything was correct when she heard a high-pitched shriek. The scream sounded like Sylvia. Louise was afraid to stand up. She didn't know if she'd find another wild animal, a crazy person with a gun, or one of Hope's neighbors.

She pushed her chair back and ventured out of the cubicle. Mr. Foley was standing, hands on hips, shaking his head at Sylvia. She was holding the Santa Claus mug, but most of the coffee appeared to be on her white shirt.

"Don't know what she was doing. Ran right into me." Mr. Foley shook his head one more time and went back into his office, closing the door.

Sylvia blinked back tears and wiped her eyes with her sleeve. Her shirt was soaked through to her lacy beige bra. "I turned around, and he was right there behind me. I don't know what happened."

"Let's go to my cube. I have an extra sweater you can wear," Louise said.

Sylvia flopped down in Louise's chair. Louise had never seen her so discomposed. Sylvia's fits of drama were always partly for show. But this time, she was really crying. Not knowing what else to do, Louise reached into her drawer for the sweater.

"He didn't even ask if I was okay. That coffee could have been hot. I'm just lucky it had been sitting around for an hour." Sylvia took a tissue from the box on Louise's desk and blew her nose. "I hate him. Hate. Hate."

"He's a goat-obsessed weirdo with a Napoleon complex. He's not worth the effort to hate." Louise held out the cardigan.

Sylvia removed her shirt and put on the sweater. It was too tight across the chest. "How did we end up with the strangest boss in the whole state of Louisiana?"

"I don't know, but I'm confident that we can deal with Napoleon Junior. He can't be any more of a challenge than our kids, right?"

Sylvia laughed. "I am going to force him to buy some DVDs if I have to go all the way to the police jury to do it."

"That might not be such a good idea." Louise told her about Mrs. Gunderson.

"Lord, girl. What have I gotten us into?"

"I don't know, but it's sure not going to be boring."

No matter what she did, the numbers on Louise's smartphone calculator wouldn't add up. Well, that wasn't exactly true. They added up to something; she just didn't like it. The numbers were telling her to sell the house.

"Mommy?" Max wandered out of his room wearing a pair of dog-patterned pajamas that hugged his slender body. "I need a snack."

"Go back to bed," Louise said automatically.

"I'm hungry."

"Oh, all right. Come sit at the table. Do you want a bowl of Cheerios?"

Max nodded and climbed onto his chair. Louise poured a bowl of cereal and sat down next to him. "Would you like to move to a new house?"

"No."

"Me neither. But we'll make sure we get one with a swing set."

"And a slide?"

"Yup."

"Okay." Max ate the rest of his cereal in silence while Louise tried to put the situation in perspective. She had two great kids, a decent job. It was going to be okay. The house was only a thing. An eminently replaceable thing. When she was a child, her father used that phrase every time something broke or got lost. *It's just a thing.*

"Come on, Max. I'll read you a story," she said, putting the empty bowl in the sink and heading to his bedroom.

"Okay. Read about the bunny with the box." Max padded back to his room, yawning.

Louise found the book and sat on the bed next to him. He pulled the covers up to his chest and tucked his teddy bear under his arm. By the time she was finished reading, he'd fallen asleep. She kissed his forehead and went back into the living room to e-mail the real estate agent.

CHAPTER 11

Louise stared at the duck painting over her boss's desk and thought about the buck taking its last breaths in the cluttered, stale-microwave-dinner-scented room. She clenched her hands into fists.

After the incident with the deer, Mr. Foley had managed to re-create his office clutter quickly. The floor was covered with new titles waiting to be cataloged, old books that needed to be discarded, and stacks of books on tape. Bookshelves lined the walls, stuffed to overflowing. Louise's feet were just inches from a dusty pile of file folders. Sylvia stood two stacks over, her stilettos grazing the edge of a collection of 1970s-era encyclopedias. They couldn't sit down because all of the chairs were occupied by folders, books, junk mail, and loose papers.

Mr. Foley hadn't offered to clear off seats for them. His attitude was so unwelcoming that he might as well have hung a "Closed for Business" sign over his door. Sylvia shoved the encyclopedias with her foot and stared down at the director. "People work from nine to five weekdays," she said. "They can't come to the library during those hours."

"Not everyone," Mr. Foley said. He glanced at the computer screen and clicked the mouse, possibly checking the date of the next goat-breeding conference. "And they can come during their lunch breaks."

"A lot of people work in Saint Jude. It's not like they can just skip lunch and pop in," Louise said.

"We're not asking you to pay us more," Sylvia said. "Whoever is working that night will come in a little later in the morning. And we can take turns so it's fair. Some of the staff might like having different hours once in a while. On Saturdays, just two staff members will be needed to work and we can do with two fewer workers on Fridays, which are pretty slow anyway. It won't cost any more money except for a slight increase in utilities for opening the library a few more hours."

"We've always been open eight to five just on weekdays and no one has complained," Mr. Foley said.

Louise almost rolled her eyes. As though anyone would be brave enough to make a suggestion to the sharp-tongued library director. Not to mention the fact that he stayed in his office all day, avoiding almost all exposure to the public. Louise had not yet solved the puzzle of how Mr. Foley had become head of the library system. He seemed to loathe the job, the employees, and the patrons. She was pretty sure he didn't even read books.

"But we've started offering computer classes at night. Matt has to stay late for those. Why not leave the library open?" Sylvia persisted.

Mr. Foley answered with a dismissive snort. "I have to get back to work."

Sylvia gave the encyclopedias another kick, and the top one slid off the stack. "We also need to talk about the collection."

"What about it?"

"This has to be the only library in the twenty-first century that has no multimedia materials. Not to mention artwork, graphic novels. We don't even have board books for the toddlers."

"Libraries are for books. Now, if y'all are finished, I have work to do."

"No," Sylvia said. "You need to understand something. This library is dying. The last time the citizens of this parish were asked to raise the millage rate for the library system, they voted against it. If that happens in this next election, you will barely be able to make the light bill. You certainly won't be able to pay your employees' salaries. If you don't do some simple things like buy materials people want to check out and offer hours that fit with their schedules, they will decide they don't need us around anymore."

Mr. Foley took off his glasses and polished them on his shirt. "In case you haven't heard, there's something called Netflix."

"There is also something called Barnes and Noble. We are here to provide materials for people who can't afford them. We will also provide educational and entertainment programming that they wouldn't otherwise have available to them. If you don't agree that this is the mission of the library, I'll resign right now and get a job at Walmart. Because I can't work like this."

"Don't quit. Fine. You can stay open later hours as long as you coordinate everyone's schedules. I have enough to do without worrying about that. I will think about your idea about the multimedia materials."

"It's a deal," Louise said, taking Sylvia's arm and leading her out before she could argue any more.

Hope put her hands on her hips. "Oh, no, you don't."

"Come on," Sylvia said. "It's just one day a week. You

come in at noon and leave at nine. And each staff member works one Saturday a month. We keep track of circulation, and if we don't get more business, we'll go back to the old hours. Besides, Louise and I will provide dinner for the first week."

"We will?" Louise knew "we" meant her since Sylvia could barely make scrambled eggs.

"Sure, you know, just sandwiches. Stuff like that."

"Oh, no, you gotta have gumbo to get me to stay." Now, Hope smiled.

"I hear you make a mean chicken and dumplings, but I won't believe it until I see it," Louise said.

"You know that won't work. I ain't gonna make my chicken and dumplings for you just for that. You gotta do something special to earn my chicken and dumplings."

"It was worth a try," Louise said. "I'll make gumbo then. I might be a Yankee, but I can cook."

"I'll believe *that* when I see it." Hope sauntered back toward her cubicle. She stopped at Sylvia's desk and picked up one of the titles waiting to be cataloged.

Unlike Louise, Sylvia didn't seem to miss academia. She claimed that after so much dry prose, reading novels about vampires and dark teenage secrets was a vacation. The paperback Hope selected from Sylvia's pile featured a pair of bright red lips and a crimson drop of blood. "Garbage," she said, thumping the book back on top of the stack. "I hear you're encouraging the teens to read this filth."

"I started a teen book club," Sylvia said. "I'm also going to the high school and junior high and giving book talks. I try to balance it between the junk they want to read and the serious stuff. But you'd be surprised. Some of the ones with the racy covers are actually pretty good."

Hope snorted. "People ain't gonna like it."

"That I'm trying to get kids to read instead of watch TV and play video games?"

"If they're reading this crap, they may as well watch TV."

"Hope, I just told you—"

"All's I know is some of this here is banned from the school libraries around these parts."

"If anyone complains, let me know," Sylvia said.

"I surely will." Hope went to her desk and started cutting out paper flowers for the children's program.

After work, Louise sat in the van with Sylvia and studied the real estate listings her agent had sent. "Are you sure you don't mind going to see a couple of houses?"

"I mind you moving," Sylvia said. "I don't mind helping you look for a house. Are you sure you want to do this?"

"I don't. But I have to." Louise started the van. "When I bought the house in Saint Jude, I didn't expect to lose my job. I mean, we're making just over half what we got at A&M. Brendan said he'd give me more money, but I can't take it, or if I do I'll put it in a college fund for the kids. I hate being dependent on him."

Sylvia ran her hand through her hair, one of her signature nervous gestures. "Yeah. We're running the well dry too. But I'm really hoping Jake will find another job soon."

"I don't want to leave the state right now," Louise said. "And Brendan would kill me anyway, since he's going to be moving here in a couple of months. I have no choice."

"You're not buying out here just to avoid him, I hope," Sylvia said.

The thought had occurred to her. The more distance between herself and her ex, the better. Aside from Brendan and Julia, though, there was no reason for her to live in

Saint Jude anymore. Her job was in Alligator Bayou. "No. I'll save a lot of money without the commute. And houses are way cheaper out here."

"Okay. Turn here. We're coming up on the first one."

Louise slowed and took a right down a newly paved street. Mailboxes lined the road, but the houses were set back so far that they were barely visible through the trees. The spacious front yards had porch swings hanging from massive live oaks. Louise imagined the kids playing in the shade while she sat in a rocking chair on a porch. Her new house might be even better than the one in Saint Jude. Highly unlikely since her budget was cut in half this time.

"This one," Sylvia said.

The street dead-ended into a fenced-off strand of trees. The house Sylvia had pointed out was the last visible one on the block. The front yard was overgrown with scraggly grass and randomly placed trees. Louise drove halfway up the unpaved driveway to get a better look. The tiny bungalow had wood siding and concrete blocks underneath for a foundation. There was a porch, but it was barely large enough for a rocking chair. Not a model of luxurious rural living. The house made her think of Adwell again. If he knew she was actually relocating to Alligator Bayou, he would conclude that she'd lost her mind.

Louise read the real estate listing. "It's in my price range, at least." She opened the door, stepped out, and sank into mud up to her ankles. "Sylvia! Stay in the car." Abandoning her shoes to the sinkhole, she slogged to the passenger side of the van.

"What?" Sylvia was preparing to place her tan three-inch platform heel on the ground. Then, she saw that Louise was standing in mud. "I didn't bring my Cajun Reeboks. You'll have to check out this place on your own."

Louise retrieved her muddy shoes and tossed them in the

back of the van. She sat down on the edge of the cargo area and stripped off her nylons. She was rolling them into a ball and searching the back of the van for a plastic bag when she saw a man walking down a long driveway at the dead end of the street.

Chapter 12

A woman was sitting in the back of a van parked in front of Trey's old place. Sal couldn't tell what she was doing, but when she jumped down, her legs and feet were bare under her knee-length skirt. He felt a little jolt of electricity when he recognized Louise. He'd meant to stop by the library, but strawberry season was approaching and he'd been busy lining up workers. In fact, it was nearly five o'clock and he was just finding time to pick up the mail from his box.

At the sight of Louise, he completely forgot why he'd hiked down the gravel driveway. Her hair was loose and floated around her shoulders when she shook her head. She hugged her maroon suit jacket around her as though she was chilly. He wondered why she wasn't wearing a proper jacket. February was one of the only cold months in Louisiana. He had a thick flannel jacket on; if she wanted it, he'd give it to her. Hell, he'd give her his shirt too, if she needed it. He stepped onto the driveway, and his work boots disappeared up to the laces. "Deep mud here."

"So I found out." Louise's shapely legs were flecked with mud. She reached up and closed the back door of the van. The movement lifted her skirt slightly.

Sal caught his breath with difficulty. "Yeah, you could do with some boots. A jacket too. Are you cold?"

She turned back around and laughed, a beautiful sound. "No, I'm from Minnesota. This would be shorts-wearing weather there."

Sal felt warm himself. He unzipped his jacket. "You thinking about buying this place?"

"I guess so. It's in my price range."

"Probably needs a lot of work. Old Trey owned it, but he let his cousin live in it for a while. He wasn't much to speak of, and I imagine he didn't keep it up too well. Sure let the driveway go, as you can see."

"I might as well take a look since I already sacrificed my shoes to the cause," Louise said.

"I'll come with you."

They walked up to the house together. She seemed surprisingly comfortable in bare feet, especially since the mud had to be freezing. Concrete pillars raised the house three feet off the ground. It was painted blue with white trim. Trey's cousin and his three rowdy teenage boys hadn't bothered to mow the lawn, let alone clean. They'd neglected the place so much that when the old man wanted to sell it, he'd had to hire a team of cleaners to scrub the walls, the carpet, everything. In fact, Trey should have replaced the carpet, but he probably hadn't. The old man's days of doing things like that himself were long gone, and he was too cheap to pay anyone competent to fix up the place. He'd hired his brother Jack, who was younger and spryer than him but not by much.

Louise stepped onto the forest green porch, her muddy feet leaving brown prints.

Sal followed, forcing himself to look at the house instead of her legs. "It's small and Trey did a lousy job painting it, but overall I think it's a well-built house. Fifty years old at least," he said. "Siding looks good. You'll have to get an inspector to check underneath for termite damage. Windows aren't great, but the caulking isn't bad."

He cupped his hands around his face and looked in the window. Just as he'd thought, Jack hadn't replaced the carpet. It was unraveling in places. He could just see into the kitchen, which was equipped with a harvest-gold refrigerator and stove that had to be at least thirty years old. The linoleum was peeling up from the floor, and a huge air conditioning unit was visible in the far window.

"Do you live around here?" Louise asked, moving her face close to the glass to see inside.

"That's my place next door at the end of the street. You can't see it from the road, but I've got a few acres back there and a mobile home I live in. I was getting the mail when I saw your van out here. Doesn't look bad inside there. Carpet's a mess and the kitchen's out of date, but I could help you retile it, if you want."

"No central A/C."

"Yeah. It has heat, though, which means there's already some ductwork. So, central air would be expensive, but not prohibitive."

"Two bedrooms?"

"Two upstairs would be my guess. Though I believe this room over here is a parlor that could be made into a third one." He walked over to the window on the other side of the green door. "Here, see what you think."

Louise peered inside. Sal couldn't read her expression. He desperately wanted her to like the place. He was already imagining driving his tractor over to mow her lawn and staying for dinner. He had to get a grip and stop daydreaming.

"I'd better get back. Sylvia's waiting in the car," she said.

"Didn't want to ruin her nice shoes, huh?"

"I was going to suggest that she take them off and join me, but she's not the slogging-through-mud type."

"And you are?" Sal raised his eyebrows in mock surprise.

She smiled. "If the situation calls for it."

He climbed down the porch stairs and held his hand out to help her. He felt the electricity again when she touched him and he didn't want to let go. Her hand felt soft and cool. Feminine. It had been a long time since he'd felt this way about someone.

"Let me know what you decide," he said as they walked back down the driveway. "You know where to find me."

"I will." Louise used the running board to scrape some of the mud off her feet and got in the van.

Sal went back to his mailbox and watched her drive away. He wanted to break into the house and replace the carpet, just to convince her to move in.

CHAPTER 13

The next afternoon, Louise's brain was going numb from cataloging when she got an e-mail alert. Eager for any kind of break from the tedium, she clicked over to her mail program.

> Dear staff,
> Due to the recent coffee spill incident, I have decided that all food and beverages must remain in the kitchen area. We cannot risk any damage to library materials. Thank you for your consideration.
> Director Foley Hatfield

Louise stood up. "Did you guys see the latest inane e-mail from our esteemed leader?"

Sylvia set down the teen werewolf novel she was cataloging. "No, what is it now?"

"He says we can't eat or drink anything except in the kitchenette."

Hope's chair squeaked, and a second later she was in Louise's cube. "Oh, no, he doesn't," she said, reading the e-mail over Louise's shoulder.

"You could actually look at it on your own computer," Louise said. "He sent it to everyone."

Hope didn't bother to respond. "This man done pushed me too far. You all come with me. This is your fault."

"How you figure?" Sylvia asked.

"You all shook things up is what. I won't say I like Mr. Foley, but we had a peace agreement until y'all arrived. Now, he's got some crazy bug up his butt. So y'all gotta help me fix this." She stomped toward Mr. Foley's office.

Sylvia pushed her cart of books out of the way and followed with Louise trailing behind. Mr. Foley came out of the employee bathroom behind the kitchen, and Hope stopped in front of him, blocking the way back to his office.

"What's wrong with you?" Hope demanded to know.

"I have no idea what you're talking about." Mr. Foley moved to the side as if to walk around Hope, but Sylvia stepped up next to her.

"Let's start with the e-mail we all just received," Sylvia said.

"I thought I explained myself pretty well. We need to keep food and beverages away from library materials."

"Mr. Foley, I done worked here with you for ten years and you never ate lunch anywhere except your desk," Hope said.

"What I do is none of your concern."

"You listen to me. I know you ain't happy about these city girls up in here. But you done hired them and you can't be taking it out on us this way. If I gotta set in the kitchen area every time I want a cup of coffee, no work's gonna get done. And you know that."

Mr. Foley pushed his glasses up farther on his bulbous nose. "Well, I suppose you'll have to drink less coffee, then."

"Then, I suppose you're gonna have to find yourself

another children's librarian." Hope reached for the coffeepot, poured herself a cup, and headed back to her cubicle.

Lily came through the open door from circulation. She hesitated at the sight of Mr. Foley standing near the kitchen with his hands balled into fists at his side. "Um, Mrs. Gunderson is here to see you."

Mr. Foley brushed past her without a word.

Lily motioned to Louise and Sylvia. "Come out here for a second. You need to see who the real boss is."

They walked through the door to circulation just in time to hear Mr. Foley welcome the police juror. "Mrs. Gunderson! It's so good to see you."

"What just happened?" Sylvia whispered. "I've never seen Mr. Foley smile. Never."

"Shhh." Louise couldn't believe it either. Not only was Mr. Foley grinning like an ape, but his voice had ascended an octave. The effusive performance was painful and comical at the same time.

"What brings you to our humble establishment?" Mr. Foley asked.

Mrs. Gunderson was a matronly woman with curly gray hair. She wore a straight, knee-length skirt and a stiff, coat-like shirt that had silver-dollar-size buttons down the front. "I heard you were extending your hours."

"Yes." Mr. Foley wrung his hands together. "We felt that our patrons would appreciate more opportunities to visit the library during times when they might be off work."

"Well, I'm in favor of it, so long as it's not too expensive. Y'all have a tight budget right now, just remember. Mr. Henry has informed me that he is planning to try to put a library tax on the next ballot. As you know, I oppose any tax increases. Government is the problem, not the solution. The last thing it needs is more of people's hard-earned dollars."

"Yes, ma'am. My new librarians, Louise and Sylvia, are changing their hours to fit the new schedule. I assure you that the extra cost will be minimal."

"You also need to keep track of your circulation. I would expect an increase from such a move, and if you don't get one, then you ought to consider returning to your previous hours of operation."

"Yes, ma'am."

"Perhaps, you should also consider ordering some multimedia materials and look into this e-book thing. Pointe Coupee library just started offering books for Kindle and so on and I hear it's popular." She made a point of looking around the nearly deserted library.

"Yes, ma'am."

Sylvia stepped through the door to circulation. "Mrs. Gunderson, I'm Sylvia Jones and this is Louise Richardson. We would like to personally invite you to our first night of extended hours Monday. We will be serving refreshments."

"Pleased to meet you. I'm afraid I can't make it, but you will be careful about food around the library materials, won't you?"

Chapter 14

Sal stood under the showerhead and let the hot water pelt his body. He'd been planting strawberries all day with his workers, and his whole body ached. There seemed to be dirt in every crevice of his skin. He scrubbed his hands again with the loofah thing that Betta had given him. Stepping out of the shower stall, he dried off with a threadbare towel and wrapped it around his waist.

His bedroom wasn't even as large as the bathroom in his Chicago apartment had been, but he didn't care. When he was in his twenties, he'd craved the big-city life. Walking down the streets in Chicago, he'd felt the excitement through the concrete. There was so much going on, all the time. He'd loved being able to leave his spacious apartment in Evanston, walk to the train, and ride into the city. He ate food he'd never tried, listened to music late at night in bars with creaky wooden floors, and spent hours in the art museums. He'd dated a few women, but they all seemed to want something he didn't—a fast life that he was already outgrowing. Eventually, it stopped being fun. Especially after the one woman he'd actually started to care about decided that she didn't want to spend her life with him. He was lonely, and time was passing. His parents died suddenly, and he came back home to Alligator Bayou.

Sal bought the trailer from a distant cousin whose mother had lived in it until she passed away at age ninety-two. He'd purchased the bed for himself, but the dresser had belonged to his father along with the pine nightstand and even some of the cuff links inside the drawer. Sal's father hadn't wanted him to quit. He'd been proud to tell his friends that his son was a big-city lawyer showing those Yankees a thing or two. Sal wished he hadn't let his worries about disappointing his father keep him away so long. Moving back to Alligator Bayou was like slipping into a cool stream on a hot day. It felt good and right.

He opened the dresser drawer and inhaled the scent of the wood that still reminded him of his father. He wanted to see Louise again, and the "Opening Night" party seemed like as good a time as any. Maybe she'd be too busy to talk to him, but he had to try. Besides, he was hungry and he'd run out of bread after feeding the workers ham sandwiches for lunch. Betta would have made him dinner, but she spent Monday nights with a group of women she'd known since elementary school. She called it the Old Maid Club, though most of them were married. Not Betta, of course.

He selected a clean pair of jeans and some boxers. A T-shirt should be fine. He didn't want to be overdressed. His clothes fit into two categories—old lawyer stuff and farm casual. He never touched the fancy clothes anymore if he could avoid it.

As five o'clock approached, Louise stared out the library's front door at the nearly empty parking lot. Sylvia straightened the napkins on the food table and arranged the drinks in the cooler for the third time.

Louise lifted the lid of the Crock-Pot and stirred the

fragrant stew. There were four more pots on the worktable in back. She'd borrowed slow cookers from everyone she could find to keep the gumbo warm. Even Hope had reluctantly contributed her prized four-quart model. She'd also allowed Louise to use her three-gallon crawfish pot to cook in, since Crock-Pots were no good for browning vegetables or reducing stock. Hope had looked surprised when she tasted the finished product. Clearly, she hadn't expected the Yankee girl to pull it off.

But no one was coming to eat it. Flashback to the time she'd planned a birthday party for herself in junior high. Only her best friend, an equally geeky girl with a passion for knitting, had shown up. They'd ended up spending the afternoon playing cards together and eating most of the cake themselves. During those awkward teenage years, Louise's mother always told her to make more friends. As if she could just call the popular kids and invite herself over.

"No one shows up on time for parties in the South," Sylvia said, slamming the top down on the cooler.

Though her tone was breezy, the way she squinted toward the door as she said it gave her away. Sylvia was as nervous as Louise. They'd put themselves and their jobs on the line for these new hours. It was the first big change they'd talked Mr. Foley into implementing. If they failed, they might never be able to convince him to try anything else. This was much more important than a junior high birthday party.

"Someone's coming!" Sylvia grabbed Louise's arm. She squeezed hard enough to leave a bruise before trotting to the door.

She swung it open and four teenage girls came in, giggling and talking. The sound filled Louise with relief. Directly behind them were two elderly women dressed in pastel colors. Louise couldn't remember their names, but she knew they liked cozy mysteries.

The teenagers—Ashley, Joan, Mindy, and Susanne—walked to the food table and examined a plate of store-bought cookies that had been Sylvia's contribution. They chose chocolate chip and bottles of fruit punch and moved off to one of the tables in the teen area. The older women paused by the gumbo, taking the lid off and sniffing with expressions of approval.

Ms. Trudy arrived along with Harry, Mike, and Jonathan, who worked for Miller Construction Company. They joined the gray-haired women at the food table and helped themselves to dinner.

"I told you this would work. I wasn't worried for a minute." Sylvia put her hands on her hips and surveyed the crowd with a possessive air.

"Yeah, right. That's why you were obsessively lining up the napkins," Louise said.

"Okay, so maybe I was worried for a minute, Minnesota girl. But I know Southerners. They won't miss a party. Let's get to work. These people need to check out books and bump up our circulation numbers."

Sylvia picked up some books and marched over to the young adult area. Once there, she tossed the novels onto the table, right in front of the startled girls, talking the whole time. The teens stared skeptically at first, but then something Sylvia said made them laugh.

More people arrived. Three preteen girls and their mother waved to Louise before getting gumbo and cookies and taking over a library table. Sylvia called the girls the B sisters because all of their names started with the letter. Louise was on her way to greet them when she spotted a skinny girl wearing thick black-framed glasses shoving cookies into a backpack. Something about the teenager captured Louise's attention. Maybe it was the methodical way she stole the cookies, almost as though she expected to be caught.

"You're going to get crumbs in your books," Louise said.

The girl gave her a look that was equal parts defiance and shame. She zipped the pack and shouldered it, seeming to dare Louise to tell her to give back the cookies.

Louise slowly took off her suit jacket and draped it over her arm, trying to show the girl that she wasn't upset. "What do you like to read?" she asked.

"My mom says the only book worth reading is the Bible. I just came because I heard there was free food. Sometimes, there's nothing for dinner at home." The girl hunched over, either from the weight of the pack or the burden of her life, real or perceived.

"Get a bowl of gumbo and let's sit down and talk."

The girl contemplated Louise. For a moment, she looked like she was going to run out the door. Instead, she ladled rice and gumbo into a plastic bowl and selected a drink. Louise led her to a table near the back of the library.

"I'm Louise. What's your name?" she asked when the teen had chosen a chair facing the emergency exit.

"Mary Hebert."

The name was pronounced "A-bear," but Louise had been in Cajun country long enough to know the correct spelling. Mary bent over her bowl and began to spoon gumbo into her mouth, not stopping until it was almost gone.

Louise watched her, trying to decide how to start a conversation. She waited until Mary paused to open her drink and then said, "What do you like to read in school?"

Mary scraped the rest of the gumbo from the bottom of the bowl. "I dunno. Most of it's old. I guess some of the books are still okay, though. I liked *To Kill a Mockingbird* and *Dicey's Song*."

"Do you like the *Hunger Games* movies? *True Blood*?"

"I'm not allowed to watch any of that stuff. My mom's kind of a religious freak. I got a *Divergent* book from the school library once, but I had to be real careful not to let her see it."

"What did you think?"

"It was good. I might try to get the next one."

Louise leaned forward, careful not to sound as excited as she felt. The girl was a potential reader, she could tell. She just needed a little encouraging. But Mary wouldn't respond to Sylvia's over-the-top personality, at least not yet. She aimed for an even tone. "How about something by Sarah Dessen?"

Mary raised her head, and a tiny smile appeared on her lips. "I've heard of her. Sounds too teen-cute. Do you know what I mean?"

Louise nodded, remembering how hard it was to be that age. The desire to be her own person had clashed with wanting to fit in and have friends. "I sure do. I have the perfect book for you. It's not teenager-y at all."

"Okay." Mary tipped up her drink and drank the dregs. Her shoulders looked less tense as she put on her pack and gathered up her trash.

Louise resisted the urge to help her. She didn't want to crowd the girl. Instead, she wove her way through the crowd to the young adult section. She found *Clockwork Angel* and turned, afraid Mary would be gone. But the girl was standing behind her, watching the other teens and Sylvia gathered around one of the wooden library tables. Sylvia was talking about a *Hunger Games*–themed trivia game party and costume contest. Mary backed away until she was leaning against the wall of books. She looked as panicked as the deer in Mr. Foley's office had. Louise understood. When she was a teen, her peers had made her feel just as confused. She touched Mary's shoulder lightly, directing her toward the circulation desk.

Once out of the crowd of teenagers, Mary dropped her pack on the floor and opened it, reaching for the book.

"Not yet. I have to get you a card and check it out," Louise said. She went behind the circulation desk and entered Mary's information quickly, still worried that the girl might change her mind and leave.

When she handed the card and book across the counter, Mary smiled. "I can check out whatever I want?"

Louise smiled back. She'd given her a gift. It felt good. "You sure can. Come back soon, anytime."

"I will." Mary placed the book in her bag, zipped it up, and put it back on. The pack on her back made her seem even smaller and skinnier. As she left, five teenagers arrived, ignoring her completely. Neither of the two boys in the group even held the door for her, a serious breach of Southern manners. Louise felt a stab of empathy so intense that it was almost physical.

Since everyone was too busy talking and eating to check out books, Louise took some gumbo and retreated to the corner behind the periodicals. She had just eaten her first bite when Sal appeared from behind the group of teenagers who had snubbed Mary. The sight of him made her shiver, and she had to work hard to swallow the gumbo. She hadn't seen him since he'd showed her around the house, almost a week ago. She'd been barefoot and muddy, so he couldn't have been impressed. But she hadn't forgotten his blue eyes and the way he'd hunched his muscled shoulders against the cold.

He took a can of Coke and leaned against the wall next to her. "Busy night."

"I can't get away from you," she said, trying to make her voice sound casual.

"Do you want to? Because I can disappear even in this little town."

"Not really. You clean up nice."

He smelled of soap and spicy aftershave. He'd made a point of showering before coming. So maybe he'd come to the library just to see her. Louise almost laughed at her own audacity. She ate another spoonful of gumbo.

"Are you still thinking about buying that house?" he asked.

"I looked at a few places with the real estate agent this weekend. But the one next to you is really the only one I can afford. I mean, that I could actually live in. You should have seen some of the dumps she showed me. One didn't even have a kitchen because someone had been using it for an office."

"I think it's nice. And I mean it—I really would help you fix it up."

"I'm warning you, my home-improvement skills are limited to replacing lightbulbs."

Sal took a swig of Coke. "That's okay. I like doing it. Another of my many hobbies."

"My hobby is cooking. You should try the gumbo I made. No one's complained yet, even though it was made by a Yankee."

"A little help over here!" Sylvia called from behind the circulation counter. The line was ten people deep.

"Uh-oh. I'd better go. I guess I'll see you around," Louise said. She'd been so distracted by Sal that she had left poor Sylvia alone to tend to the masses.

Sal wished he'd asked Louise on a date. He'd been working his way up to it, but he was too slow. The last time he'd really let down his defenses with a woman it hadn't worked out very well. Still, he couldn't let his stupid insecurities stop him from trying. He'd been lonely long enough.

He went to the food table. A group of teenage girls in too-tight T-shirts were standing in a circle, giggling about something. The girls were like colts—long-legged and awkward. All three were daughters of his high school classmates. How had they gotten to be teenagers already? Time moved too fast. Sometimes, Sal felt like he'd wasted it.

He took one of the last plastic bowls and spooned in gumbo and rice. Louise had used parboiled rice. Smart move, because even though it had been sitting on the table for a while, it wasn't sticky. He shook in a little hot sauce and took his bowl to the periodical area. The chairs were occupied by four clerks from the Piggly Wiggly. He nodded in their direction and rested his back against the wall, setting his Coke on a nearby shelf.

Sal had eaten a lot of gumbo in his life. His mother had made it for special occasions. After she was gone, Betta took over the tradition. Usually, it was chicken and sausage, sometimes with okra if the slimy vegetable was in season. The dish required hours of cooking, and some people even let it rest overnight before serving. Louise had done something to hers that seemed to wake up every taste bud on his tongue. Even though she'd used frozen okra and tomatoes—an ingredient that some purists rejected—he couldn't stop eating it. As soon as the bowl was empty, he pushed away from the wall and went back to the table, but the pot was scraped clean.

Louise stood behind the circulation desk, checking out a stack of books for Ada Gautreaux. Sal wanted to try to talk to her again, but the crowd was getting bigger. He took a cookie and left.

CHAPTER 15

The next Monday, the library still smelled like the most recent party food: chicken and dumplings made by Louise. The residual odor reminded Louise that she had a new mission. By Sylvia's count, two hundred people had come in each day for the new hours. They didn't just eat, either. The patrons talked to Sylvia and Louise about ideas for the library, filled out surveys, and borrowed hundreds of books. Even Hope attended the party on Friday, helping check out books and declaring Louise's chicken and dumplings "good, but not near as good as mine." By the end of the week, Louise felt like all the people she'd met were, if not friends, at least neighbors. For the first time, she realized how important the library was, especially for a town like Alligator Bayou that had no bookstore, no movie theater, no college. She owed it to the residents to make it as useful and welcoming as she could.

As she turned on her computer, she glanced out toward the parking lot. A green van with a mismatched red passenger-side door pulled in and parked near the entrance. "The B sisters are here."

"I'll open early." Sylvia tapped past Louise in her blue

patent leather pumps and went out into the patron area. The girls came in, sounding like a herd of elephants. Except that elephants were supposed to be highly intelligent animals. Maybe the B sisters were more like hippos. Sweet, friendly hippos.

Sylvia returned a few minutes later and poured herself another cup of coffee. "Can you watch them? I need to make a few phone calls about my book talks at the high school tomorrow."

"Okay. I'll make sure they don't overdose on the cute animal videos." Louise pushed the cart of books out of the way and went to circulation. One of the girls was standing at the desk. She had frizzy hair, glasses, and fifty extra pounds packed around her midsection. "Bonny, right?"

"No, I'm Belinda." The girl didn't smile. Louise remembered that she was the serious one. The second-oldest.

"How come you guys aren't in school?"

"The furnace in the building broke down. Second time this week." Belinda dropped her backpack on the floor. She slid her library card across the desk along with a pile of novels with photos of crying teenagers on the covers.

Louise checked out the books, and Belinda stuffed them into her pack before rejoining her sisters at the bank of computers. The sisters chatted and surfed the Internet, occasionally switching seats when one found an especially funny cat video. The three girls and their mother were built the same—like doughy fire hydrants—but their faces and personalities were different. Louise felt bad that she couldn't keep their names straight.

Mary pushed through the glass front doors and put *Clockwork Angel* on the counter. Her khaki uniform pants rode two inches above her ankles. Instead of a jacket, she wore a voluminous black sweatshirt that fell halfway down her thighs. The sleeves were rolled, revealing skinny wrists.

"Did you read it already?" Louise asked.

"Yeah. I liked it. It's really . . . cool. Um, do you have the other ones?" The girl ducked her head and smiled shyly, like Louise was a friend she was sharing a secret with.

"I sure do." Louise led the way to the young adult section. "So I hear your school is closed today. You must be glad to be off."

"Not really." Mary studied her high-top sneakers. The right one had a hole by her big toe. A bit of white-gray sock showed through the opening.

"Why's that?" Louise stopped by the *C*'s and found the next two novels in the series.

"My mom's working anyway and there's nothing to eat. At school, at least I get breakfast and lunch."

"What do you do in the summer?"

"I get pretty hungry sometimes." The girl adjusted her backpack as they walked back to circulation.

"Just a minute," Louise said. She left the books next to the checkout terminal and hurried to the refrigerator in the workroom. Her lunch was in a plastic grocery bag and Sylvia's was right next to it—a turkey sandwich and carrot sticks. Louise thrust all of the food into the bag, brought it up front, and handed it over the counter. "Don't look inside, just take it."

"Thanks." Mary squatted down and placed the bag in her open backpack.

Louise scanned her card and the books. "If school doesn't open tomorrow, stop by, okay?"

Mary put on the pack and stared at her feet again. "I might come after school anyway. I mean, if you don't mind."

"Of course not. You're always welcome here. You can stay now and read if you want."

"I might come back later."

The girl left, heading back to an empty house, probably. Or, more likely, a trailer or apartment building. She might live in the trailer park on Lowell Lane that was filled with dilapidated mobile homes slowly being eaten by black mold. A ten-year-old boy had accidentally fallen into the park's swimming pool the previous Friday and drowned. The picture in the newspaper had made the place appear menacing, even in the afternoon sunlight.

Lily arrived and shook her head at the girls using the computers. "I see the B sisters are off school."

"Furnace broke down yet again," Louise said, still trying to banish the image of the creepy trailer park from her mind.

"Let me get my coffee and I'll take over circulation."

When Lily returned with her cup and the latest Alligator Bayou Historical Society newsletter, Louise went to her cubicle. She had a cart of books to catalog, a prospect that would have brought on nostalgic thoughts about her lost academic career just a few weeks previously. Now, she didn't mind. She knew that the cozy mysteries were for Ms. Trudy and her friends, the thrillers would be read by Mr. Gaberdine, who taught at the high school, and Ada Gautreaux was waiting for the new romances.

Sylvia popped her head over the cubicle wall on Louise's side. "You know what I want to do? Zumba classes on the nights I'm scheduled to stay late and on the Saturdays when I'm working."

"What's that? A new kind of knitting for the younger set? Are you going to teach the teens to Zumba themselves some sweaters?" Louise said.

"No, my chronically out-of-touch friend, it's like Latin dance." Sylvia swayed and executed a hip bump. "I'm sick of being out of shape. And I know a lot of people around here could use some exercise."

"Y'all are crazy," Hope said from her corner.

"I'm going to the certification class this weekend."

"Don't you have to ask Mr. Foley?" Louise said.

"Nope. I asked Mr. Henry and he said it was fine. Women pay big bucks in health clubs for Zumba, and we're gonna offer it for free." Sylvia did another dance move that involved a lot of arm swinging and almost knocked her computer to the floor.

"Okay, good luck with all that." Louise took a book from her cart. "Oh, this is probably the time to tell you that I stole your lunch."

Sylvia stopped dancing. "Why's that?"

"A girl named Mary."

"Mary Hebert," Hope said. "Skinny. Long hair."

"That's her."

"Her momma bags down at the Piggly Wiggly. She used to be a cashier, but she had sticky fingers, if you know what I mean. Only reason they let her stay is because of Mary. You still gotta pay attention if she packs your stuff. Get home and your nice steak might be missing. Bring your receipt back and complain, and old Jude'll give you another one, though. Don't know why he puts up with her. Some people say they have a thing going on, but I reckon he just feels sorry for the daughter. I seen her go in there with a quarter for a gum ball and leave with a loaf of bread." Hope came out of her cube and stretched her arms above her head.

Louise opened the book to the title page. "She said school was off and she had nothing to eat, so I gave her my lunch and Sylvia's."

"What's wrong with her mother?" Sylvia asked.

"Lazy, drunk, dumb. Too busy chasing some guy or a bottle of something to take care of her own daughter or even show up to work half the time," Hope said. "I gotta warn you, that Mary's like a stray cat. You feed her once and she'll keep coming back."

"I hope she does," Louise said. "I lent her some books, for one thing. Plus, I like her."

"She's a good kid. Better than her mother, I'll say that." Hope went back into her cubicle. "I'll call Anthony's and order us some lunch."

Louise sat at a table in the patron area, staring at her plate of homemade brownies. Even though she was committed to making the library relevant, she wasn't thrilled about the book club idea. Studying some cheesy pop culture book with a group of daytime TV watchers wasn't her favorite activity. But the library patron survey had revealed that it was one of the most popular program ideas, so Sylvia had pushed her to organize one.

While Louise waited for the book club members to arrive, Sylvia and a group of high school kids decorated the young adult section with lava lamps, beanbag chairs, and paper stars. Sylvia had bought the supplies herself because Mr. Foley refused to contribute any of the library's funds. He'd only reluctantly agreed to let her go ahead with the project using her own money.

Mary sat at a table in the corner, pretending to read a book and stealing glances at the group. Louise wanted to tell her to just join in, but she knew firsthand how hard it could be. Finally, Sylvia sashayed over and placed a lava lamp directly in front of Mary. The girl smiled but stayed where she was.

"Is this the book club?"

Louise set down her coffee cup. She hadn't heard anyone approach, but now Ms. Trudy and two other women were in front of the table, regarding her with motherly concern. All three wore reading glasses around their necks and polyester blouses. They were like old-lady versions of the B sisters.

"Yes, sorry, I was just daydreaming. Would you all like some coffee?"

"That would be wonderful," Ms. Trudy said.

Louise trudged back to the work area. This was going to be exactly what she was afraid of: a bunch of women who wanted to read Nicholas Sparks.

At the coffee machine, she chose three mugs and added cream and sugar to the tray. She'd brought real half-and-half, since she hated Mr. Henry's chemical powder.

On her way out to the table, she was watching the coffee, thinking she'd filled the mugs a little too high. When she glanced up again, her hands shook and the cups overflowed onto the tray. In the few minutes she had been gone, the table had filled up with people. Two women she recognized as clerks from the Piggly Wiggly. One man was the father of a teenager who often came in after school. The mother of the B sisters—Brianna?—was already helping herself to a brownie while she talked to a dark-haired man who looked a lot like a certain strawberry farmer. Louise held her breath and waited for him to turn his head. She was sure it was Sal. But who was the woman next to him with the Betty Boop figure and the big hair? His wife?

Louise headed back to the kitchen with the tray of spilled coffee. She tried to compose herself as she cleaned up the mess and poured six more cups. So what if Sal was married? They'd had a few friendly conversations—that was all. Besides, she hadn't even seen him since the opening-night library party, a whole week ago. Not that his absence had stopped her from thinking about him. She took a deep breath and carried the loaded tray out to the patron area.

She set the tray down on the table and took the last available seat. Next to Sal.

"We ought to all get acquainted," Ms. Trudy said, taking a cup of coffee and a brownie. "This here's Louisiana Richardson, and she's supposed to be running this thing."

"Yes," Louise said. "Though you're welcome to take over if you want, Ms. Trudy."

"Nah. But I'll introduce myself. I'm Trudy and these are my friends Eloise and Eleanor."

The two white-haired ladies nodded, their reading glasses swaying identically.

One of the Piggly Wiggly clerks looked like she lived on Twinkies and Coke. Her friend apparently stuck to Pall Malls and breath mints.

"I'm Amber," the larger one said, reaching for a brownie.

"I'm Tina." The thin one had a whiskey voice that matched her leathery face.

The man with the teenage daughter spoke up next. "Michael. My wife made me come. She says I don't read enough." He loosened his tie and reached for his coffee.

"I think you know me," the B sisters' mom said. "Brianna."

"Sal," Sal said. "And this here's my sister Betta."

Louise almost collapsed with relief. Sister, not wife. She should have guessed since the two had matching black hair and blue eyes. She drank her coffee and tried to look casual.

"I can introduce myself, you know," Betta said, nudging her brother in the ribs. Sal's appearance didn't scream Italian, but his sister's certainly did. Barely five feet tall in her high-heeled boots, Betta was big in all the right places. Her helmet of roller-curled hair wouldn't move in a strong wind.

"Ow." Sal rubbed his side. "Watch it there, sis."

A young couple approached the table. He was dressed in business casual—khaki pants and a button-down shirt—and she wore a fitted dress and high heels. They looked like actors playing young professionals.

"Are we late?" she asked. "I'm Catherine and this is Steve."

"Not at all." Louise got two more chairs. Sal scooted closer to her to allow room for the newcomers. She sat down, her elbow almost touching him, and nibbled on a brownie. She was having trouble concentrating. Her mind was focused on Sal and the proximity of his body. Had he come because he really wanted to read books? Or did his sister force him? Or was there some other reason? And how could someone smell so good?

Sal was glad there were two other men in the book club. That way it wouldn't look like he was just there to meet women. Which he was. Except that he was only interested in one particular woman. He'd been too busy to drop by the library again since the party. When Betta called and asked him to come with her to the book club, he'd agreed with an eagerness that surprised his sister. Attending the club probably wasn't the best way to get Louise's attention, but he couldn't just waltz into the library and ask her out. Maybe Chicago Sal would have done that. These days, he wanted to be more careful, especially with his sister and cousin watching his every move.

In fact, Betta was sitting a little too close to him. Even though she was short, his sister took up a lot of room with her big hair and loud voice. People who didn't know her would never guess how Betta had lost herself when their parents died. She hadn't cried at the funeral, but then she completely broke down while the lawyer was reading the will. They'd left her the house. She and Sal had spent a week cleaning it out. Most of the time had been spent arguing over whether it was okay to throw away old ticket stubs, dried-up ink pens, and expired spices. She'd insisted on keeping their mother's clothes, even though they were all too small for her.

For three years, she had been casting around for something to do. She latched onto Sal, helping him on the farm whenever she wasn't working and cooking dinner for him almost every night. He loved her, but she needed to get her own life.

Sal inched his chair away from his sister and closer to Louise. She was staring into her cup of coffee as though deep in thought.

"I think we could go ahead and start," Ms. Trudy said.

"Oh, yeah, sorry. Um, what do you guys want to read?" Louise met Sal's eyes for a moment as she glanced around the table.

Sal reached over and took a brownie. It was rich, chewy, and delicious. He must have made a sound because Louise looked at him again.

"Something good, but not too depressing. No Khaled Hosseini please," Eloise said.

"I agree." Eleanor set her brownie on a napkin. "I mean, I guess I understand why everyone raves about his books, but life is too short to read about horrible childhoods."

"Y'all are so anti-literature," Ms. Trudy said. "We are not reading Nicholas Sparks."

"No one suggested that," Eloise said.

"Well, if you don't want anything horrible . . ."

"I said no horrible childhoods," Eleanor said.

Ms. Trudy laughed. "So horrible adulthoods are okay."

Sal leaned back in his chair and finished the brownie. He loved eating Louise's food. Either she was a great cook or the brownie tasted wonderful just because she was sitting so close that he imagined he could feel the heat of her body.

"My brother reads a lot. Maybe he has some ideas," Betta said.

Sal hadn't been paying attention to the bickering old ladies. He narrowed his eyes at his sister. Did she know the real reason he'd come? Betta had always been able to read his mind. The skill had been useful when he was three years old and still unable or unwilling to talk, but ever since then it had been mostly just annoying.

"I like Michael Chabon. Richard Russo, at least his early stuff. Ed McBain, Elmore Leonard," he said.

"Guy books," Betta said.

"I'm a guy. What do you want?"

Betta punched his shoulder. She seemed determined to give him a bruise.

"I have an idea," Louise said. "We'll take turns choosing the book. Each month, someone else gets to pick."

"Great idea. Let's go oldest to youngest," Ms. Trudy said.

"That means I'm first," Eleanor said.

"I know, darling."

Eleanor crumpled her napkin. "Then, I choose *The Longest Ride*."

Ms. Trudy groaned.

"Just kidding! Seriously, *East of Eden*."

"Depressing," Ms. Trudy said.

Eleanor shrugged.

"Okay. There's just one problem. Mr. Foley—that's the library director—won't buy enough books for the club. So I don't know how many copies we have. I'm guessing one," Louise said.

"Don't worry, honey. We all read on Kindle now, anyway," Ms. Trudy said.

Business concluded, the meeting devolved into social hour. Sal folded his hands behind his head and let the chatter flow around him. He was not going to miss the opportunity to ask Louise on a date this time. He touched her shoulder. "Can I talk to you over there for a minute?"

Louise nodded and followed him to the periodicals. Sal leaned against a chair and studied his scuffed work boots. "I have a confession to make. I know this sounds crazy, but I can't afford to buy the book. I don't want Betta to know. I sank all my money into these new strawberry plants. They're a special variety from Germany. I don't know how they're going to work. They all might die. But I want to be in the club." He raised his eyes and gave her a sad puppy dog face.

"You can have my copy," Louise said. "No problem. I've already read it, but I'll want to reread it for the club."

"We can share," Sal said. "I read fast. I had to, for law school. We can pass it back and forth."

"Sure."

Sal heard a note of disappointment in her voice. Had she been hoping that he'd ask her out? Clinging to that idea, he plunged ahead. "I want to ask you on a date, but since I don't have any money, you'd have to endure my cooking and a movie on TV."

"It's a deal," Louise said. "I can get a sitter for tomorrow night."

Chapter 17

Louise didn't know what she expected from Sal's farm, but certainly not a pack of Chihuahuas. The dogs attacked her as soon as she stepped out of the van. She didn't fear for her safety since the assault consisted of licking and attempted leg humping by animals no bigger than her cowboy boots.

Sal appeared from behind the trailer wearing his usual faded flannel jacket, jeans, and John Deere cap. Louise was relieved that he hadn't dressed up. She liked him in his farmer clothes. Besides, she'd considered one of the "date" dresses that she never got to wear anymore but settled on jeans and a T-shirt instead.

"Let's hurry, it's getting dark," he said.

"Hey, I thought this was dinner and a movie," Louise said, but Sal was already leading the way around the trailer. The sun had gone down, and the floodlights attached to the side of the mobile home made circles of light that didn't illuminate much except a few feet of grass. In the darkness ahead, she could make out a greenhouse with a single bulb burning above the entrance.

Keeping the dogs back with his muddy work boot, Sal held the door open for her and shut it quickly after they were both inside. He turned on the lights. The greenhouse had seen better days. The greenish glass was covered in a thin layer of dirt, and a few of the panes were cracked. Still, the place was obviously loved and cared for. Plants in pots were lined up in rows, and gardening tools, bottles, and cans neatly filled a metal shelving unit against the wall.

"Look at these." Sal stopped in front of a row of tiny plants. He squatted down to touch the leaves, caressing the plants gently.

Louise pretended to examine the plants, but she wasn't thinking about agriculture. She was still worried about whether she was doing the right thing. Even if they liked each other, how would they find time to be together? Besides, Sal didn't have any children, so he couldn't possibly understand the constant chaos of her life.

Sal stood up. "These are the ones. The strawberry plants I bought. Seeds, actually. Incredibly expensive seeds. They are finally growing. The first few I planted died almost immediately. I tried a bunch of stuff and figured out I had to elevate them and make sure the soil was dry, but not too dry."

"Interesting," Louise said. The tiny green shoots didn't look particularly special. She knew nothing about gardening or plants. Brendan had always mowed and landscaped. Her yard was mostly crabgrass and weeds now that she had to maintain it herself.

"I just hope I can get a few to grow big enough to produce strawberries. I have no idea what they'll taste like, but everyone says they're really good. Have you eaten a Louisiana strawberry?" Sal said.

"I think so."

"They taste like nothing. Do you know why? Because the farmers breed them for fungus resistance, not flavor. Also size. People like big red strawberries. But they're tasteless. All the ones I grow out there are just garbage." He gestured toward the fields behind the greenhouse. "I hate to even sell them, but I have to. It's the only way I can pay my bills. Someday, though . . . Let's go inside."

Louise watched his broad back as he walked along the stone path back to the house. Sal was the polar opposite of Brendan. Her ex was trim and compact, as though he'd been made using exactly the right amount of material. In contrast, Sal's shoulders and chest were wide and muscular, the body of a man built for physical labor.

She caught up to him in front of the mobile home, and he opened the door to let her inside first. The smell of red beans and sausage made her stomach growl.

"Betta didn't trust my cooking skills," Sal said. "She came over and fixed up beans in the Crock-Pot this morning. I even have rice in the rice cooker."

"It smells really good," Louise said.

Both appliances were plugged in on the cream-colored Formica countertop. The kitchen had a two-burner stove, a three-quarter-size refrigerator, and a scaled-down sink in front of a window with yellow flower curtains. Sal looked like a giant as he reached into the refrigerator for beer. He opened two bottles and offered her one.

The living room was small, but at least the furniture was man-size. An overstuffed beige couch faced the TV. A few library books were piled up on the coffee table. All in all, the place was amazingly tidy for a bachelor pad.

Five dogs had come inside, and now they all jumped on the couch and arranged themselves in a pile.

"How can you keep track of all these dogs?" Louise asked, drinking some of the cold beer.

"I only have ten: Saul, Buffy, Jackie, Maestro, Caesar, Joan Jett, Winston Churchill, Cherry, Duke, and Gumbo." Sal went back into the kitchen and opened the refrigerator again. "I picked these string beans this morning. Problem is, I can grow stuff, but I can't cook it."

The green beans he casually dumped on the countertop were beautiful, like paintings of vegetables rather than the real thing.

"These are the most gorgeous beans I have ever seen," Louise said.

"You're kidding, right?" Sal walked over and looked, his hips nearly touching hers. "You're beautiful. These beans are . . . beans."

Louise could feel the warmth of his body, close, too close. She had to fight to control her voice. "Nope, you're wrong. This is vegetable perfection. Cooking them is the easy part, though. I'll teach you. Get me a sauté pan and some butter or bacon. Do you have chicken stock?"

"I don't know what a sauté pan is, and I might have some bacon. Stock, no way."

"How about a knife? Can you handle that? Chop the ends off and halve them while I see what we have to work with here."

Louise found a pan, bacon, garlic, and a wrinkly lemon and set to work. She chopped the bacon and fried it in the pan.

Sal watched her while he cut the ends from the beans, one at a time.

"Don't look at me. You'll cut your finger off," Louise said. "Let me show you. You're holding the knife wrong to begin with. Plus, this is dull. Do you have a sharpener?"

"I don't know," Sal said.

Louise found a sharpener in the drawer, ran the knife through it a few times, and tested the blade with her finger. "Okay, that's better. Now watch how I hold it. You try."

Sal grasped the knife in his fist. "Like this?"

"No, your index finger should be on top of the knife.

Choke up." She guided his hand to the right place on the knife, trying to ignore the burst of electricity that ran up her arm when she touched him.

Sal grinned. "Maybe I'll get this."

"Hang on." Louise scooped the bacon onto a paper-towel-lined plate and turned off the burner. "Now line up three beans and put the tip of the knife on the cutting board. You've got it."

Concentrating on the task, Sal looked like a kid learning a new skill. Louise felt a rush of guilt. Her children were spending yet another evening without her. The worst part was that she was having far more fun than she'd had in a long time.

"Okay, they're done, chef." Sal set down the knife.

"Good." Louise turned on the burner again and put the garlic in the pan. She stirred in the beans, then put in a cup of water and covered the pan. "Ten minutes or so and then we add the lemon juice, salt, and pepper."

"Guess I should feed the dogs." Sal opened the door and whistled. Five more Chihuahuas tumbled in and stood at attention on the kitchen floor with the five from the couch. Sal opened a plastic bin of kibble and scooped out ten bowls.

"How'd you end up with so many dogs?" Louise asked.

"When I first moved back to Alligator Bayou, that big one, Saul, showed up at my door. He about licked me to death, and I kind of fell in love with the breed. So anyone around here finds one, I end up with it. Oh, hey, I almost forgot. I got a movie for us to watch." Sal bounded over to the TV and held up a DVD. "*East of Eden*, in honor of our book club."

Watching the movie with Sal, Louise felt twenty years old again. She wasn't a mom or a librarian, just a girl with a boyfriend and a life of her own. It was nice to pretend. Soon, she'd wake up and be the overworked single mom again. Thinking about it made her tired.

"These are the best beans I've ever had," Sal said.

"The red beans?"

"No, the string beans. I mean, my sister's a pretty good cook, but you're amazing."

"I told you they were beautiful beans."

"No way. Betta cooked these exact same beans before and they didn't taste like this."

"Thanks." Louise savored a mouthful of the wine Sal had opened with dinner. It wasn't any better than the cheap stuff she usually bought, but the atmosphere made it seem vastly superior. Two dogs were lying on the couch next to her, their tiny heads nestled against her leg. Winston Churchill was between Louise and Sal, stretched out with his feet against her thigh and his head on Sal's leg. Even though they were in the way, Louise liked the dogs. They added to the homey feeling.

"You know what? It's going to be really late for you to drive all the way back to Saint Jude. Why don't you just stay here? I have an extra bedroom."

Louise didn't want to go back home. She missed her kids, but at the same time she wanted to keep pretending a little longer. Besides, the wine and food were making her sleepy. It would be nice to fall into bed without wrestling kids into pajamas, brushing their teeth, making them take their vitamins, getting one last snack and drink of water. More than nice—it would be a dream come true. Not forever, but for one night. "Wouldn't people talk? This is a small town."

"The great thing about small towns is that people might talk about you, but at least you know exactly what they're going to say." Sal set his empty plate aside and moved Winston Churchill to the end of the couch. He slid closer to

Louise until their legs were almost touching. "I wanted to ask you on a date the first time I saw you, but I wimped out. Then, things got crazy around here for a while, but when I heard about your book club . . ."

Louise finished her wine. "Okay, you talked me into it." She got her phone and called Sylvia.

CHAPTER 18

Sal woke to Joan Jett licking his face. It was almost eight. He hadn't slept so late since first coming back to Alligator Bayou. He and Louise had stayed up past midnight talking. He'd told her about his time in Chicago, his parents, his sister, and how his hometown fulfilled and stifled him at the same time. She'd confessed her worry that he wouldn't be able to deal with her rowdy children and the drama with her ex-husband. He'd responded that he was ready to try. He was more than ready. The need he felt when he was with her consumed him. If he told her how much he wanted to be with her, she'd probably run the other way. It had taken an act of willpower to show her to the guest room when they were both too tired to stay up anymore.

A frenzy of barking erupted from the living room. Joan Jett exploded off the bed along with Gumbo and Winston Churchill, who had been sleeping at the foot. Sal pulled on jeans over his boxers and walked into the kitchen.

His sister set a repurposed Christmas cookie tin on the table and took off her coat. "Sal! I brought muffins. Are you still asleep? How did it go last night?"

"Fine." Normally, Sal didn't mind Betta dropping by

unannounced. Usually, he was lonely anyway and welcomed her company. But he would have liked a few minutes alone with Louise before she had to leave. He scooped some coffee into the machine and got out three mugs.

"You don't sound too . . . Oh! I'm sorry, Louise. I wouldn't have dropped by if I'd known you stayed the night. I just had these muffins and I needed to use them up before they got stale," Betta said, getting the butter from the refrigerator.

Sal turned. They'd only been apart for a few hours, but he was eager to see Louise again. She was wearing one of his T-shirts. It barely skimmed her knees and the sight of her bare legs made him lose his breath for a second.

She sat down at the table and brushed the hair back from her face. "Good morning, Betta."

"Muffins, right. Like you didn't come because you wanted the scoop on our date," Sal said. "Betta's a hairdresser. All she does all day is gossip."

"That is not true! I take my beauty treatments very seriously." Betta opened the tin, selected a muffin, and took a dainty bite.

Sal sat next to Louise and stretched his legs out under the table. "What kind of muffins are these?"

"Blueberry, of course. My freezer's still full from summer."

"Oh, yeah. I grow some blueberries too. They're pretty good," Sal said to Louise as he chose a muffin, broke it in half, and slathered it in butter. "Do you have any questions, Betta? Since you're here and all."

Betta toyed with a strand of her roller-curled black hair. "No. Come on, Sal. Be nice."

Sal got up and poured three cups of coffee.

"We enjoyed your beans and the movie. Thanks," Louise said.

"You're welcome. Have a muffin."

Sal brought mugs to the women, got the half-and-half from the refrigerator, and returned to the table with his own coffee. He hoped his sister didn't think he'd slept with Louise. Betta needed to know that this was no one-night stand. He couldn't exactly make the declaration over the breakfast table, though. He finished his muffin and washed it down with black coffee.

Louise poured half-and-half into her cup and took a muffin. "I have to go in a minute. I'm already late for work. My boss might slap my hand with a ruler."

"I have to leave too. Ms. Trudy's coming in at nine for her weekly appointment. Why don't you drop by sometime, Louise? I'll give you highlights to die for," Betta said.

Sal saw a look of horror cross Louise's face for a brief second. He stifled a laugh.

"Sure, um, maybe I will," she said.

"Bring the kids. I'll do them up too. Not highlights, I mean. Just cuts. I have suckers."

"Okay. The muffin was really good. Thanks, Betta." Louise stood up and put her mug in the sink. "I hate to go, but Mr. Foley really does get mad if we're late. I'm going to change and then I'd better leave."

Once she was gone, Betta clapped the top on her tin. "I really messed things up, didn't I?"

"No, you didn't. I'm glad you came by. But I don't want you to get the wrong idea. I really like Louise. A lot," Sal said.

"Good. Good for you." Betta grabbed her coat from the chair and put it on. "I have to go."

His sister banged the door shut behind her. Sal had been worried about the wrong thing. He should have known that Betta would be jealous. If he started seriously dating Louise, she wouldn't be the only woman in his life anymore. Then she'd be lost all over again.

CHAPTER 19

Sylvia's head floated above the cubicle wall like part of a disassembled Barbie doll. "You have to come."

"I can't dance. I told you that." Louise straightened the stack of books she was cataloging. She hadn't danced since gym class in eighth grade, when she'd stumbled through the waltz with sweaty-palmed Danny Stuart. The bitch girls—her private name for the gang of her three most vicious tormentors—had rehashed the episode for weeks. She became Left-Foot Louise.

"You're going to be here watching the desk anyway. You might as well join in," Sylvia said.

"I can't if we're busy," Louise said.

"What about you, Hope?" Sylvia moved to the other cubicle wall. "Are you coming to Zumba tonight?"

Hope snorted. "Y'all are crazy. You didn't clear this with Mr. Foley, did you?"

"Nope. I'm doing it on my own time," Sylvia said. "It's a public service."

"Don't worry, I ain't gonna tell. But I'm just letting you know. He won't be happy when he finds out."

"I put an announcement in the newsletter and sent a

press release to the newspaper. Not to mention the sign on the front door. It's not exactly a secret."

"Your funeral," Hope said.

"Ahem. Good morning, ladies."

Louise was startled at the sound of Mr. Henry's voice. Had he heard Sylvia's comments about Mr. Foley? He never said a bad word about the director. The two men behaved oddly around each other, hardly ever having a conversation and yet seeming to communicate somehow. Either they were mind readers or they secretly texted back and forth.

Sylvia showed no embarrassment at being caught discussing her boss. She turned to the assistant director. "How are you feeling today, Mr. Henry?"

"I've been better, but I'll survive." He drank from his coffee mug and coughed before continuing. "I have a little project for y'all. We have been trying for a couple of years to get a millage increase passed so we could have more funding for the library. Not much, just a little property tax that would cost the average homeowner around a hundred dollars a year. I've asked the police jury to put it in their meeting agenda next week. I think it would be nice if we had a little presentation about the improvements y'all have made."

"We're on it, Mr. Henry," Sylvia said. "Don't you worry about a thing. Louise and I will make it happen."

"I really do think y'all are doing a great job. Time was, I would have made the report myself, but I'm an old man now."

"Don't say that. You're as young as you feel," Sylvia said.

"I feel about a hundred and ten," he said, shuffling in the direction of his cubicle.

Hope stood up and watched him until he went through the door to circulation. "This is it, y'all. Mr. Henry don't want to admit it, but Mrs. Gunderson wants to shut us down. I done told y'all about her, right?"

"The police juror who basically runs the parish. Ms. Trudy filled me in," Louise said.

"The little fat lady that Mr. Foley genuflected to when she came in? She wants to close the library?" Sylvia said.

"She hates Mr. Henry because he didn't support her campaign for police juror. She's gunning to become mayor of this here town. Reckon she sees him as her enemy. She ain't overly fond of me, neither." Hope put her hands on her hips and scowled as though Mrs. Gunderson were standing in front of her.

"She can't really shut down the library," Sylvia said.

"Not if the dedicated tax passes. But she aims to make sure it don't and then let the library slowly bleed to death." Hope sat back down in her cubicle.

"What do we do? How do we beat her?" Louise asked.

"I don't know. Seems like no one wins against that old bat."

From her place behind the circulation desk, Louise watched the women arrive for Zumba. Sylvia had insisted that the conference room was too small, so she and Louise had moved the tables from the center of the library to clear a space. By the time the class was scheduled to start, fifteen women were standing in the middle of the library, self-consciously pretending to stretch. The B sisters' mom was there along with her oldest (Belinda?); Amber, the Piggly Wiggly clerk; Cheryl, Gina, and Tracy, mothers of little kids who often came for story time; and Jennifer, Michelle, Stacy, and Tomika, who all attended nearby Bayou Parishes Community College. Some of the others seemed familiar, but Louise couldn't remember their names.

Sylvia had badgered Louise until she changed into her

workout outfit. The week before, she'd dug it out of the bottom of her dresser and signed up for a free trial membership at the local gym. She didn't want to admit that her sudden interest in getting in shape might have something to do with Sal. Or that he was the reason she'd retrieved her nearly dried-up mascara and fingernail polish from the highest cabinet in her bathroom, the one she was too short to reach without standing on a chair.

Mary walked in and regarded the Zumba women with a hint of amusement. She put her books on the counter. "What's up with this?"

"Zumba. The latest fitness craze." Louise checked in the books. "Sylvia's trying to convince me to do it, but I can't dance."

The girl raised one shoulder under her huge sweatshirt. "Most of them probably can't either."

"You're right. Did you like the *Divergent* series?"

"Yeah. A lot."

"Have you read *The Hunger Games*?"

"No."

"I haven't either, but Sylvia says they're really good. Have you thought about joining her book club?"

Mary shook her head. "Those kids think I'm weird. I always say the wrong thing and they look at me funny. They're all into TV shows I haven't seen and makeup and stuff like that. I guess they're nice enough, but they don't get me."

"You have to keep trying. It took me a long time to learn that. I'm giving it to you for free."

"Easy for you to say."

"I know. I was picked on a lot as a kid."

Mary's eyes widened. For the first time since Louise had known her, the girl seemed completely awake. "You?"

"I guess I was different. Quiet. Dorky. Who knows? So I

married the first guy who paid attention to me, got divorced, and now I'm raising two kids on my own."

"That sucks."

"It could be worse. I'm not scared of people anymore. I go after what I want now. All they can say is no." That much was pretty much true. She still felt awkward sometimes, like around the Southern belles. But she was okay with that. When she was a teenager, a situation like Trish's disastrous baby shower would have left her binge eating and hating herself. These days, it was worth little more than a shrug.

"Yeah." Mary glanced at the Zumba class again. "Can I get those books? I should go home and do my homework."

They walked to the young adult section. Louise's story might not have made any difference to the girl. Mary had a lot more problems than she had faced as a teenager, like worrying about having enough food to eat. Getting into college would be a good first step for her to break out of her situation. Louise made a mental note to tell Sylvia they should have some college-prep programs at the library.

"All right, ladies. Let's get started!" Sylvia punched a button on her portable CD player as Louise and Mary returned to the circulation desk.

"Do it," the girl said. "I mean, if you want to."

"I guess." Before checking out the books, Louise got her extra lunch out of the fridge. She'd gotten into the habit of bringing food, just in case Mary stopped by. She came back to the counter and checked out the books. "Would you like a babysitting job? I'll bet Sylvia would love a night on the town with her husband and I'd like an evening with a good book in a coffee shop."

"That would be great. I used to watch our neighbor's kids sometimes before they moved away," Mary said, putting the food and books in her backpack.

"How about Monday?" Louise said. "Come by at four

thirty and I'll drive you to my house. You can stay overnight and I'll get you back here in time for school."

"Yeah, that would work." Mary zipped up her backpack and slouched toward the exit. She stopped in front of the door, raised her eyebrows, and inclined her head toward the Zumba group.

Louise shrugged.

The girl nodded, pulling her back a little straighter as she walked out the door.

Sylvia turned out most of the lights and activated a disco ball she'd hung from the ceiling. The first song was "Thriller," which made some of the women giggle. But they gamely followed Sylvia's moves. Sylvia was not a great dancer, but her enthusiasm was infectious.

Louise came out from behind the desk and found a place at the back of the group. The women gyrated and shimmied along with Sylvia. When the song was over, the clapping and laughing was nearly as loud as Michael Jackson had been.

The next song was something in Spanish. Louise forgot to be awkward and lost herself in the music. The beat was fast, and most of the women had trouble keeping up.

"Just move," Sylvia shouted. "Don't worry if you can't get the steps right!"

By the second verse, some of the better dancers were getting the moves down. Louise was always kicking the wrong foot or stepping right instead of left. For once, she didn't care about looking silly.

The song was almost over when the music abruptly cut off. Everyone froze. In the half-dark, Louise saw a troll-like person near the CD player. It took her a moment to recognize Mr. Foley. Hands on hips, he glared out at the crowd. "You can't do this in here! Stop right now!"

The silence following his outburst made Louise's ears

ring. It seemed as if every woman in the group was holding her breath.

The library director pointed a trembling finger at Sylvia. "You did this without my permission. You can't turn my library into a dance hall!" He yanked the CD player cord out of the wall and waved the plug in the air. "Sylvia Jones, you are a menace to this community. Pushing our children to read trashy vampire novels, sullying this institution of literature with noneducational DVDs, and bringing your crazy big-city ideas to our town. This isn't New Orleans, and we don't need your kind here."

"You can't talk to our Sylvia like that!" Brianna shouted.

"No, sir. We won't stand for it," one of the others said.

Amber and some of the other women started to move forward, as if they might fall upon Mr. Foley in an angry mob. The director held his hands out in a gesture of surrender. A tall African American woman in a hot-pink sweat suit marched up and wagged her finger in his face. "Mr. Foley, I don't know what your problem is, but it seems to me that you're out of line. This young lady is doing a service to this community. Most of us don't get enough exercise. And if you don't mind me saying so, you could probably stand to drop a few pounds too."

The woman's speech drained the tension from the room. There was tittering from the assembled ladies, and the ones who had advanced toward Mr. Foley went back to their original places. The director ducked his head, defeated.

Louise crept forward and tapped a short blond woman on the shoulder. "Who is that?"

"Oh, Marty Pratt. She's on the police jury. I don't guess Mr. Foley would have shut us down if he'd known she was here." The woman laughed. "He's such an old fuddy-duddy."

That was a nice way of putting it. Louise's own thoughts

about her boss were much less charitable: *Bitter, pathetic little man.*

"I'm sorry. You're right, Ms. Marty. I apologize. I just got a little carried away. Please continue." Mr. Foley tiptoed out the emergency exit.

Sylvia cranked up the music again. Louise joined in the next number, even though her good mood had evaporated. Mr. Foley might have been thwarted this time, but he wasn't going to give up.

When her phone rang that night after the children were in bed, Louise contemplated smashing it against the wall. She answered it on the premise that otherwise she'd have to listen to one of her ex's interminable voice mails and then call him back.

"Did you get the check?" Brendan asked. "I wanted to make sure since you didn't write me an e-mail or anything."

The anger in his tone was obvious. Louise pretended she didn't hear it. He might think her world still revolved around him, but it didn't. "Sorry, I just got the check yesterday and I haven't had time to e-mail you."

"Well, the wedding is only a week away. And I gave you an advance on your child support so you could make an offer on that house."

"I know, and I really appreciate it. They accepted the offer and we're closing at the end of this month. We also had a serious offer on the old house, so it's all coming together." Louise had a sudden attack of acid stomach. Brendan had been uncharacteristically helpful by lending her the money, but she still didn't want to see him. Trying to act normal around him for the children's sake was going to be painful. She couldn't let Zoe and Max know how much she disliked him and Julia. They'd torn the family apart, and she wasn't sure she could ever forgive them for it.

"I assume you have the wedding clothes all taken care of," Brendan said.

"I got Zoe a dress. I think it fits. I haven't tried it on her yet."

"What about the tux? You have to get it fitted, you know."

"I was going to do it last weekend, but I ran out of time." Louise sat down on her bed and rolled her eyes at her own reflection in the mirror. Brendan didn't need to know that Max had wandered off while she was buying the dress for Zoe. By the time she'd found him mooning over Batman figurines in the mall toy store, she'd been too relieved and worn out to deal with the tux or the dress for herself. If he knew, Brendan would only conclude that she was a lousy mother. Which he probably thought anyway. "We'll go tomorrow."

"I hope so."

"I have to go." As she hung up, Louise heard him say something, but she ignored it. She scrolled to Sylvia's number. She answered on the first ring as usual.

"Do you want to go to the mall tomorrow?" Louise asked.

"I always want to go to the mall. Why?"

"I need a tux for Max and a dress for myself, and I can't take the kids there by myself again." Louise felt like she might cry just thinking about the misery of dragging Max and Zoe on errands. She'd started making hurried grocery runs before picking up the children from school because shopping with them invariably left her exhausted and embarrassed. Stores turned the kids into tiny destruction machines. She choked back tears, making a little sad squeaking sound into the phone.

"What's wrong?" Sylvia said.

"I just talked to Brendan."

"That would do it. Don't worry. We'll get the tux together and a dress for you. It'll be fun."

"Sure," Louise said. It was possible. If the kids behaved and if she could forget that she was shopping because of Brendan's wedding. She tossed the phone on the bed and went into the kitchen to pour herself a glass of wine.

CHAPTER 20

Sylvia arrived at Louise's house dressed in a pair of stretch pants and a long, flowing shirt that somehow still accentuated her curves. Max hugged her legs in an unusual show of affection. "Jimmy mommy!"

"Hi, darling. Are you ready to go to the mall?" Sylvia crouched down. "We're getting you a suit. Won't that be fun? Jimmy's waiting in the car."

Max went outside and waved at Jimmy. Louise gathered her arsenal of sippy cups, diapers, and wipes and installed Zoe's car seat in the back of the SUV. The only sign that Sylvia felt the pinch of her reduced income was the car. It had once stayed remarkably clean, but now the floor was littered with Cheerios and stray fruit snacks. Sylvia must have had it professionally cleaned before Jake lost his job.

"How goes it with the househusband?" Louise asked.

Sylvia put Max's car seat next to Jimmy's. "Girl, it's a mess. I come home from work every day, and there are dishes everywhere, toys on the floor, laundry overflowing the baskets. I can't yell at him about it because he's so depressed. He's good with Maddy, but watching a baby all day is killing him. I hated to leave her with him today, but she was sleeping when it was time to go."

"What does he do all day?"

"Please, girl. You forget what a baby is like. And men can't multitask. He is desperately looking for jobs online. Even calling friends from college. Suddenly my man is a networker." Sylvia got into the driver's seat and checked her lipstick in the mirror. "It's made him appreciate me, though. He asked me how I kept from going crazy when Jimmy was a baby. I said wine and *Days of Our Lives*."

"Right. More like coffee and mystery novels."

"Overpriced lattes from Starbucks. I used to load Jimmy into the car and drive there every morning." Sylvia backed the SUV out of the driveway. "So, you have to go to Brendan's wedding. God, I can't believe he's moving here."

"Me neither. It's my worst nightmare come true."

"Shut up. It won't be that bad. Maybe he'll help with the kids. Give you a break once in a while."

"Mary's coming over to watch them Monday. I'll have to pay her, but at least she won't criticize my parenting skills." Louise glanced back at the children. Max and Jimmy were hitting each other and Zoe was staring out the window. She wanted help with them, but at the same time, she didn't want to share her children with Brendan.

"You should milk it for all it's worth. Get him to take them every other weekend or something. Maybe you can have some dates with your strawberry farmer. I hope you called him to take you out on Monday." Sylvia waggled her eyebrows.

"No, I'm just doing a grocery run by myself. That's exciting enough for now." Louise wanted to see Sal, but she convinced herself that going to the store was more important. They were running out of everything. She'd used the kids' blue bubble-gum-flavored toothpaste that morning because hers was completely gone. In the back of her mind, a little voice asked whether she wasn't just afraid of a new relationship, but she ignored it.

At the mall, Sylvia miraculously found a parking spot near the door. When they got out of the SUV, they headed for the tuxedo store.

"Does he have shoes?" Sylvia asked.

"Spider-Man and *Cars*," Louise said.

"Yeah, no. We'll have to rent those too. Unless you want to buy some."

"God, I don't know." Louise was glad that Sylvia had decided to take charge. Left to her own devices, she would have let Max go to the wedding in his light-up sneakers. She found it difficult to make even the smallest effort for Brendan. Why should she? She didn't owe him anything. Maybe she'd feel different if he sent the child support on time, just once. Or if he'd made some effort to see his children in the past year other than for his own wedding.

Once inside the store, Sylvia told the salesman what they needed while Louise tried to keep the kids from touching anything with their sticky hands. After Sylvia finished briefing him, the man went into the back room and returned with a miniature tux and a pair of shiny black shoes.

"Crap, I don't remember what color bow tie Brendan wanted him to wear and if he's supposed to have a vest or a cummerbund," Louise said.

"It doesn't matter. Everyone will think he is so cute that they won't notice if he doesn't match the groomsmen." Sylvia held the suit up to Max. He backed away.

"You don't know Brendan. He'll have a fit."

"You could call him."

Louise got out her cell phone. "Sylvia, can you please

stop Zoe from touching all the bow ties?" She got Brendan's voice mail. "He's not there."

Sylvia strapped Zoe back into her stroller. "Black vest, black bow tie. You can't go wrong with that."

The salesman nodded. He took a measuring tape from his pocket and held it up to Max's arms, legs, and waist. The boy watched him with wide eyes.

"Now, Max, you need to try on these shoes," Louise said.

"No." Max joined Jimmy again. They ran around one of the clothes racks, pretending to shoot each other.

"Max, if you don't come and put on these shoes right now, you're not getting any ice cream later."

"Ice cream!" Jimmy stopped running.

Max came over and looked at the shoes. "I don't like them."

"Try them on." Sylvia pulled off his Spider-Man sneakers and stuffed his feet into the patent leather ones.

"Too tight!" Max wrenched the shoes off.

"Do you have a size bigger?"

The salesman shrugged. "I'm sure those are right."

"I don't care if they're elephant-sized, as long as he'll wear them," Louise said.

He shrugged again and left.

"Men." Sylvia rolled her eyes. "Jimmy!"

Jimmy was trying to pull down a dress coat. He gave the jacket another yank. The rack tilted toward him, and instead of letting go, he pulled harder. Sylvia and Louise both ran to grab it. Too late. Jimmy jumped out of the way, and the rack crashed to the floor.

The jackets looked like dead bodies squashed flat and heaped into a pile. Louise and Sylvia pushed the rack upright and began to rehang the coats. The salesman came back with a pair of two-toned shoes. He stared at the coats on the floor but didn't say anything.

Sylvia took the shoes, leaving Louise to finish the cleanup. "Is this all you have?"

"In the bigger size." The salesman's shoulders did their thing again.

"Max, try these on," Sylvia said.

Max was wearing one of the suit jackets. The sleeves dragged on the floor. Louise took it off and hung it on the rack. "Quit with the Charlie Chaplin impression."

Sylvia helped him put on the shoes. "Do you like them?"

"Yes," Max said.

"We'll take them."

"Fifty dollars," the salesman said.

"I thought they were rentals," Louise said.

"Not these."

"Okay," Sylvia said. "We are going to the play area. We'll meet you at the food court in forty-five minutes. Think that's enough time for you to find a dress?"

"Are you sure you can handle all three of them?"

"If there's a crisis, I'll call you."

"If you insist." Louise hurried toward the nearest department store, trying to ignore Zoe crying for her to come back. The sound echoed in her ears, even after she was out of hearing range.

As she walked through the women's section, Louise fought to suppress her anger toward Brendan. She shouldn't care that he was marrying Julia. She hadn't expected otherwise and she certainly didn't want him back. So why was she upset? Because she was alone? On impulse, she got out her cell phone and called Sal.

"Hey," he said. "Look, I'm sorry I haven't called. My stupid expensive strawberry plants are dying. I'm trying everything, but nothing works. And the crop of strawberries I actually sell is in, so I've been working like crazy."

"I'm sorry." Louise let out the breath she'd been holding. It had only been a week since their date, but she'd still been worried that he hadn't called or stopped by the library. "I want you to take me out. Please."

"Okay. I mean I hate to ask, but why?"

"I have to go to Brendan's wedding and I don't want to buy a dress for it. If I knew I could wear it on a date with you, I might be able to actually choose something." Louise flipped through a rack of dresses that reminded her of the polyester nightmares her mother favored. She moved on.

"I'm going to see the first profits from the strawberries next week, so yeah, let's do something. I'm sorry about the wedding."

"Oh my God. I just had a thought."

"What?"

"You should come with me. I mean, you can always bring a date to a wedding, right?"

"Yeah, I guess so. I'm not an etiquette expert."

"You have a suit, right?"

"A bunch. From my fancy, high-powered lawyer days."

"Please?"

"Okay. Hey, we'll make it fun. Dance a little."

Louise spotted a royal blue calf-length dress.

"Perfect."

CHAPTER 21

Monday morning at work, Louise spent the first few hours in an exhausted haze. Zoe had woken up at two a.m. and refused to go back to sleep until five. Louise resorted to watching late-night TV, catching up on all the reruns of shows that she never had time to watch. Then, she fell asleep in Sylvia's SUV on the way to work despite the dance music blaring from the radio. She felt like her brain was stuck in first gear, grinding along slowly despite the five cups of coffee she'd forced herself to drink.

During her turn on the circulation desk, she sat in Lily's chair and nodded off for a moment. When she awoke, a sour-faced woman with platinum-blond hair was standing in front of her. "If you are finished with your nap, I'd like to talk to you."

"Sure." Louise straightened up. "Sorry, my daughter kept me up last night."

"Uh-huh." The woman was clearly not impressed with Louise's excuse. "I am outraged that you are encouraging children to read this garbage." She held up a book with a red-lipped young woman wearing a halter top on the cover. "This is despicable. My daughter brought it home from school. She said that one of y'all let her check it out. I don't like the idea that my child can get a book from the library without my permission. You are violating my right as a parent to control what my daughter reads."

Louise still hadn't woken up completely from her unintended nap. She stared at the teenager on the book cover as though the sultry-looking girl might speak up and give her an answer. "Um, well, I believe our librarian Sylvia discussed that book at some of the high schools . . ."

A rough hand squeezed her shoulder. She glanced up to see Hope, her mouth set in a hard line. "Ms. Ursula."

"Ms. Hope. Do you know about this?"

"About Ms. Sylvia going into schools and trying to get our young people reading again? I surely do."

"So, you approve." Ursula made a face that suggested she smelled something rotten.

"Well, this is how I see it. If you're gonna get kids to read, you gotta give 'em something they're interested in. You can't just hand over *Moby-Dick* and 'spect a teen to get all hot in the pants about it. This here book is not as bad as it looks. See, they put this kind of cover on these things to draw the kids in, you know. 'Sides, Ms. Ursula, I were you, I'd be more concerned about what your little angel's getting up to behind the bleachers with that Krasky boy."

"Hmpf. Mrs. Gunderson will hear about this." Ursula dropped the book on the desk in front of Louise and stalked out the door.

"I thought you didn't like these young adult novels," Louise said.

Hope folded her arms across her chest and watched Ursula leave. "I don't like her neither. I hope you and Sylvia are working on your presentation to the police jury. That there's what you're up against."

"What *we're* up against," Louise said.

Hope glanced at her, and for a moment, Louise was afraid she was going to argue. "You're right. All of us are in this thing together," she said.

Louise made a fresh pot of coffee for lunch. She bounced on her heels as she watched it drip, another desperate attempt to wake herself up. Listening to loud music with headphones in her cubicle helped a little, but now her ears were ringing. She got her cheese sandwich and apple from the refrigerator and sat at the table. After a couple of minutes, Sylvia and Hope took out their own lunches and joined her.

Mr. Foley poked his head out of his office. Louise had the distinct feeling that he was trying to find something to reprimand them for, but the best he could do was, "Y'all keep it down out here."

"Yessir." Sylvia gave a mock salute, and the bald head disappeared. The miniblinds banged as Mr. Foley slammed the door.

"Don't know what y'all done to him," Hope said. "He used to be a pain in my behind, but now he's a hemorrhoid."

"Did you tip him off about the Zumba last Friday?" Louise asked, biting into her apple.

"No, I done told you I wasn't gonna tell. He probably saw the flyers or something. Why? He show up and shut it down?"

"Tried to, but Marty Pratt was there and she stopped him."

Hope stirred her leftover red beans and rice. "Hoo! You know she's on the police jury. She's basically his boss. One of them, anyhow. No wonder he's in such a state."

"Did you make those red beans?" Sylvia asked. "They smell good."

Her overly sweet tone of voice gave her away: she was up

to something. Louise shot her a questioning look, but Sylvia just smiled.

Hope didn't appear to notice. "Grow my own kidney beans. That's the start of it. Then, I don't use anything but Richard's brand andouille. Don't care what anyone says, that's the best sausage around. Fry it up, then cook up your trinity—that's onion, celery, and green pepper to y'all Northerners—and a bit of garlic in with the grease, and put the whole mess plus your beans in the Crock-Pot. 'Cept you leave out the sausage until you make your rice. Put meat in the pot too early and it gets mushy."

"That's interesting." Sylvia sipped her Diet Coke and appeared to think for a moment. "See, I want to have sort of a wellness campaign at the library."

Hope bit into her cornbread. Her expression was pure skepticism.

Sylvia pushed on. "We have the Zumba. But I think the problem with people today is that no one cooks anymore. That's why they're so fat."

"You right about that," Hope said. "Don't no one know how to cook these days. Act like they don't got time, but they got plenty to watch TV all night. Takes just a few minutes to make up my beans in the morning and I got dinner when I get home. That restaurant food is just garbage."

"The only problem is, I can't cook." Sylvia held up her turkey sandwich. "I can make this, but not much else."

"Girl, your momma didn't teach you?"

"She never cooked much either."

"Too bad."

"So, we could offer cooking classes. But we need someone to teach them. And Louise is already doing the book club."

"No one 'round here wants to learn to make Yankee food anyway. You need someone who can make Southern food,"

Hope said. "But where you gonna get a stove? You can't do it here."

"Why not? Mr. Henry's got a camp stove he can bring. I'm sure we can round up a few more or maybe some hot plates."

"I got a camp stove too. Good for when the power goes out."

"I wonder if Lily can cook," Sylvia said.

Louise had to stop herself from smiling. Sylvia was really laying it on thick.

"That woman can't make nothing but whump biscuits," Hope said, glancing out toward circulation to make sure that Lily was in the patron area shelving books. "And she'd mess those up too 'cept they got directions on the can."

"What about the women at the other branches? Maybe Glenda could do it."

Hope snorted. "You shoulda seen that mess of a cake she brung to the last bake sale. I was embarrassed, and I didn't even make the blessed thing."

"Well, I don't know, then. Maybe we'll have to do something else. Like blood pressure screenings. I think the Red Cross will send someone out."

"That won't get no one excited about the library. Since y'all got me working late Wednesday, I could do it then. But you gotta round up some stoves."

"Hey, that's a great idea! We'll get you whatever you need." Sylvia swept up her trash and threw it away. "I'm going to make some calls right now. While I do that, can you look over the draft of the presentation to the police jury I started?"

"You want me to read it?" Hope said.

Sylvia went into her cubicle and returned with a stapled packet. "Sure. You know all these people. You can tell us how to impress them."

"I don't know about that, but I guess I can try." Hope got a red pen and sat back down at the worktable. She placed the pen behind her ear and began to read.

Mary arrived at exactly four thirty toting her huge backpack. Her pants had a rip in the knee. She put two books in the pile to be checked in and then leaned against the wall.

Louise scanned the books and turned off the circulation computers.

"Don't just stand there, help us close up," Sylvia said. "Shut down these patron computers, please, while I go get my purse."

"Okay, sure." Mary circled the computer tables, setting each of the machines to shutdown mode.

"Your mom is okay with you staying the night at my house?" Louise said.

"Yeah. She just said to be good."

"Come on, gals, let's motor." Sylvia breezed through circulation, and they all went out through the front door together.

Louise was glad it was Sylvia's turn to drive. She was still exhausted, and besides, the van was a minefield of sippy cups and snack containers. She leaned her head back against the seat and half listened as Sylvia and Mary discussed the newest teen novels.

By the time they got home with the kids, Louise just wanted to crawl into bed with a glass of wine and a good book. Instead, she showed Mary around the house and told her where the kids' pajamas and toothbrushes were.

When they got to Max's bedroom, Mary held up a hand. "If you spend any more time explaining stuff to me, the evening will be over. Don't worry, I can figure it out."

"You're right. Okay, there are chicken nuggets in the freezer. Do you know how to operate the stove?"

"If I couldn't do stuff like that, I would have starved a long time ago. Just go. Have fun. Go shopping or whatever."

"Sure, okay." Louise got her reusable bags for the grocery store and the novel she planned to read at the coffee shop. "Bye, kids!"

"See you later, alligator," Max said.

She went out to the van, got in, and started it. Something felt wrong. She looked around at the empty car seats, discarded cups, and forgotten toys. She missed her kids already.

CHAPTER 22

After work the next Thursday, Sylvia drove Louise out to look at the new house. Louise had signed the closing papers, but she hadn't had time to even drive by in the two days since. The movers were scheduled to come the next day, and she wanted to make sure that the place was in acceptable shape. Sylvia had dipped into her savings, and her moving present to Louise was a crew of housekeepers who had spent that morning scrubbing away the previous tenant's dirt.

As soon as Louise walked in the door, she was assaulted by lemon-scented fumes from the cleaning products the crew had used. The place looked spotless. She didn't care that the carpet was unraveling and the kitchen cabinets were painted Pepto-Bismol pink. The price was right, and the quiet neighborhood was just five minutes from the library. She strolled through the house, planning where everything would go. The two upstairs bedrooms would be for her and Zoe, she'd decided, and Max could have the parlor.

"Louise, I think you have a trespasser," Sylvia called from the kitchen.

Louise went back downstairs. From her friend's tone of voice, she expected something harmless—a lizard or a cat maybe.

She joined Sylvia at the kitchen window. She'd bought the house in spite of the backyard. It was nothing special—an unpainted wooden fence surrounding a half acre of weeds. Her promise to get Max a swing set had been weighing on her mind. Even though money was tight, she couldn't let him down.

Looking out the window, she thought she must be dreaming. The grass had been neatly trimmed, and someone had installed a swing set complete with a slide and a sandbox. Sal stepped out from behind a bush he'd been pruning.

"Did he do this?" she asked, still in a daze.

"I don't know," Sylvia said. "But it seems like the most reasonable explanation. And the most reasonable response would be to go out there and thank him."

"Yeah, I guess so." Louise shook her head, trying to clear it. Sal must have spent all day in her yard. He'd given her the best gift she'd ever received, and she hadn't even asked. Even though he didn't have children, he understood her. She felt her throat tighten, but there was no way she was going to cry in front of Sylvia.

Sylvia pulled open the screen door and held it for Louise. "Come on, girl. I doubt he bites."

Sal set down the trimmer, took off his hat, and wiped his forehead with a red bandanna. "Hey, y'all. This was supposed to be a surprise."

"It is," Louise said. "It looks great. I can't believe you did all this."

"Me neither. I'm supposed to be working on my strawberry crop. But Betta told me I needed to do something with this old swing set, so here I am. Figured I'd mow too while I was at it."

"You could teach my Jake a few things," Sylvia said. "When he mows the lawn, it looks like a bad haircut."

"I like doing it. I guess the same reason I like farming. There's real satisfaction in seeing the results of your work. I didn't get that as a lawyer at all."

"I wish I could take you out to dinner, but I have to go pick up the kids," Louise said.

"That's okay. Betta's got some of her gumbo going, and she'll tan my hide if I don't go help her eat it. But I wouldn't say no to a rain check."

"It's a deal," Louise said.

At home, there was a package waiting for Louise on the front steps. She regarded the neatly taped box with suspicion.

"Mommy, can you open it? Please?" Max tried to lift it, but the package was too heavy and he dropped it immediately.

Louise unlocked the door and dragged the box inside. "It's from your daddy."

"Daddy!" Zoe said.

Max jumped up and down. "Open it! Open it!"

"Okay, okay. Hang on a second." Brendan had used far too much tape, and Louise had to saw through the mess of plastic with scissors while Zoe climbed on her back. She resisted the urge to shake the girl off like an oversize fly.

Louise dug through the packing material and found a shirt for Max with a picture of a truck on the front. It was big enough for him to wear as a dress. She gave it to him, and he tossed it to the side. For Zoe, there was a T-shirt that Louise could tell was a size too small. Naturally, Brendan didn't include a receipt. If he had asked, she would have told him the kids' sizes, but of course he hadn't. Brendan always thought he knew everything. When they were married, she hadn't really noticed that he never asked her opinion. It wasn't until after he left that she realized what a doormat she'd been.

He'd sent a plastic doll for Zoe. She wasn't interested in dolls. Predictably, she shoved it into the corner and went into the kitchen to play with the canned goods in the pantry.

Meanwhile, Max was trying to open a package of monster trucks. At least Brendan had gotten something right. Louise freed the trucks from their box after five minutes of hacking at the packaging, and Max raced them across the floor. He was easy to please, at least temporarily.

Louise poured herself a glass of wine before reading the enclosed note: "We hope the children enjoy their presents. I trust everything is ready for the wedding. Brendan and Julia." Louise sipped her wine and started the oven for chicken nuggets while Zoe removed cans from the pantry, lining them up on the kitchen floor. She wished Brendan had gotten Zoe some pretend kitchen accessories.

Louise stuffed the packing peanuts and the note in the trash. She didn't have a wedding gift for Brendan and Julia, but she wasn't really a guest. Max and Zoe were the real invitees, not her. Still, she was probably supposed to bring something. Why couldn't Brendan and Julia just get married in Vegas by an Elvis impersonator?

The stupid staticky peanuts were difficult to corral into the dustpan. Zoe found one and started tearing it into tiny pieces that would be impossible to sweep up. Louise was too tired to stop her. She sat down and finished her wine. She hoped that someday she would stop resenting Brendan and Julia. The anger was not good for her or the kids—she knew that. But every time she thought about them, her whole body tensed.

The oven beeped, and she got up to start the kids' dinner. From the corner of the room, the discarded doll regarded her with sightless eyes.

CHAPTER 23

Louise walked through the old house in Saint Jude, making sure the movers hadn't forgotten anything. She had kept her vow not to go into the backyard. Even through the window, the sight of the tree swing and the little shed where she'd kept the inflatable pool and various balls and toys made her sadder than the empty house. It was just another reminder that her life was changing against her will again.

Max and Zoe didn't even remember the bigger house in Iowa, back when their parents were married. When they first moved to Louisiana, Max sometimes mentioned Brendan, but then he seemed to forget. Louise had been secretly happy when that started happening. Since he didn't do any of the work for the kids, he didn't deserve any love from them. Now that he was moving to Saint Jude, she was going to have to change her attitude, fast. It wouldn't be easy.

Louise locked the house and got into the van. Saint Jude had started to feel like home in the past year. She wasn't sure Alligator Bayou ever would. When she'd first moved to Saint Jude, she'd thought that it was too different from the Midwest and that she would never get used to the South. But Alligator Bayou was something else entirely. Saint Jude was a major metropolitan area compared to that little backwoods town. She was moving somewhere rural and insular. Everyone knew everyone else. She would be even more of an outsider than usual.

When she got to the new house, Sal was out front trimming the bushes with a manual hedge clipper. Ms. Trudy and Betta were kneeling on the ground, planting flowers. Louise parked the van behind Ms. Trudy's Oldsmobile and stared in wonder. The move to Saint Jude had been lonely. No one had helped her unpack, mow the lawn, or fix the holes in the wooden fence. Until she met Sylvia, she'd felt lost. But Alligator Bayou was welcoming her.

Inside, she found Hope and Brianna in the kitchen making lunch. All these people working for her benefit made her feel wanted. She was really going to be part of this town. "I can't believe you all are here just for me," she said.

"Don't nobody move to Alligator Bayou without a proper welcome," Hope said. "Your library patrons been dropping off goodies all morning. Come see."

The countertop near the refrigerator was covered with baked goods: bread, cookies, pralines, pecan pie, pound cake. Each of the homemade gifts came with a handwritten note.

"I feel like I'm marrying into a huge family," Louise said, reading the card attached to a plastic bag of chocolate chip cookies. Clearly, the people in town appreciated what she and Sylvia were trying to do. It was important to them. Without the library, where would Mary go for free lunch, books, and companionship? How would the B sisters keep up with their online friends and find other kids who liked to talk about C. S. Lewis? How would the long-haul trucker get the books on tape to play as he struggled to stay awake on his cross-country rides? Where would Ms. Trudy go for her coffee and *People* magazine? She put the cookies back on the counter and turned to face Hope. "We have to win against this Mrs. Gunderson."

Hope's eyes widened even more than usual. "True enough. Now set down and I'll fix you a plate before we start unpacking these boxes," she said.

Someone had set up a white plastic table and chairs in the kitchen. Louise sat down and watched Brianna dip catfish fillets in egg and then cornmeal and place them in a cast-iron frying pan. She moved nimbly despite her oversize body. Hope stood next to her, loading plates with catfish, white bread, and coleslaw. Louise didn't want to relax when the others were so busy, but she knew better than to argue with Hope.

Hope brought the plates over to the table along with plastic flatware and napkins. When everything was ready, she opened the front door and called out, "Y'all come and eat!"

Sal, Betta, and Ms. Trudy came in, taking off their dirty shoes and washing their hands before crowding around the table. Hope poured paper cups of iced tea, and everyone started eating. Louise poked her plastic fork into the crispy coating on the fish. The flesh was creamy and moist. It was even better with the tangy coleslaw.

Hope stopped the movers as they brought in the first load of boxes. "Y'all find Louise's dining room table and some chairs and set them up before all this gets cold. I reckon y'all want some iced tea anyway after all that lifting."

The two young black men hurried outside to get the table while Belinda filled their paper plates.

Louise looked around at the crew: Sal with his rumpled, curly hair matted down from his John Deere cap; the lanky, gold-toothed movers taking off their leather gloves; Betta in her tight-fitting gardening coveralls; bubbly Brianna bringing over a plate of extra catfish; and Hope forking coleslaw and fish into her mouth like a starving dog. Louise felt almost at home with these people. She'd never be a Southerner, but maybe she could be the eccentric Yankee librarian in town. That might not be so bad.

"I'm glad you're here," Sal said. "We all are."

"You may be from the frozen north, but I reckon you're still good people. We'll keep you," Hope said.

"Serve me food like this and you won't be able to keep me away," Louise said. "What should we have for dessert?"

"Pound cake." Betta brought her empty plate to the kitchen. "I brought my homemade canned strawberries to put on top."

When they'd finished two of the cakes and a jar of sweet strawberry preserves, everyone got back to work. With so many hands unpacking things and putting them away, almost everything was set up by the time Louise had to pick the kids up from their new school. She wished she could find a way to thank everyone. She hugged the women and shook hands with the men as they headed to their cars.

Sal was the last to leave. "Let me take this trash out for you."

"Thanks for everything. I can't believe y'all did this for me."

"My motives aren't all that pure." Sal tied the garbage bag and carried it to the front door.

"What do you mean?"

"I still want that second date with you."

"Me too," Louise said.

CHAPTER 24

Louise sat in her cubicle, drinking a third cup of coffee from the pot she'd made after lunch. Another day of being tired. Just once, she wanted to sleep through the night. Usually Zoe was the one who woke her up, but Max had been plagued with nightmares the last few nights, probably because of being in the new house. He generally went back to sleep with a little reassurance and a story on his iPad, another present from Brendan. Sometimes, though, he'd wake up again just a couple of hours later. Louise was so sleep-deprived that her eyes hurt. She'd even tried napping in the van during her lunch break. It didn't work.

Sylvia popped her head above the cubicle wall. "Ten people," she said.

Louise blinked hard, trying to focus. "For what?"

"Hope's cooking class. I think that's pretty good, for the first one."

A squeak of sneakers and Hope was standing outside Louise's cubicle. "I don't want him shutting us down like he tried to do to y'all's Zumba thing. I want this on the up-and-up. I'm going to tell him right now."

"Okay, but Mr. Henry already approved it," Sylvia said, pushing a cart of new young adult books into her cubicle.

Louise gulped some more coffee and managed to finish cataloging her cart of new mysteries. A few minutes later, she was on her way to the patron area with the cataloged and labeled books when Hope came out of the director's office. She slammed the door and the miniblinds slapped against the glass. She stomped out the back exit without saying anything to Louise and Sylvia.

"We've got to catch her." Sylvia speed-walked to the door and pushed it open. "Hope, wait."

"No, I've had enough. I'm getting out of here. That man done pushed me too far." Hope waved dismissively over her shoulder and kept walking.

"At least tell us what happened," Louise said.

Hope climbed into her pickup truck. "Y'all want to know, come with me."

"Where are you going?"

"Sal's farm."

"We can't just leave," Louise said. She liked the idea of seeing Sal again, but abandoning the library would be completely against her work ethic. She'd never even snuck out on the cafeteria job she'd hated.

"Suit yourself." Hope started to close the truck's door.

"Why not? We're off in an hour anyway," Sylvia said. "Let that lazy bastard check out someone's books for once."

Hope grinned. "Nah, Lily's there. She'll take care of it. 'Sides, she's on the late-night shift today."

"Wait, I have to get something. Don't leave without me." Sylvia rushed inside and came back out with her laptop. She was amazingly fast in her three-inch stilettos.

They squeezed into the front of the cab, Louise in the middle with her thigh pressed against Sylvia's.

"Will you wear my letterman's jacket?" Sylvia said.

Louise laughed. High school probably was the last time she'd been wedged so tightly into a vehicle. "Only if you ask me to prom. I'm not as easy as I look."

Hope started the truck and put it in gear. They were all the way past the Piggly Wiggly before she said, "He told me to get my fat behind out of his office. Only he didn't say it that nice. I've known him since we was kids. He's got no right to talk to me like that." She shot Louise a sideways glance. "Y'all really got him worked up."

"We didn't do anything," Sylvia said.

"Well, you done changed the hours, started these teen programs, book clubs, and then this Zumba thing. He don't like y'all changing things. He's comfortable in his easy little job. He don't want nothing different. Hates it. He and I both remember when you knew everyone's car when they drove down Route One, which used to be Hatfield Lane, named after his daddy. His house was the first one built on his street. Backed up onto an empty field. Now, he can't hardly get out of his subdivision in the morning for all the traffic. Same with me."

"That's no excuse for him acting like a miniature dictator all the time," Louise said.

"Heck, no, it sure isn't. And I'm mad as a treed 'coon. I'm 'bout ready to quit and go back to working at the day care. Little kids give me less trouble than he does."

Sylvia slid against the door as Hope took a hairpin curve too fast. "Why are we going to Sal's farm?"

" 'Cause maybe he'll be able to calm me down. Plus, if his sister's there, we might get us some dinner in the bargain."

"They won't mind us dropping by?" Louise said, bracing herself for another hard turn.

"Nah. He's family. 'Sides, I know he'll want to see Minnesota girl again."

Sylvia nudged Louise in the ribs a little too hard.

"Ow," Louise said.

Hope drove into Louise's new neighborhood and slowed in front of her house. "You liking your new home?"

"Yeah. It's kind of nice to be out here. I didn't even realize how much noise the highway made until we were away from it." Aside from Max's nightmares, the children had quickly taken to the new house. They spent hours in the backyard, swinging and playing in the sandbox. They didn't notice that the house was smaller than the old one or that the carpet was worn down and the kitchen linoleum was peeling in the corner.

Hope came to a complete stop. She hooked her thumb toward the house across the street from Louise's. "You met the Pettigrews?"

"Not yet."

"Old lady's watching us right now. She done moved into that house with her first husband around 1956, and I reckon she ain't hardly budged from that there window since. Hilda goes by to take them a cake now and then, and she says they got one of them console TVs and chairs like you see in *Leave It to Beaver*. Inch of dust on everything." Hope turned the truck onto the dirt road leading up to Sal's. "Harmless enough, I suppose. You oughta stop by and introduce yourself sometime. Once a week, Sal drives his mower over there and does the lawn."

Louise nodded, but she wasn't really listening. This was only the second time she'd been to Sal's place. Was he really as busy as he said? Or was he taking it slow for some other reason? Clearly, he liked her. His sister couldn't have really pushed him into spending all day fixing up her lawn. It had to have been his own idea. Or maybe she just wanted to believe that.

When Sal heard a vehicle crunch up his driveway, he walked around the mobile home to see who it was. February was his busiest month. The strawberries had begun to ripen, and Betta had basically closed down the salon to help him with the school tours and open weekends. Kids came to pick berries, play, and learn about farming. He loved having his property full of children, workers, friends, and family, but there was so much to do that he barely had time to think. He kept meaning to call Louise and never seemed to get around to it. The only reason he was even at the trailer was to feed the dogs and check on his greenhouse strawberries.

The visitor was Hope. He recognized her red pickup truck. Sylvia was the first to get out, and the dogs ran toward her from all directions. She squatted on the ground, and the Chihuahuas tried to lick her face.

After Louise and Hope also stepped down from the truck, some of the attention turned to them. Louise wore a navy-blue jacket and skirt with low-heeled black shoes. She was still gorgeous, but Sal preferred her jeans-and-cowboy-boots ensemble. For one thing, she seemed uncomfortable in the dressy clothes, discreetly tucking her blouse back into the skirt and adjusting her nylons.

Hope cleared a path through the dogs with the top of her black, rubber-soled shoe. "Sal, your Chihuahuas are attacking."

Sal whistled. Two of the dogs ran to him and the rest continued to sniff the visitors. "Y'all have to excuse my animals. They don't have the best manners. I see you brought the whole library."

"Nah, Lily and Matt ain't here," Hope said.

"True. Y'all want to come inside? It's a little cold out here today, especially without jackets." He raised an eyebrow. "Mr. Foley run y'all off?"

"You guessed it," Hope said. "And you better talk me into going back there tomorrow or you and Betta will be feeding me every day."

"She wouldn't mind that a whole lot." Sal held open the door of the trailer, and they all went inside. The dogs followed, knowing it was time for their dinner. He was glad to see Louise and cursed himself for not calling her. Sure, he was busy, but he could have found a minute. Was he afraid? Nervous that he would somehow mess up with her or that she would break his still-bruised heart? "I got white beans for a crowd if y'all want to stay. Betta came over and put them in the Crock-Pot for me this morning. Like I said, she's into feeding people."

"What I want right now is beer," Hope said.

"Help yourself." Sal scooped out food for the dogs, and they lined up to eat, tiny tails wagging.

Sylvia and Louise sat at the kitchen table while Hope rummaged in the fridge.

Sal took the chair next to Louise. He wished that they were alone so he could apologize for being out of touch. "So, y'all haven't told me what you're doing here," he said, accepting a beer from Hope.

"That SOB we work for was rude and obnoxious to me. I had enough of his attitude," Hope said, drinking half of her beer before sitting down next to Sylvia.

"Well, that's nothing really new, is it? Come on, Hope, we've known Foley long enough to expect that kind of thing."

"No, this is different. Ever since Louise and Sylvia here started, he's been a real pain in my behind. Yelling at everyone for talking, sending out nasty e-mails. I told him that I wanted to start offering cooking classes and he said my food stunk. He knows that ain't true! I don't appreciate being treated like a third grader."

"Louise and I are trouble, no question about it," Sylvia said.

Hope snorted. "Y'all aren't the problem. He is."

"The police jury meeting is tonight," Louise said. "Mr. Foley might think we're problem children, but we have to show his bosses that we aren't."

"I done completely forgot about that. Good luck to you. Mrs. Gunderson is tough as they come. She don't vote for nothing that she didn't dream up her own self."

Sal leaned back in his chair. He wanted to help them save the library somehow, but he knew how powerful Gunderson was in town. The woman dealt in favors, and those in her disfavor were punished. They might find themselves pulled over for driving two miles an hour over the speed limit or in front of the police jury in violation of a zoning ordinance they didn't know existed.

"We just have to blow her away," Sylvia said. "In a matter of speaking. Louise and I have worked like crazy on this presentation."

"What I saw of it looked good." Hope raised her beer bottle in a toast. "I truly wish y'all the best."

"I take it we can count on your help." Sylvia batted her eyelashes at Hope.

"Oh, hell, yes. Especially after today. Y'all may be city folk, but you're on the right side of this thing, no question."

The dogs perked up their ears. A moment later, Sal heard a car coming up the drive. He'd lost track of time. He'd promised to help Betta close down the strawberry patch. She must have already counted the money, supervised the workers, made sure all the toys and things were put away, and locked everything up. He owed her one.

He finished his beer and opened the door. Betta came up the steps carrying a chocolate cake. She set it down on the table and shrugged off her brown, furry jacket while the dogs jumped at her knees. “I see you have company. Good thing I made the full batch of beans.”

“They have to eat quick and get off to that police jury meeting,” Sal said.

“Oh, Lord, you have to go to that? Those folks will talk all night about nothing.”

“Well, it’s the library tax. You want string beans to go with this? The ones you put up last month?”

“If that’s all you got.” Betta sat at the kitchen table.

“ ’Course that’s all I got. What do you expect? Goat cheese and miniature arugula?”

“Maybe once.”

“Can we help with anything?” Sylvia asked.

“Nah, I got it.” Sal grabbed a jar of home-canned beans from the cabinet and dumped them into a pan.

Betta got up. “Let me make the rice. You burned it last time.”

“You set there. I’ll make it.” Hope bustled past her cousin and grabbed a large saucepan.

Sal sat back down and watched the women take over. The story of his life, it seemed.

By the time they’d finished slices of Betta’s homemade chocolate cake, Louise wanted nothing more than to lie down on the couch for a long nap. But she was nervous about the meeting. Would a Yankee and a Yat from New Orleans really be able to beat Mrs. Gunderson at her own game?

“I’ll tell you what, Betta,” Hope said. “Your cake makes me feel like I could almost face that bastard again. And Mrs. Gunderson too.”

"I guess you'll be seeing both of them," Betta said, crossing her dainty feet at the ankles.

"Yeah, I imagine our boss will be at the meeting. Not that he's exactly jumping up and down about what these here two are trying to do. We best be going. Thanks, y'all." Hope patted her belly and stood up.

When everyone else was outside, Louise turned to Sal. "I still owe you a date for fixing up my lawn, and my ex's upcoming nuptials don't count."

"You sure do," he said. "But if I remember right, there's also a leaky faucet in your bathroom."

"So it's my place."

"You name the time."

There was no good reason Louise couldn't invite him over on Friday night. But she hesitated. The way her pulse raced when he was near scared her a little. She didn't want a man walking all over her again. "I'll call you," she said.

The sun had gone down, and a cold wind churned up the dirt in Sal's yard. Louise hurried to the truck and got into the front seat next to Sylvia.

"You sure took a long time," Sylvia said. "We almost left without you."

Louise didn't bother to answer. She should have told Sal how much she liked him and that she really wanted him to come over for dinner. She couldn't let her experience with Brendan destroy any possibility of another relationship. Now was not the time to worry about her love life, however. She needed to focus on the presentation to the police jury. "Sylvia, are you ready to do this thing?"

"Of course, girl." Sylvia undid the top button of her blouse. "The presentation is loaded on my laptop right here. We're going to make it really hard for these people to say no."

Hope drove down the street and turned on Main. They passed the post office and the elementary school before coming to city hall. The squat, nondescript brick structure was a mirror image of the library building. The parking lot was already full of pickup trucks and cars.

"Is this the entertainment for the entire town? Don't y'all have cable?" Sylvia said.

Hope cut the engine. "Beats me. I know I got things I'd rather be doing."

The windowless beige room was just as cold as the chilly evening air. An empty table in the front had a nameplate and a microphone for each of the police jury members. Almost all of the audience seats were full. Louise recognized many of the faces on the right side of the room, although she didn't know all the names. She spotted Ms. Trudy, Eleanor, Eloise, and the B sisters and their mother clustered near the front. Mr. Foley and Mr. Henry were a few rows back.

She didn't like the look of the group on the left-hand side of the room. None of them were library regulars, and judging from their glowering faces, they weren't supporters.

A man wearing khaki pants and a press badge motioned them over to a group of empty seats near the back.

"Hey, Breaux," Hope said as they sat down. "I brought our new librarians, Louisiana and Sylvia."

"Y'all are in for a treat. These meetings are never boring."

"Gerald Breaux writes for the *Alligator Bayou Gazette*. Heck, he writes the *Alligator Bayou Gazette*."

"Now, that's not fair. I have a staff of two." Breaux flipped open his reporter's notebook, took the pencil from behind his ear, and wrote something on the page.

The police jury members filed in and took their seats. Marty Pratt and Delilah Perkins could have been sisters.

Both had frizzy, gray-streaked black hair and stood taller than most of the men on the jury. But while Pratt's dress was a conservative navy blue, Perkins wore a puffy polka-dotted frock and knee-high boots. The only jury member taller than the two women, Reverend McDonald, wore a three-piece suit. Beau Foster, the jury president, was balding and corpulent, like a taller version of Mr. Foley.

When Mrs. Gunderson entered the room, all talking ceased. She wore the same jacket-shirt and skirt she'd had on when she'd visited the library. She walked to the table in her chunky heels and adjusted the chair before sitting down.

"There's the Gund. Hattie Gunderson. She runs the show here. Those other folks are just for looks," Breaux said.

"Yeah, I know who she is." The sight of Mrs. Gunderson made Louise's stomach sink. This woman had the power to fire her, cut off all the funding to the library, even close it down if she wanted to. And, if Ms. Trudy was right, she wanted to.

Foster banged a gavel. "I call this meeting to order."

Breaux passed Louise an agenda. "They're gonna discuss Redlight before your thing. I hope your seats are comfortable."

"Juror Reverend McDonald will lead us in the prayer, and then Mrs. Gunderson will lead the Pledge of Allegiance," Foster said.

"Oh, great, the Reverend Cheeseburger," Breaux said. "He'll ask God to bless the entire blessed state before he's done."

McDonald stood and bowed his head. "Our Heavenly Father, we thank you for all the great blessings we have received. We ask you to protect the men and women of the armed forces who are fighting for our freedom around the world. We ask you to bless all the children. All the children, Lord, who are hungry and helpless and homeless in this world. And let us not forget the unborn children. Lord Jesus, we must remember those innocent lives that have yet to begin. And thank you for the free market system, Lord, that wonderful system that has heaped so many blessings on our blessed country. Help us here tonight to make good decisions for our little part of this great country, Lord. Guide our steps and our hearts in all we do. Lord Jesus, we ask for your help in the decisions that will affect all the good and worthy people of our town, your town."

Louise opened her eyes just enough to glance over at Sylvia. She was shaking, trying not to laugh. Who would he bless next? The catfish farmers? The prostitutes in New Orleans? The meeting might never begin.

The reverend sucked in a great quantity of air before continuing. "Lord, help us to make the right decisions in this room. Help us do the right thing for the people of the community, and especially the children whom you knew before they were even born, Lord. In your name we pray. Amen."

Louise and Sylvia both missed saying the "Amen." Sylvia put on an expression of studied seriousness as they turned toward a flag in the corner and recited the Pledge of Allegiance.

"First item on the agenda: Approving the agenda," Foster said when everyone had returned to their seats. He proceeded to read the document in a slow, halting voice.

"Is he actually going to read the entire thing?" Louise asked.

"Word for word," Breaux said.

By the time Foster was finished, Louise's palms were sweaty. She obsessively rehearsed the presentation in her head, not sure whether it was good enough. Too bad there wasn't a magically foolproof way to convince all the skeptics to support the library. They would need powerful voodoo to win over the frowning left-hand side of the room. Even the force of Sylvia's smile might not be enough.

"Do I have a motion for approval?" Foster said.

Pratt spoke up. "So moved."

"That's my snitch," Breaux whispered.

"I know her. She came to Sylvia's Zumba class," Louise said.

"Really?" Breaux looked at Sylvia over his wire-rimmed glasses. "That would have been a sight."

"Second," McDonald said.

"All in favor let it be known by the sign 'aye,' " Foster said.

The jurors ayed.

Foster picked up the agenda and held it in front of his face. "Item two. Redlight. Mrs. Gunderson."

Mrs. Gunderson cleared her throat. "Yes, as you all know, I feel that we made a mistake entering into a contract with this firm. When I get calls from people in the community about people running red lights or speeding, it's through neighborhoods. And we all know why Redlight won't put their radar equipment in subdivisions. They aren't concerned about safety. They're about making money. The sheriff's department needs to have its own traffic division to issue tickets, not this private company."

"We still have two years on the contract," Foster said. "There isn't anything we can do."

"We need to explore our options."

"None of us signed this contract. It was before we all were on the police jury. But we're bound to it now."

"There are always options," Mrs. Gunderson said. "What if we moved their equipment to a dead-end street?

Or set it to only ticket people at twenty miles over the speed limit?"

"They talk about this every meeting," Breaux said. "The horse is long dead and they're still beating on the poor thing." He fixed the pencil behind his ear and leaned back in his chair.

"We can't do that," Foster said. "The contract states that we have to leave the equipment where they put it."

"We need to meet with their representatives. I make a motion that Mr. Foster and I hold a meeting with Redlight and our lawyer and discuss our options." Mrs. Gunderson stabbed her finger into the table.

"Second," McDonald said.

"All in favor, let it be known by the sign 'aye,' " Foster said.

The council ayed. Breaux rolled his eyes.

"Item three. The library budget. Mr. Foley?" Foster said.

Mr. Foley approached the lectern in front of the jurors and pulled the microphone down to his level. "Yes, sir. You all have copies of the budget for this month. You should also have a copy of my projected budget for next year. I always like to get a head start."

Mrs. Gunderson flipped through her packet. "Mr. Foley, in future, if there are this many pages in something, I would prefer them to be numbered. It is hard to refer to a page when there are no numbers."

"Yes, ma'am," Mr. Foley said, his shoulders slumping. "I'm sorry."

Even though she'd witnessed it before, Louise couldn't get used to Mr. Foley's change in attitude around the police jurors. Her boss's voice sounded completely different—polite and placating as opposed to cynical and dismissive. He was like an ape in the presence of an alpha male.

"So, if you turn to, let's see . . ." Mrs. Gunderson made a

show of counting. "Page nine. You have budgeted a thousand dollars more for supplies than last year. Do you really need that many pencils?"

"No, ma'am. But the cost of everything will go up next year. My supplier told me—"

"Cut back, then. And make sure the employees don't steal anything. Lord knows, those people you hire . . ."

"Yes, ma'am."

"Moving right along. On page three, you have budgeted an increase for utilities as well."

"I expect our costs to rise. And we are keeping the library open slightly longer hours and on Saturdays."

Mrs. Gunderson cut him off. "I notice that there are windows in the workroom. Perhaps, you could leave the lights off during the day and have your employees open the blinds. At least in the winter, when it wouldn't make the room much hotter."

Breaux slapped his forehead. Mrs. Gunderson glared at him.

"Yes, ma'am," Mr. Foley said.

"And what about these longer hours? Do patrons actually take advantage of them?"

"Yes, ma'am. My employees report a twenty percent increase in gate traffic since we have expanded our hours."

Sylvia looked at Louise. They had provided Mr. Foley with the increase in patronage. He'd acted unimpressed, but now he was reporting it to the board without mentioning that he'd fought the extended hours until Sylvia threatened to quit. A jerk move. But maybe he'd finally come over to their side.

"That's good, I suppose. Except that more patronage doesn't bring in more money unless they forget to turn in their books on time." Mrs. Gunderson turned the page with unnecessary force. "What about this line for 'multimedia equipment'? I don't recall this from last year's budget."

"Well, ma'am, technology is changing. We all need to stay in the loop."

Louise and Sylvia exchanged glances again. Another surprise. Mr. Foley seemed to be considering buying DVDs and CDs for the library. The goat farmer might actually be smart enough to realize that he'd been wrong.

Louise daydreamed as Mrs. Gunderson picked through the rest of the budget. Maybe they should talk more about the children's programs during their presentation. Mentioning the Zumba classes could be a mistake since Mr. Foley had been so against the idea. Also, Mrs. Gunderson would probably be scandalized by Sylvia's proposal to hold a dance at the library. What about e-books? Should they talk about that more since it was something they actually agreed with her about?

Sylvia elbowed her. "Wake up. They're talking about the tax."

" '. . . to allow for the following to appear on the May 14 ballot. A one mill property tax to be levied by the parish in effect for ten years beginning in September.' " Foster was laboriously reading from a legal document.

Louise's mind wandered again. She came back to reality when Mrs. Gunderson's aggrieved voice replaced Foster's weak one. "I feel that the library has not shown us what it can accomplish with the money it already has. Why should we ask the people of our parish to give more?" she said.

"The library is an important educational tool for our children," Pratt said.

"Please. Everyone knows that most people just go over the border to Saint Jude Parish and check out books there. The people that still even use libraries, that is."

"But as our libraries here get better, people will use them."

"Really? I doubt it. Who even reads books anymore? Who has time?"

Foster banged his gavel. "I hereby open the floor for public comments. Is there anyone wishing to speak for the library?"

The board secretary, Regina Lewis, stood up from her chair next to the police jury table. Regina was a library regular and reader of cozy mysteries and gardening books. It made Louise feel a little more optimistic to see a library supporter.

"I believe we have a request to speak from two of our librarians, Sylvia Jones and Louisiana Richardson," Regina said, smiling encouragingly at Louise.

"Please come forward," Foster said. "State your names and addresses for the record."

Sylvia dimmed the lights and plugged her laptop into the projector. "We just want to give y'all a taste of what we have been doing."

"Name and address, please," Mrs. Gunderson said.

"Sylvia Jones, 5990 Whitehorse Way, Saint Jude."

Mrs. Gunderson made a disgusted noise, her comment on Sylvia's outsider status.

Louise recited her own address while Sylvia punched a button on the laptop. A photo of the B sisters filled the screen.

"This is your community," Sylvia said. "We'd like to think that it's now our community as well. And we are here to serve it—to serve you—any way we can."

Louise took over projection duties, switching to a picture of a group of high school students around a table of books in the library.

"Education doesn't stop with the classroom, or when the kids leave school, or when they reach a certain age. We provide a variety of different programs for children and adults in a variety of different areas—fitness, art, reading, and more," Sylvia said.

Louise advanced to photos of the adult book club, the Zumba class, the children's story time, and Sylvia teaching a group of teenagers to make memory books.

Sylvia continued, "We all have things to learn every day. To help us advance our careers, make more money, have better lives, and have more fun. All of these things are important. And we can do it all. This library is not just about books. Libraries are about expanding opportunities for everyone. No one is excluded because they are too old, too young, or too poor. We serve everyone. But right now, our budget is stretched. Last year, the voters didn't approve our tax. Louise and I were hired using a grant from the feds. That grant expires this year. If this tax doesn't pass, we'll both be laid off. There wouldn't be enough staff left to continue the expanded hours in the main library or to try doing the same at the other branches. In fact, all the branches of the library would have to start closing on Mondays to save money. The book-buying budget would be frozen. Essentially, this library would slowly die and we'd lose everything we worked for."

Sylvia paused and Louise clicked ahead to a photo of the outside of the building. "The passage of the tax would mean we could make a few improvements. We need to do maintenance on our building, which dates back to the 1980s. We need money for new technology—updated computers, software, CDs and DVDs, e-readers, e-books. We also need more staff to help us expand our hours, our programs, and our outreach to those who can't come to us. The extra hundred fifty thousand dollars per year we expect to receive from this tax isn't a lot, but it would allow us to at least move forward rather than backward."

"If that is all, Ms. Sylvia, we will go to a vote," Foster said.

"Now hang on here one minute." Hope came up the aisle, went to the microphone, and stated her name and address. "I didn't support these two troublemakers when they got here, nohow. Thought they were just a couple of Yankees looking to stir things up."

"Hey, I'm no Yankee," Sylvia said.

Hope held up her hand. "But I've come around. These here ladies care about this community. I reckon Ms. Louise woulda rather stayed at Louisiana A&M at first and maybe even Ms. Sylvia too. But then, they fell for the place, the people here. Louisiana even bought that place up by my cousin Sal's. 'Cause we are good people. And we want to better ourselves in all the ways she done talked about and some she didn't. We can't be depending on Saint Jude and New Orleans to carry us on their backs no more. We got to do for ourselves. And these two here are gonna help us with that. That's all."

Ms. Trudy and her friends, the B family, and a few others around them clapped. Louise felt a tiny sliver of hope return.

Ms. Trudy came forward, told her name and address, and cleared her throat. "I just want to speak for myself, Ms. Brianna, Ms. Eloise, and Ms. Eleanor . . ."

"Please get to the point, Ms. Trudy," Mrs. Gunderson interrupted.

"All of us who use the library. We have been enriched by all these ladies have done, and I believe they have earned our support." Ms. Trudy returned to her seat.

"We have a few more requests to speak," the secretary said.

Ursula, the woman who had complained about her daughter's book selection, stood up. She wore a gray suit and a grim expression. Louise's hope wavered.

"Please approach the microphone and state your name and address," Foster said.

Breaux leaned over and whispered, "That's Ursula Broussard. She runs this group called Tax Free Louisiana. She's against everything."

Ursula recited her name and address. "I just don't see why we need a library at all. Kids have libraries in their schools. The rest of us got the Internet and Books-A-Million. The time I went in the library, I just saw a bunch of old ladies getting romances and trash like that. I mean, really, they could start a book swap or something. We already pay too many taxes for things like this. People need to take care of their own selves and not expect the government to do everything for them."

"Thank you, Ms. Broussard, for your opinion," Foster said. "Anyone else?"

A parade of taxpayers followed Ursula Broussard's lead. Most of them said basically the same thing. Louise slumped farther down in her chair. The whole town seemed to be against the library.

Breaux leaned over again. "Don't think too much of this. They're all on the same team, if you know what I mean."

"No, I don't."

"I mean, they're all friends of Gunderson. She trots them out whenever she's opposed to something. Gets them to sound off and make it look like the whole community's against whatever it is."

A man in work boots and jeans that sagged in back

concluded his speech about welfare parasites and returned to his seat.

Foster banged his gavel again. "I declare the public hearing closed. It is time to call the question. Do we have a motion?"

"I make a motion that we pass this. I mean, we should try to get this tax on the ballot," Pratt said.

Mrs. Gunderson folded her arms over her ample chest. The other jurors stared at the table. Pratt nudged her friend, but Delilah ignored her.

"Motion dies for lack of a second," Breaux said, writing in his notebook.

Sylvia stood up. "Wait, you can't do this."

Foster fixed her with his emotionless blue eyes. "The public hearing is over. Please sit down."

Sylvia obeyed, looking a question at Breaux.

He shrugged. "There's nothing we can do right now."

"I make a motion that we revisit this at our next meeting," Pratt said.

"By then, it will be too late to get it on the ballot in May," Mrs. Gunderson said.

Foster put the agenda in front of his face again. "Next item."

Hope made a "huff" noise before heading for the exit. Louise and Sylvia followed. Back in the truck, Louise was colder than ever. "What are we going to do?"

"Nothing," Hope said, fiddling with the dashboard heat control. "It's over."

"No, it's not," Sylvia said. "The May election isn't the last one ever."

"Might as well be. They ain't gonna put it on the ballot."

"I wish you'd told me that our jobs were paid for by a grant that's about to expire before I bought a house out here," Louise said.

"I just found out." Sylvia put her laptop on the floor between her feet. "Mr. Henry didn't give me the numbers until this afternoon. I don't know why. Could be he forgot, or maybe he and Mr. Foley didn't want us to know."

Hope revved the engine on the truck. "I knew things was tight, but I didn't know about no grant either. Y'all better start working on saving your jobs."

"Thanks for the tip. Got any ideas?" Sylvia asked.

"Nope. You might could try praying."

CHAPTER 25

Sal stood on Louise's porch holding his father's old canvas tool bag. He kept it in the truck for quick fixes around the farm. Until he came back to Alligator Bayou, he hadn't realized how much he'd missed being surrounded by familiar, old things: his dad's tools, his mom's wooden spoons, the land itself. All of it gave him a sense of identity, of home. Louise didn't have any of that. She was starting over, just like he did when he went to Chicago. It was no easy thing.

He shifted the bag to his left hand and rang the doorbell. Nothing. Well, there wouldn't be a shortage of jobs for him to do for her. He took a screwdriver out of his bag and detached the doorbell from the siding.

Sal was so engrossed in the job that he forgot to knock. When the door swung open, he was startled. Louise stood in the doorway wearing her usual jeans and black T-shirt. Her hair was pulled back into a messy ponytail. She looked stunning. "Your doorbell's broken," he said.

"I know." She tucked a strand of loose hair behind her ear.

Zoe peeked at him from around her mother's legs. Sal winked at her and she disappeared again.

"This thing's pretty old. I think I'll just pick up a new one for you." Sal replaced the doorbell and put the screwdriver back in the tool bag.

"You don't have to do that," Louise said, stepping aside so he could come in.

"I want to. Anyway, strawberry season's over so I need a project."

"So, I'm your project?"

Inside, the house smelled like butter and cinnamon. Sal's stomach grumbled. "Just to be fair, I can be your project too. Especially if the project involves your cooking."

Louise walked through the living room to the kitchen and grabbed an apron from a hook on the wall. "It's nice to have an appreciative audience. The kids won't eat most of what I make. I end up having leftovers for lunch until I get so sick of the stuff I can barely stand it."

Sal straddled one of the cane-bottomed kitchen chairs. Next time he came, he'd bring some paint for the hideous pink cabinets. He'd ask Louise, but he thought chocolate would match the floor and walls and wouldn't show too much dirt.

Zoe tiptoed in from the hallway and stared. Sal patted the chair next to him, but she didn't move.

Max ran into the kitchen. "Hey, what's that?"

"My tool bag," Sal said. "Do you want to see what's inside?"

The boy nodded. Both children crept forward as he took things out of the bag—screwdrivers, a hammer, wrenches, a towel rack.

"What's that?" Max asked.

"The towel rack we're going to put in your bathroom."

"Let's do it."

"Don't get in Mr. Sal's way," Louise said. She poured rice into one of the pots on the stove and then turned to stir something in another pan.

"They're going to help, right, guys?" Sal said.

"You might get more than you bargained for." Louise opened the refrigerator. "I suggest you take a beer with you."

"I can't say no to that," Sal said. He accepted the bottle and picked up his tool bag.

Max and Zoe followed him to the bathroom. The room was so small that Sal had to wedge himself between the toilet and the wall. The kids stood by the pedestal sink, eyeing him as though he were an exotic and possibly dangerous animal.

"Where should we put it?" he asked.

"I don't know," Max said, taking a step forward.

The only place to put the rack was right over the toilet. As soon as Sal turned on the drill, Zoe ran out the door. Max watched with his mouth hanging slightly open.

"Can I do that?" the boy asked.

"No, but you can find a screwdriver for me," Sal said.

By the time they were finished installing the rack and fixing the sink, Sal had explained the function of every item in the tool bag twice.

"Dinner's ready," Louise called from the kitchen.

Sal gathered up his beer and tools. Max trailed him to the table and insisted that they sit next to each other. He put his napkin on his lap, copying Sal.

Louise set out bowls of rice, applesauce, and coleslaw. There was a platter of thick pork chops right in front of Sal's place setting. He lifted the largest one onto his plate.

"I want one too," Max said.

"Okay." Sal put one on his plate and began cutting it into small pieces.

"I want it big like yours."

"I'm going to cut mine up as soon as I finish yours," Sal said.

Louise passed the applesauce across the table. “I haven’t cooked like this since . . .” She trailed off, scooping rice onto Zoe’s plate.

“I know,” Sal said. “You don’t need to say it.”

“Yeah.” Louise pushed the rice bowl toward him. “But I don’t miss him. Not even a little bit.”

“Miss who?” Max asked.

“Hey, buddy, tell your mom what we did,” Sal said.

“We used a drill. It was loud.”

“Loud.” Zoe put her hands over her ears.

During dinner, Sal learned the names of all Zoe’s friends at school and Max’s favorite superheroes. Zoe wished she were a dog. Max wanted to be an astronaut when he grew up. Sal found all their views and ideas hilarious. Louise had clearly heard it all before, but she still smiled.

After dinner, Sal volunteered to get the kids ready for bed while Louise did the dishes. The relief in her face when he offered made him sad. He worked hard all day, but after dinner he could watch TV and go to bed rather than tend to the endless needs of small children.

By the time he’d finished getting the kids into their pajamas, brushing their teeth, finding Zoe’s misplaced stuffed rabbit, and reading Max three Spider-Man books, he was ready for another beer. Instead, he sat on Zoe’s bed, his legs stretched out on top of her princess comforter. The girl was wary of him at first. By the time he finished the second book, she’d crept up from the end of the bed and snuggled up next to him, pressing her bony shoulder against his side.

“One more book! One more book!”

“I think I’m falling asleep.” Sal put his head down on something that was either a pillow or a fat purple unicorn and made snoring noises.

“Wake up, Mr. Sal! Wake up!”

Sal opened his eyes. "Okay, just one more. Your brother's already asleep, you know."

Zoe reached into the bookshelf above her bed and grabbed a book, apparently at random. Reading the story about Minnie Mouse and friends, Sal held onto the moment. Somewhere in the back of his mind, he'd always pictured himself as a dad putting his kids to bed. Along the line, it had gone wrong somehow. The opportunity had passed by without him even realizing it.

When he came back to the living room, Louise was opening a bottle of wine.

"I'm ready for a glass of that for sure," he said, leaning against the counter.

"They don't stop, do they?" Louise poured two glasses. "I mean, they're great, but it's exhausting."

"I see that. It took me five minutes to convince Max to open his mouth so I could brush his teeth."

"That's not bad. It usually takes me at least six."

"So, what's going on with your job?" Sal sat down on the couch and sipped his wine.

Louise lowered herself onto an armchair. She had dark circles under her eyes, and her ponytail was falling out of its elastic holder. "I don't know what we're going to do. Sylvia and I are paid with a grant. If we don't get that money next year, we'll be laid off."

"I'm pretty sure there's a way to work around the police jury and get the tax on the ballot. You should be able to get the citizens to sign a petition. I think if you get enough signatures, they have to put it on the ballot. Talk to Gerald Breaux. He knows just about everything about this town." Sal knew the answer was lame. Ever since he'd heard about what had happened at the police jury meeting, he'd been trying to think of a way to get the library system the money it needed. He had an idea, but he'd need help to make it work. Even then, it might not be enough. Gunderson was too powerful. If she didn't want something to happen, generally it didn't.

"Breaux was at the meeting," Louise said.

"Oh, of course. Did you ask him what to do?"

"No, we left right after the vote and I haven't talked to him since. I just bought this house, and I really don't want to leave now. I was an idiot. I didn't know our salaries were dependent on this grant. I guess Sylvia and I were so busy trying to make the library better that we didn't think about it."

Sal set down his empty glass on the end table. He'd drunk the wine too fast without noticing. "This fight is not over. You, Sylvia, and Hope are smarter than Mr. Foley and Mrs. Gunderson. I've lived here most of my life and I can tell you that the people will vote for this. Y'all just need to get it on the ballot."

"Yeah, I hope so."

"I have to get home. The dogs will be looking to be fed, and I have some new heirloom strawberries I need to check on." He stood up.

"Okay," Louise said. She stepped toward him and then hesitated.

Sal took both her hands in his, leaned forward, and kissed her lightly on the cheek. Louise pulled him closer and looped her arms around his neck. He put his arms around her waist and brought his lips to hers again. Holding her felt as good as he'd dreamed it would.

CHAPTER 26

The *Alligator Bayou Gazette* operated out of a corrugated-steel building set far back from the road. Louise knocked while Sylvia tried to peek in the window.

"Hey, what're y'all doing here?" Breaux answered the door with a biscuit sandwich in one hand and a cell phone in the other.

"We thought you might could help us out," Louise said. After the words left her mouth, she realized she'd used the weird Alligator Bayou expression without even thinking about it. She was going native.

Breaux didn't appear to notice. "I was just talking with the mayor. Police chief is being asked to leave and I was trying to find out why. Turns out some of his subordinates claim he creates a hostile environment. Even his own daughter-in-law says he's a mean old coot. Can't get the mayor to tell me anything about it, though. Come on in. It's not much, but it's home. Rest of the building is the distribution warehouse. I get this little corner."

The office was barely big enough for two desks. One had a computer on it, and the other was piled up with papers and notebooks. Industrial beige walls were decorated with comic strips cut from the newspaper and framed photos of scenes from the early days of Alligator Bayou, including one of a man with a handlebar mustache standing in front of a two-story-high log pile.

Sylvia and Louise sat in the spare office chairs. Breaux balanced his sandwich on top of a stack of newspapers and took a seat in front of his computer.

"We need to know how to get a library tax on the ballot," Louise said.

"Well, according to the parish charter, if you get a thousand signatures, you can put anything on the ballot," Breaux said.

"Really? Well, that's a useful piece of information that you could have told us at the meeting," Sylvia said, uncrossing her legs and planting her black boots on the floor.

"Y'all left so fast, I didn't get a chance to tell you. Plus, I thought maybe your lawyer turned strawberry farmer friend might know."

Louise wasn't too surprised that Breaux knew about her and Sal. "I don't think he's studied the parish charter."

Breaux retrieved his sandwich and took a bite. "I guess not. Anyway, you can't do it yourselves, of course. Being public employees and all. I can write you an editorial. Then you might have the votes of my three readers."

"Thanks," Louise said.

Breaux washed down another mouthful of sandwich with coffee from a *Gazette* mug. "Y'all remember all those people the Gund had talking at the police jury meeting when they nixed the bond?"

"The concerned citizens against the library, yeah."

"They'll probably cook up something else too. Last time the tax was on the ballot, they made up some barely literate flyers and passed them out in the trailer parks. 'Course, nobody did anything for the library that time since it was just

Mutt and Jeff—your director and his lackey—in there and they didn't seem to give a rat's behind what happened. You gotta use their methods. Get the word out."

"Ms. Trudy can do it. She can form a Friends of the Library group or something," Sylvia said. "That way she can raise money as a nonprofit organization."

Breaux nodded. "Don't underestimate that old bird. She'll take on the Gund and her clan without blinking an eye."

CHAPTER 27

The morning Brendan was scheduled to arrive, Louise wanted to just stay in bed. The day he had packed up his clothes and left, he'd accused her of letting herself go after the children were born. "You could join the gym at least," he'd said. Louise hadn't bothered to remind him that he refused to help with the kids enough so that she could get adequate sleep let alone work out. She also didn't point out that he never set foot inside a gym. Being thin didn't make him fit. As he walked out the door with his suitcase, she allowed herself to notice his scrawny arms and skinny neck. She'd stupidly hoped it might be the last time she saw him, even though she knew that the children made that impossible. And soon he would be back in her life for good.

While she was fixing Zoe's hair, Max ran in wearing nothing but a stocking cap. "Can I watch TV?"

"Not until you get dressed. Underwear, pants, shirt, socks, and shoes. No hat."

After he ran off to his room, Louise managed to laugh and calm down enough to make halfway decent pigtails. Zoe had an amazing amount of hair, and even though it took five minutes to style every morning, Louise couldn't bring herself to cut off the bouncy curls.

She selected an outfit for Zoe. The pants were too small and the shirt rode up over her belly. "You're going to be tall like your daddy," she said.

"Daddy," Zoe repeated.

Hearing her say the word almost made Louise cry, but she tried to smile back at Zoe as she got out a dress for her instead. "Let's wear this one."

"Dess." Zoe grabbed the matching leggings and tried to put them on herself. She ended up with both legs in the same hole.

Max came in with his clothes on backward. "Can I watch TV?"

"Not yet. You have to put your shirt and pants on the right way. The picture goes in front, remember?" Louise said.

Max looked down at his chest and pulled off the shirt. Now, it was inside out. Louise reversed the tee and handed it back to him. She decided not to bother making him fix the pants. They were sweats anyway, so no one would notice.

While Max and Zoe watched TV, Louise straightened the living room. The children had decorated the kitchen cabinets with markers and stickers, the table and floor were sticky, and the stove was crusted with runover from the previous day's spaghetti sauce. There was no way she could get it all done before going to work. Dishes were the first priority. She got a load going and swiped at the stove with a sponge.

Once at work, Louise couldn't concentrate on her cataloging. Brendan's wedding had been in the back of her mind, but she'd had trouble believing that it was really going to happen. Now that he was on his way, it finally seemed real. All the work she'd done to put distance—emotional and physical—between them had been for nothing. Seeing him again might reduce her to her former state of spineless doormat. She couldn't let that happen. She had to stand behind her decisions about her job and the children no matter how much he criticized her.

She had cataloged half the books on the cart and gathered her things to leave for her lunch-break workout when he called.

"Hey, we're here."

"I'm at work and the kids are in school." She tried to drink some coffee, but the mug shook in her unsteady hand. She set it down carefully.

"I'll pick them up," Brendan said.

"You're not on the list of people they're allowed to leave with."

"I'm their father."

"It doesn't matter. You still have to be on the list and I forgot to add you, I'm sorry. Look, just wait until I get off work at five thirty."

"What am I supposed to do until then? We were going to take them swimming in the hotel pool."

Louise wanted to reach through the phone, grab her ex, and shake some sense into him. Not that it would do any good. "Zoe is two and Max is three and a half. They can't swim. I told you that."

"It's not my fault that you haven't taught them."

In her fantasy, Louise switched from shaking him to choking him. "Max had lessons this past summer. But that doesn't mean he can really swim. Those hotel pools are deep."

"So what? We'll be watching them."

"They are my kids. And I don't like it."

"They're mine too."

"You could have fooled me. You've never shown any interest in them."

"Why do you think I'm moving? Because I like heat and mudbugs?" Brendan emphasized the word "mudbugs."

"I'm sure Louisiana A&M gave you more money," Louise said.

"Maybe, but I never would have bothered to move if you hadn't dragged my kids down here."

"This was the only place I could get a library science professor job. You know that."

Louise was shaking so hard that she was afraid she was having a full-blown anxiety attack. She closed her eyes and began to count: *One, two, three, four, five . . .*

Brendan sniffed loudly into the phone. "Look, I don't want to argue. I just want to see the kids."

Louise opened her eyes and stared at Zoe's drawing of different sizes of circles pinned to her cubicle wall. "How about tomorrow? You and Julia have a relaxing day at the hotel and pick them up in the morning."

"Louise, we're only going to be in town for a few days."

"Yes, but—"

"Six o'clock? That'll give you time to get them ready. We'll take them out to dinner and bring them back in time for bed."

Louise glanced up and saw Mr. Foley leaving his office. If he heard her talking on the phone, he would go into lunatic mode. She didn't feel like dealing with another jerk. "Okay. Fine." She hung up the phone, tossed it into her bag, and left.

Despite her still-precarious financial situation, Louise had kept the gym membership. Not because of Brendan but for herself. After some calculation, she'd decided she could afford it if she cut out fast food and drive-through coffee. By the time the weight-lifting class ended, she was sweaty and starving but relatively calm. She ate a cheese sandwich and drank iced tea on the way back to the library.

"Where have you been, girl?" Sylvia asked when she walked in the back door.

"The gym. Lunch break." Louise slipped into her cubicle. "I thought you were doing book talks."

"The kids are all at lunch right now, but I'm going back in a few minutes. I've been trying to call you. Your ex is here."

"Brendan? In the library?"

Sylvia nodded. "With his cute little fiancée. I shouldn't say little. She's skinny, but almost as tall as I am. Gorgeous too."

"I know, I know. Rub it in a little more, would you, please? What the heck are they doing here?"

"He said he wanted to see where you worked. The girlfriend didn't look so thrilled. What does she do?"

Louise felt nauseated. She drank some tea. "She's a graduate student in English."

"Robbing the cradle, is he?"

"I think she's twenty-five."

"Barf." Sylvia tossed her hair. "Do you want me to tell them to leave? That you had to go home or something?"

"No. I'll go out there in a few minutes."

Sylvia picked up her bag and a pile of paperbacks with sad-eyed teenagers on the covers. "I have to go. Good luck, girl."

Louise finished the tea, trying to calm herself down. Knowing that Julia was coming, she'd worn her highest heels. Even with the lift, the graduate student would have a couple of inches on her. Not to mention a mane of wavy blond hair and perfect skin and teeth. The first time Louise had seen Julia looking at Brendan during that fateful English department party, she'd known she was in trouble. At the time, she hadn't even known that Julia was also brilliant and shared Brendan's love for nineteenth-century British literature.

Louise stood up and looked into Mr. Foley's office. It was dark. He'd left early. The director didn't clock forty hours a week anymore. Not that he actually had to use the time clock like the rest of them. She continued past his office and got a glimpse of her ex through the doorway. She took a deep breath and walked through the door to circulation.

Brendan leaned against the front desk. He couldn't believe that Louise had sunk so low. Alligator Bayou wasn't much more than a wide place in the road, and the library was a dreary box. He felt like he should be wearing a cowboy hat and boots in this hick town. He'd dragged Julia out here against her will. She didn't understand why he wanted to see where his ex-wife worked. Well, he was curious, that was all. Louise hadn't even told him about her new job. He'd had to call A&M and chat up the English department secretary to get the news.

Julia was showing her disdain for the whole trip by engrossing herself in her smartphone. Big surprise. Brendan turned around just as Louise walked out from the employee area. She looked the same as the last time he'd seen her. Louise never dyed her hair or kept up with current fashion trends. He recognized the geometric-patterned red-and-white skirt she wore. He'd helped her pick it out on a long-ago shopping trip. Julia never kept a piece of clothing for more than two seasons. Brendan never bothered to ask what she did with them. Anyway, Julia always looked fantastic and she paid for her clothes with her own money so it was none of his business.

"You finally came back! I thought you worked here," he said to his ex-wife.

"Lunch break." Louise met his eyes, her expression unreadable. "Hi, Julia."

"Hi." Julia didn't glance up from her phone.

"So, what's there to do in Alligator Bayou?" Brendan asked.

"Not much." Louise's face was still closed. She hated him; he could see that. He couldn't blame her too much, but it had been almost a year since their divorce. Couldn't she at least treat him like a human being? Be civil in front of Julia? Not that his fiancée cared. She probably wasn't even listening to the conversation, if you could call it that.

He lowered his voice. "Seriously, this is the best job you could get?"

Louise visibly clenched her teeth. "I have to go back to work now."

A brown-haired, mousy librarian lady pushed an empty book cart across the floor and brought it behind the circulation desk. "Can I help y'all?"

"No, thanks," Brendan said. "We were just going. Actually, do you know a good place for lunch?"

The woman's eyes darted between Brendan, Julia, and Louise. She was clearly trying to assess the situation and failing. Louise shrugged and walked back to the employee area.

"There's Anthony's just around the corner and Main Street Café down the road a ways. That's pretty much it unless you want gas station fried chicken," the woman said.

"Thanks," Brendan said. He'd already decided to head back to Saint Jude.

After Brendan and Julia left, Louise found it impossible to get anything accomplished. She cataloged for two hours, but only managed to work through half the books left on the truck. She couldn't stop thinking about Julia, in all her breathtaking perfection. In contrast to Louise, the underemployed rural librarian, Julia was a promising young scholar. Once she finished her PhD, she'd have job offers around the country. Of course, if she wanted to stay with Brendan, she'd be stuck in Louisiana like Louise. Though the state had started to not seem so bad, at least until Brendan arrived.

"I should have just taken the day off," Louise said, opening a new best seller to the title page.

Sylvia's head appeared above the cubicle wall. "You should have come to my book talks. Those teenagers are a hoot. They're so excited about the mystery game I'm planning at the library. They were asking me all these questions about costumes and how it works. I think it was a great idea, if I do say so myself."

Louise tossed the novel aside. She doubted high school students would cheer her up. Right at that moment, only three people came to mind with that power and two were in day care.

"I know something that might make you feel better," Sylvia said, raising her eyebrows suggestively. "Sal just walked in."

"How do you know? Do you have special powers I don't know about?"

"Extrasensory hunk detection." Sylvia's head disappeared, and her bracelets clacked against the keyboard. "No, I hear Lily out there mooning over him."

"She's a little old."

"Give the girl a break. She can flirt if she wants to."

Just knowing Sal was in the library lifted Louise out of her funk. She put down the novel, pushed the book cart out of the way, and left her cubicle.

When she came through the doorway to the circulation

area, the crow's feet around Sal's eyes crinkled. "Do you have some book recommendations for me?" he asked.

"Um, I'll have to think about it."

"Lily here only reads teen romances," Sal said. "She's no help at all."

Lily looked at him like he was lunch, chocolate, and Bradley Cooper all rolled into one. "Sal's such a card."

"I'll watch the desk if you want to take your lunch break," Louise said.

Lily hesitated but gave in. "I'll be in the kitchen if y'all need me. See you later, Sal."

Sal saluted and leaned against the counter again. "Full disclosure. I don't really need any more books yet."

Louise looked down at her hands. Short, stubby fingers, no manicure, not even any fingernail polish. She could never compete with Julia. If Brendan's fiancée were here, would Sal be talking to her instead? "So, why are you here?"

"Since your ex is in town, I thought you might want to go out to dinner."

"I'd love to. He wants to take the kids tonight. I can hardly stand him and his perfect fiancée. She was here two hours ago using her powers of blond gorgeousness to destroy my self-esteem."

"I got the impression this visit wasn't going to be a whole lot of fun for you." He produced a red rose from behind his back. "I know it's not Valentine's Day, but I thought you needed it. I grew this in my greenhouse. Tell you what, it's not easy to grow roses here. I don't even know why I planted them. Maybe I was just hoping I'd meet someone I wanted to give them to."

Louise took the rose and stroked one of the soft petals. "Thanks. I should tell you that I have a bad history of killing plants. Not on purpose."

"Don't worry. Just put it in some water. I think Hope has a vase back there in the kitchen. And enjoy it."

"It's beautiful."

"Not as beautiful as you."

Just like that Julia was gone from Louise's mind. She was going to focus on the positive, especially this incredibly handsome farmer in front of her.

CHAPTER 28

Louise and Sylvia went out to the parking lot after work and stood in the late-afternoon sunlight.

Sylvia put on her sunglasses and leaned against the door of her SUV. "I still can't believe you're dating the hot farmer. I love Jake a lot, but I'm still going to live vicariously through you."

"God, please don't call him the hot farmer to his face. Hunky Strawberry Man would be much better." Louise scanned the street for Sal's car. He was going with her to get the kids from school and bring them back to her house. Brendan and Julia were supposed to come by later and take them to dinner. She didn't know where they were going, but she wasn't giving advice unless he asked. Which he wouldn't. "I can't believe he is actually interested in me."

Sylvia looked at Louise over the top of her sunglasses. "Shut up! Why not? You're cute, funny, interesting, personable when you want to be."

"Yeah, that's why Brendan left me for the leggy blonde with the Einstein brain."

"He left you because he is a jackass. Besides, you and Sal

have been dating a few weeks now and things are going well, right?"

"Yeah. It's just that having my ex around makes me miserable."

"Well, he's not as cute as Sal, I'll tell you that. That farmer is smart, funny, good-looking, and crazy about you. Forget about stupid what's-his-name."

"I'm trying, but him being around all the time isn't helping. Maybe I'll get used to him. Like an ache in my toe."

Sal's truck pulled into the library lot, and Louise felt a little rush of excitement. Seeing him did make her almost forget about Brendan.

He rolled down the window and leaned out. "Ready to go?"

"Yeah. What about the truck?"

"I'll leave it here for now." Sal got out of the pickup and followed Louise to her van.

After waving good-bye to Sylvia, Louise buckled herself in and tried to relax while Sal adjusted the seat to accommodate his long legs.

"I hate seeing Brendan. He always made me feel bad about myself. Here I am with a PhD, working in an outdated library in the middle of nowhere with two kids I can barely handle. I'm a complete failure," Louise said. She adjusted the mirror unnecessarily.

"You can't let him make you feel that way," Sal said.

Louise started the van and pulled onto Route 1. "I know. But I can't just turn it off. He also makes me feel short, fat, and ugly. It doesn't help that he left me for Miss Tall, Blond, and Stunning."

"He's an idiot. I can't imagine she is prettier than you."

"Thanks. I'm sure you're the only person in the world who thinks that."

"Sometimes I pretend to be someone else. Like the

Rock. Or Superman, I don't know. An actor following a script. It doesn't always work, but it's worth a try."

"It's hard to imagine you feeling weak or insecure."

"Because I'm a big, strong man." He took off his hat and ran his hand through his flattened curls. "Right. How do you think I felt coming back to Alligator Bayou after being a lawyer in Chicago? I knew everyone would think I was a failure. That I couldn't hack it."

"But you chose to be a strawberry farmer. I got laid off and now I'm underemployed."

"So what? You like your job, right?"

"Yeah. This hick backwater grew on me. Who knew?"

"So don't worry about what Brendan thinks."

Louise turned into the day care parking lot and stopped. "Why did you come back to Alligator Bayou, really?"

"Family, partly. But there is something special about small towns. I'll bet you never lived in one before."

"I do now and I'm still not sure I fit in."

"You don't have to fit in. Just be yourself. It's going to be great. You'll see." Sal smiled, reminding her exactly why Alligator Bayou was great. Because he lived there.

The look on Brendan's face when Sal opened the door of her house was priceless. He stood on the porch and stared at Sal. Even Julia glanced up from her smartphone and actually acknowledged Louise. It was just a moment of eye contact, but enough to let Louise know that she was impressed.

"You must be Brendan and Julia," Sal said, putting on a convincingly good-natured grin. "Please come in. I'm Sal."

Zoe ran up to Louise and hugged her legs, trying to hide. Thinking about leaving the kids with these two made Louise's stomach hurt. She didn't like the idea of Brendan and Julia even setting foot in her house, let alone watching her children. Sal put his arm around her waist and whispered, "They'll be fine."

He was right. Brendan and Julia would not let anything happen to the children. The likely worst-case scenario was that all four of them would be unhappy for a few hours. Louise stood up straighter. "Y'all coming in?"

Brendan ignored her. "Is this really Zoe? She's so big."

"She was barely a year old last time you saw her," Louise said, reaching down to try to loosen the girl's grip on her knees.

"Yeah." Brendan examined his daughter, no doubt looking for Louise's parenting failures. His critical eye would zero in on any flaws, from plaque on her teeth to delayed language development.

Julia put her smartphone back in her purse. "Let's get going. Where's their stuff?"

Louise stepped out of the way, and Brendan and Julia finally came inside. Louise had packed one backpack for each child, and Max was wearing his. He ran out of his room, saw Brendan and Julia, and immediately retreated again.

"Max, it's me. Daddy." Brendan started toward Max's room.

Julia put her hand on his shoulder. "Don't. He'll come out when he's ready."

"But he should remember me. I'm his father."

"He's three. He doesn't understand that."

Louise gaped at Julia. Along with all her other skills and attributes, this impossibly perfect woman understood children.

Julia saw her expression. "I have five siblings. The youngest one is twelve now."

"Oh." Louise felt stupid again. She should be glad that Julia would be able to handle Max and Zoe. But it was just another thing for Brendan's fiancée to be better at. Not that she was trying to compete.

Sal went into Max's bedroom and patiently told Max that he was going to spend some time with his father. Brendan sat on the couch and tried to convince Zoe to get onto his lap.

"No," the girl said. She walked over to her play stove and started banging pots and pans around.

Somehow, the action seemed very adult. Zoe was looking more like a girl and less like a baby every day. She also tried to repeat everything her mother said. Louise had never been sad about Max growing up because the older he got, the easier her life became. But sometimes she dreaded Zoe's milestones.

Sal and Max emerged from the bedroom. "This big guy is going to have dinner with his dad. Right, buddy?"

Max nodded.

"I'll switch the car seats," Louise said.

"We went ahead and bought some," Brendan said. "Julia installed them already. I'm hoping you can keep them here for us after we leave."

"Yeah, sure," Louise said. Julia was now choosing and installing car seats for her children. She'd probably managed to get them in right the first time too. When Louise had first installed a car seat, the operation had used up twenty minutes and she'd been covered with sweat by the time it was done. Julia was proving to be superior in every way.

"How is the house-hunting going?" Sal asked.

"We found a nice place in University Heights," Brendan said. "We have a few more to look at tomorrow, but I think that might be the one."

"I'm just going to check out your new car seats," Louise said. Zoe followed her outside and ran her hand along the door of Brendan and Julia's rental. Naturally, the seats were the right ones for the kids' sizes and Julia had installed them correctly. The straps felt tight when Louise pulled on them, and the installation indicators on the sides of both seats were green.

Louise opened the door, and Zoe climbed in. She put her in the seat and kissed her cheek. This was worse than leaving her at day care. Much worse. Now, she was going to have another car seat, another family, another house.

Sal came up to the car with Max trailing behind. "Let's strap these guys in before they get too hungry."

Louise shut Zoe's door and returned to the house, leaving Sal to get Max into his seat. She was angry at Brendan, at herself, at the world. He was taking her children, and she was letting him do it.

Brendan was standing on the steps. He reached out to touch Louise's arm as she passed, and she instinctively recoiled.

"Thanks for doing this," he said.

Louise backed up farther and studied her ex. He wasn't joking.

"I mean, you didn't have to. I did everything wrong. I abandoned all of you. So, thanks for giving me another chance to have a relationship with them."

"Yeah. You're welcome." Louise felt some of the resentment lift, but not all of it. Not by a long shot.

Louise felt lost driving to the restaurant without the kids, almost like she'd left one of her limbs behind.

But then she glanced over at Sal. His flannel shirt was unbuttoned over a faded T-shirt, and his arm rested comfortably against the van window. At least she wasn't alone.

"Take a right here," he said, indicating the street that led to the courthouse.

"Where are we going?" Louise asked. Until that moment, she'd been so distracted by Brendan and Julia taking the kids that she hadn't thought to ask.

"My favorite restaurant in Alligator Bayou, if that's okay with you."

"Sure. The only places I know are Anthony's and that gas station that sells fried chicken."

"Yup, the chicken at the Stop 'N' Gas is pretty good, but the atmosphere leaves something to be desired."

They passed the post office and the town hall. Up ahead, there was another gas station and a yellow clapboard building with a lot full of cars. The sign read, "Main Street Café."

Sal took off his hat and put it between the seats. "This used to be the grocery store, before the Pig went in. Then, Stephanie bought the place and turned it into a restaurant. As far as I can tell, she and her daughters do everything."

Louise was glad that the Main Street Café looked casual, almost shabby. Fancy restaurants made her nervous. Brendan had liked going to places where all the menu items had prices in the double digits, but Louise hated the fussiness of it all.

Sal held open the screen door for Louise. At first, she had the crazy idea that he'd arranged a surprise party even though it wasn't her birthday. She knew almost everyone in the restaurant. Ms. Trudy waved from her table in the corner; Regina, the police jury secretary, occupied a spot by the window with a man Louise assumed was her husband; and a few other library regulars sat at the other plain wooden tables. Seeing them made Louise think about the library. She and Sylvia were concentrating on providing programs and services that people wanted. Ms. Trudy had started a Friends of the Library group, and she was raising money as well as spreading the word about everything new at the library. It seemed to be working since the library was becoming the center of life in the town. People came for the cooking classes, teen programs, new books and multimedia materials, book clubs. Louise was working harder than she ever had, but it didn't feel arduous. It was fulfilling.

Sal chose a booth in the back, waving and exchanging greetings with the people he knew. "Only problem with a small town," he said as they finally took their seats. "No anonymity."

"That's okay," Louise said. She picked up the menu, a laminated card listing the dishes she'd come to expect at almost any restaurant in Louisiana: gumbo, red beans and rice, crawfish étouffée, crab cakes, catfish po'boy.

"I always get the special," Sal said. "It's listed on the chalkboard over there. Thin fried catfish topped with crawfish étouffée today."

An African American woman with hair clipped military short appeared at their table. "Hi, darling."

"Hi, Stephanie," Sal said. "How's business?"

"Can't complain. We got some nice catfish today. You know how I feel about deep-frying, but this come from my cousin's brother's farm and there's no other way to do catfish right."

"Well, I'll take some for sure."

"How about you, Louisiana? You ever had thin fried catfish?"

Louise had ceased to be surprised when people in Alligator Bayou knew her name, even her given name. "I'm not sure. I've had fried catfish."

"This is special. You'll like it, honey. I hear you bought that place by Sal's. You met Mrs. Pettigrew yet?"

"So far, I've just been watched through her window."

Stephanie put her pad in her apron pocket and rested her hand on her hip. "Let me give you some advice. Make you some cookies or a cake or something and bring it on over there. Take the children with you. That's all you gotta do."

"I will," Louise said.

"All right. Beer?"

"Yes, please."

A minute later, Stephanie returned with two sweating pint glasses. She hurried away when a table of seniors with walkers parked next to their chairs signaled for more drinks.

By the time their food arrived, Louise had drunk half of her beer. She knew that if she finished it, she wouldn't be able to drive.

Sal seemed to sense her dilemma. "Let me be the responsible one for tonight. It's got to be hard being in charge all the time."

"It is," Louise said. "Sometimes, I want to let someone else be the mom, just for one night. Is that terrible?"

"No. My dad was gone a lot, and it was tough on my mom. Even as a kid, I got that. I think that's why Betta never had children. She saw how hard it was on your own, and she didn't trust any man to stick around."

"Was she ever married?"

"No. She dated this guy Jack for a long time after high school, but he eventually married someone from Saint Jude. I don't know what Betta wants. She sort of feels like she takes care of me, and I guess I let her. Since our parents are gone, I'm all she has left."

Stephanie dropped off their food unceremoniously. The restaurant was nearly full, and she seemed to be serving all the tables herself.

The thin fried catfish was addictively crunchy and the creamy crawfish on top provided a mellow contrast. The side dish of bacon-flavored green beans was perhaps even better than the fish.

"I guess you like it," Sal said, draining his beer.

"Huh?" Louise straightened up. She'd been hunched over her food like a starving person.

"You haven't said a word for ten minutes now."

"Sorry, it's just so good. How does she get the catfish so thin?"

Sal prodded his remaining étouffée with a fork. "Don't know. I never learned to cook since Betta has appointed herself my personal chef."

Louise sipped her beer. "Do you ever get irritated with her?"

"Maybe a little. Sometimes I feel like she doesn't have her own life. Except during strawberry season. Then she's plenty busy."

"She could teach, if she likes kids."

"Betta has a fear of commitment. Come to think of it, maybe that's why she never got married. Afraid of something new too. Me, she knows. Shoot, she knows everyone in town. That's the way she likes it. Doesn't want change."

"Sometimes, change can be good," Louise said.

Sal paused, fork in midair. "Yes, it can."

The rental car was in the driveway when Sal pulled up in front of Louise's house.

"They told me eight thirty," Louise said. "It's only eight fifteen."

Sal cut the engine. "Don't worry. They can't be mad."

"Yes, they can. This is Brendan we're talking about, not a reasonable person." Louise held her breath and went up to the car. Max spotted her through the window and waved. Zoe was asleep in her seat, head cocked to the side at an uncomfortable-looking angle.

Brendan got out and handed Louise the two backpacks. "We went to Mexi Palace, but Max kept sawing at the table with a steak knife and had a meltdown when we took it away. Zoe refused to sit in a high chair, but when we let her out, she jumped up and down in the booth. We ended up eating in the car."

"I never take them to sit-down restaurants," Louise said.

"Well, that explains it."

"Brendan, they're little kids. You can't expect them to be patient. That's why I packed their toys and coloring books."

"Max threw his cars across the room, and Zoe dropped all the markers on the floor."

Sal put his hand on Louise's shoulder. "Let's get the kids to bed. Y'all can talk about this later."

Brendan opened the door and let Max out.

"We ate in the car!" the boy said. "I love this car."

Louise went around to the other side and lifted Zoe from her seat. She shifted her head from side to side before settling it on Louise's shoulder. "We'll talk tomorrow," Louise whispered to Brendan.

Sal helped Max brush his teeth and read him a story while Louise put Zoe to bed. Afterward, she poured herself a glass of wine. A few minutes later, Sal came out of Max's room and sat down on the couch next to her. "Give Brendan a break. He hasn't been around kids much."

Louise let her head fall back against the cushions. "I guess. But it's pretty frustrating that he won't listen to me about anything."

"Just give it time. He's going to see that you have experience. I mean, look at tonight. If he'd asked you, you could have told him that the kids are too young for restaurants."

"No, he thinks this is my fault. That if I had trained them properly, they would sit still. That's how he sees it. I know him."

"He'll learn. Since he's here now, he'll have more time with them. He'll try stuff and he'll fail. Or maybe he'll succeed and you'll reap the benefits. Think about it—what if he could make it easier for you to get Max's teeth brushed and things like that?"

"I don't understand why he does it for you now. It still takes me ten minutes to get him to open his mouth."

"Right, so I can help you. He and Julia can help you. You have to realize, Louise, you're not alone in this anymore. And that's a good thing."

Louise reached for his hand and held it. This was what she'd wanted. Just a little support. She'd never gotten it from Brendan, even when he was around. Now, she had this great guy and a whole town behind her. Just that day, a library regular had brought her a box of hand-me-down clothes for Max, and Brianna had baked cookies for the staff. "Thank you," she said.

"Hey, I'd better take off. I don't want to confuse the kids by being here all night."

"Yeah." Louise wanted him to stay, but she knew they needed to take it slow for themselves as well as for the children. "What about your truck?"

"I'll walk home now and get Betta to drive me to the library in the morning. Give her something else to do for me." He kissed her lightly, then deeply. "Sorry, I know I have to stop with the kids in the other room."

"We don't have to stop forever," Louise said. "Just for now."

CHAPTER 29

Sal leaned back in the van seat. It felt strange to be wearing his tux again. Betta had altered it for him because his shoulders were broader now than they had been during his lawyer days. He never went to the gym anymore, but all the lifting around the farm had given him some bulk. The scratchy feeling of the fabric brought back memories of the last time he'd worn the penguin suit. He'd been standing in front of the altar in a freezing-cold church, listening to the string quartet play through every piece they knew. The poor musicians had been killing time waiting for the bride's father to convince her to come down the aisle. It hadn't worked. A blessing, he later realized.

Louise parked in one of the last spots in the church's lot. First Episcopal was a towering brick building with dark windows. Sal didn't understand why Brendan and Julia couldn't get married in Saint Jude. Louise had told him Julia's parents wanted to see the sights or something. They were having the reception at some famous hotel; he couldn't remember which one. People had a romantic view of New Orleans that he, as a country boy, didn't understand. If he ever had another wedding, he'd do it on his own farm. Let the kids play on the swings while they said their vows.

He took Louise's hand and kissed it. "You look beautiful."

"Thanks. I'd say the same to you, but men are funny about compliments."

"I know I look like a hick in a monkey suit," Sal said.

"See? You're impossible." Louise got out and unbuckled the kids.

Sal took Max's hand. "Come on, buddy. We're going to see your daddy."

"Can I take the jacket off now?" Max asked.

"Not yet. After the ceremony."

"Can I take the jacket off after the cer-moony?"

Sal laughed. "Yes."

"That will be a great idea." Max smiled and jumped out of the van.

"Zoe, wait for me!" Louise said.

Sal turned to see the girl running after him. He lifted her up with his free arm. "Come on, sweetheart. You can't run away from Mom."

At the church door, Sal set down both children, and they raced inside, nearly knocking over a young couple who gave them identical nasty looks. Sal smiled apologetically, and they looked away.

The bridesmaids in their rose gowns and the black-suited groomsmen stood in an awkward group outside the sanctuary doors. Within seconds, the children were surrounded by fawning bridesmaids. Max was handed a pillow and Zoe a basket, and both received whispered instructions from the women.

"We need to go sit down," Sal said. "They're going to start in a few minutes."

"Will they be okay?" Louise asked, watching Max grin at his admirers.

"We'll sit on the aisle so we can get out and help if we need to." Sal looped his arm around Louise's and led her to a pew near the front. She'd barely talked during the hour-long drive. Now, she was tight-lipped and pale. He wished she'd relax a little. Not that he was comfortable himself. The church bore too much resemblance to the one he'd almost been married in. Until that day, he had somehow overlooked all the signs that Chloe didn't love him the way he loved her. Maybe she had tried, but if she had, it was for the wrong reasons. Her family loved Sal. Her father especially seemed to see him as the son he'd never had. The old man was part of the reason he'd put off telling Chloe about his decision to quit the law firm. He'd hated to disappoint Mr. Henderson. He'd even allowed him to teach him golf, a sport he'd never cared about and hadn't played since. Spending so much time with Mr. Henderson had made him realize how much he missed his own father. But by the time he found his way back to Alligator Bayou, it was too late for that. Sal clenched his hands into fists.

The last empty seats were next to a group of disheveled men that he pegged as professors. They were talking about the best bars in the French Quarter. Apparently, the most important criteria was the price of the drinks, followed by the number of good-looking women likely to frequent the establishment.

Sal turned to ask Louise whether she knew the men, but she didn't seem to hear him. She stared straight ahead at the forbidding dark wood of the pulpit. The entire place dripped with gravitas: kneelers in front of the pews, weighty candlesticks, dark-red carpeting. Even the organ music seemed more serious than festive. The melody changed, and everyone stood to look down the aisle.

Max came through the doorway and took a few tentative steps. Zoe followed, scattering rose petals from her basket.

She bent down to pick some back up again. After putting the petals in the basket, she walked toward the altar, but stopped when Max came to a standstill in front of her.

Max glanced around for a minute, his eyes big and scared; then he broke into a run. He sprinted up the aisle and threw the pillow at the startled priest. "Here you go!" he yelled and ran back past the processing attendants. Zoe raced after him, squealing with delight. Her basket swung wildly, and the petals flew out.

After a moment of startled silence, everyone started laughing.

CHAPTER 30

Sal knocked on Louise's door holding a chilled bottle of champagne. She wasn't happy that Brendan and Julia had decided to keep the kids in New Orleans overnight, so he wanted to make the evening special for her. Since there weren't any fancy restaurants in Alligator Bayou, they'd have to make do.

"Just happened to have this in the fridge next to the caviar and lobster," he said when she came to the door. She had a pink apron tied over her jeans and T-shirt, and her hair was in a ponytail.

In the kitchen, he grabbed a towel and twisted off the champagne cork. "Do you have glasses for this?"

"Nope. We'll have to use jelly jars." Louise hefted a pot off the stove and drained some kind of curly pasta into a colander.

"Works for me." Sal poured and sipped while she tossed the pasta with butter, sautéed mushrooms, and Parmesan cheese.

"How are the strawberry plants doing?" she asked.

"Not great. It's the end of the season anyway. I might have to try again next year." He didn't tell her that he was spending a lot of his time plotting how to get the library tax on the ballot. She knew that he was meeting with the Friends of the Library, but he had another idea that would have to be a secret. "Can I help with anything?"

"You could set the table."

Sal reached into a cabinet above the refrigerator and found two candlesticks fitted with brand-new candles. He rummaged in her kitchen drawer for matches. "I'm sure the kids are having fun."

Louise's shoulders slumped. "I know. I shouldn't be thinking about them. I should be just enjoying this time with you."

"Don't worry about it. We have the rest of our lives." Sal immediately wished he could take the words back. He was presuming way too much.

"Yeah," Louise said. "We're neighbors now."

"I'd like to be more than your neighbor," Sal said. Why not? He'd already stepped in it; he might as well jump in with both feet.

"I know. I want it too. But after the mess with Brendan, I guess I'm a little scared." Louise turned away to grind pepper onto the pasta.

Sal came up behind her and put his arms around her waist. "I'm not Brendan."

"Yeah."

"And you're not Chloe. She's the one who left me on the altar five years ago. It's taken me that long to get over it. But once I met you, I decided that I was ready to stop hurting. You tell me when that time comes for you."

Louise turned around and hugged him back. "I'm ready for it to stop now."

Sal felt like a switch had been flipped in his body. Every part of him was awake. He didn't want to let her go, but he pulled away long enough to ask, "Do you think that pasta would be good cold?"

Chapter 31

When Louise woke up, she was alone. She glanced at the clock and panicked. It was eight o'clock. The kids never slept that late. She was just going to run to their rooms when she remembered that Max and Zoe were in New Orleans with Brendan and Julia. Sal had stayed overnight.

As she slowly got out of bed, Louise continued to ride the emotional roller coaster. She'd impulsively led Sal to her bedroom and they'd made love. Afterward, they'd eaten the pasta and drunk the champagne, talking until after midnight. The warm glow from the previous night was dulled by the knowledge that Sal had left before she'd woken up. Had she done something wrong? Scared him off somehow?

But as she walked downstairs to the kitchen, she caught the scent of coffee. Sal was here. Or he'd made a pot and left. She rounded the corner and saw him at the table, his muscular shoulders hunched as he read something on his smartphone. He put it away quickly.

Louise wished she had more exciting pajamas than her old T-shirt and ratty flannel pants. She ran her hand through her hair in a belated effort to make it look presentable.

"I would have made breakfast, but I figured you didn't want burnt eggs," Sal said. "Coffee is the only thing I know how to cook."

"That's all I need anyway," Louise said. She poured herself a cup and sat across from him. The night had been perfect. She'd been too happy and excited to sleep at first, and then she'd rested better than any time she could remember. Did he feel the same way?

Sal finished his coffee. "I wish I could stay, but I have to supervise my workers, mend about five holes in the fence, and do ten or so other things that I can't remember right now."

"That's okay. I have a bunch of stuff to do before the kids get home." Louise stood up, gulping down half her coffee.

"Wait." He pulled her close and kissed her. "I'll call you later."

Louise nodded. She was still holding her coffee mug and she sipped from it distractedly as he opened the door and left.

After finishing her grocery shopping and other errands, Louise paced the house, waiting for the kids to get home. She went into the living room, opened the blinds, and watched the street for a moment. Maybe a glass of wine would help her relax. She poured some cheap merlot into a jelly glass and sat in front of her computer, momentarily forgetting that she still didn't have an Internet connection. She picked up the novel she'd borrowed from the library instead and read the first page three times without understanding any of it.

She gulped some wine and scrubbed the dried food and marker from the cabinets. Why weren't they back? Hadn't Brendan said six o'clock? The timer beeped, indicating that her rice was done. She turned off the burner and looked out the window again. Nothing.

Her arm was aching from the furious cleaning when she heard tires crunching on the driveway. She sprang up and saw the rental car pull in behind the van. Julia got out, her long, thin legs covered by skin-tight black jeans with rhinestones on the pockets. She lifted Zoe out of her car seat and set her down on the front lawn. Watching from the window, Louise hoped Zoe would run toward the house, excited to be home, but she squatted down and examined a yellow dandelion instead. She was wearing a new purple dress and had a matching bow in her hair.

Louise went outside and ran to embrace her daughter. "Zoe!"

"Hi, Mommy."

"Did you have fun with your daddy and Ms. Julia?"

"Yeah." Zoe picked the weed and held it in her fist. "Flower."

Julia unhooked the car seat. "Where should I put this?"

"In the house," Louise said. She tried to take Zoe's hand, but the girl pulled away.

Max jumped out of the car and hugged Louise. "Can I watch a show?"

"Okay." Louise couldn't say no to anything he wanted right now. Did he feel abandoned by her? Confused that his dad was back in his life?

Max ran across the lawn and up to the front door. "That will be a great idea," he said, employing one of his favorite phrases. Louise didn't know where he'd picked it up, but she'd given up trying to explain that it wasn't quite correct.

Brendan got Max's car seat and followed Julia toward the house. "We have to get going. We had a great time, didn't we, buddy?"

"Yeah," Max said in his usual deadpan voice.

Julia went back to the car and got the kids' bags, leaving them in the hallway with the safety seats. Brendan watched her with affection and desire, just like he used to look at Louise. Louise would have to get accustomed to that, like all the other new things in her world. There were good things, though. Sal especially.

"We're closing on our house on the thirtieth," Brendan said. "It's right by A&M, in University Heights."

"I know where that is," Louise said. It was an expensive area, but they could probably afford it because of Julia's family inheritance, trust fund, or whatever. So, maybe now that they were married, Louise could expect more child support. Sylvia was right; she should try to enjoy the advantages of having Brendan and Julia around.

"We're hoping to move in right after school ends, in May. I'll let you know."

"Great," Louise said.

"I wish you'd gotten Max's hair cut before the wedding. It sticks up in the back," Brendan said, descending the stairs to his car.

All Louise's good feelings melted away. As soon as they moved to town, everything she did would be examined under the Brendan microscope.

CHAPTER 32

Louise backed the van out of her long, still muddy driveway. The rain had lasted for three days, delaying Sal's plan to have a load of gravel delivered. He had repainted the cabinets and replaced the kitchen linoleum with plain but beautiful deep-brown tiles. She'd rewarded him with a dinner of lasagna and pie, feeling like it wasn't nearly enough. He seemed to enjoy the work, though. Max was fascinated with his every move, from laying tile to eating salad. Sal endured the attention with grace, answering every question, no matter how convoluted or personal. Louise liked having him around the house. Even when they were in different rooms—she did laundry and cleaned the bedrooms while he worked on the kitchen—his presence made her happy. She didn't want the weekend to end, but now it was Monday and time to go back to work.

Turning down the street, Louise saw a sign in front of the Pettigrew house. She pulled in front and stopped to read it.

"Let's GO!" Max said from the backseat.

"Just a minute." Louise read the sign again, out loud this time. " 'Sign petition to close library. Book-burning party! CitizensAgainstHedonism.com.' "

"I like parties," Max said.

Louise continued down the street, driving slowly so she could think. The sign had to be the work of the Gund's minions.

On the way to the day care, she counted ten more signs: "Burn *The Hunger Games*!" "Burn *Harry Potter*!" "Burn *Fahrenheit 451*!"

At the library, Hope was standing in Sylvia's cubicle, looking at the computer screen over her shoulder.

"The book-burning crazies have a Facebook page," Sylvia said. "Take a look. It's unbelievable."

Louise clocked in, poured a cup of coffee, and went into her cubicle. When the computer finally booted up, she found the page. At the top was a photo of orange flames. "If it's the Bible, read it. If it's not the Bible, burn it." "Come to the party—burn the books." The other posts were lists of bands and other entertainment for the book-burning party. There was going to be a bouncy house and a clown. Louise leaned back in her chair and pressed her fingertips to her temples. Her phone rang.

"I hope you did your hair this morning," Breaux said.

"What does that have to do with anything? And who's putting up those signs everywhere?" Louise said.

"I don't know, but there's going to be a TV reporter from Channel Six at your library before lunch. Be warned."

"How'd they find out about this already?"

"I called them. Don't you see? This will help you. People will get mad and take your side."

"Do you really think so?"

"Nobody likes book burners." Breaux hung up.

"I'm gonna find out who these nutjobs are and tell them where they can put those signs," Hope said.

"I just talked to Breaux. He says a TV reporter's coming."

"Shoot, and me one day from my beauty appointment. I

need me a lipstick touch-up." Hope took her purse into the bathroom.

"Got a comment on the Facebook page," Sylvia said. "Brianna Rogers writes, 'Y'all are sick.' "

"Is she in the library right now?"

"I think so. She came in this morning like always."

"We should go see if she'll stick around to be interviewed by the TV reporter." Louise left her desk and went into the patron area. Brianna was at one of the computers, surrounded by Ms. Trudy, Eloise, and five other people that Louise didn't recognize.

"They can't do this," a man wearing coveralls said. "Close the library and burn books? I mean, that's illegal, right?"

"If they get one thousand signatures, they can put it to an election," Ms. Trudy said. "That's what we're trying to do right now, except that we're *for* the library. We need signatures to get a library tax on the ballot."

"Where do I sign?" the man asked.

Everyone in the library gathered around to put their names on Ms. Trudy's petition. As they were finishing, a woman wearing heavy makeup and a tiny skirt came in, followed by a man carrying a camera. Louise went in the back and announced, "The media is here."

Sylvia and Hope practically ran her over in their rush to get to the patron area.

The following day, Hope arrived at the library two hours late, lugging her giant-size Crock-Pot. "Made y'all my famous chicken and dumplings."

Louise poured water into the coffeepot. "Smells great."

"Thanks. Reason I'm late is my nutbird neighbor Hilda. She got a big old dead tree in her yard. Can't afford to get it cut down 'cause she sends her whole social security check to that useless son of hers in Alexandria. Never got him a real job. Runs an art studio or something up there. She showed me pictures once, and I'll tell you what, I wouldn't let my momma look at that stuff. Anyways, like I was saying, that tree dropped a branch in the wind last night. Knocked out the power to my house. Had to get Louisiana Power out, then call Winston this morning to come and cut off all the branches hanging over my place. I had enough of that tree."

"I can imagine," Louise said. She needed caffeine. The coffee was dripping much too slowly.

"So I brung the chicken and dumplings because I want to teach the recipe for my first cooking class tomorrow. Sylvia got a bunch of camp stoves lined up."

"You're still going to risk the wrath of our Zumba-hating boss? Even after he told you your cooking was crap or whatever?" Louise said.

"Yup. I called Marty Pratt, and she wants to bring some of her friends. Mr. Foley can't say nothing. Anyway, I've had it with him. He wants, he can fire me. Probably he's one of those book burners." Hope dragged the worktable closer to the wall and plugged in the Crock-Pot.

Lily came in and poured herself a cup of coffee, not appearing to notice that Louise was about to grab the carafe. She stirred in some artificial sweetener and walked over to examine the slow cooker. "You put carrots in there?"

" 'Course," Hope said. "Who makes chicken and dumplings without carrots?"

"Adds a nice splash of color," Lily said.

Hope rolled her eyes at Lily's back. "Don't matter to me how it looks. I'm making food, not a painting or something."

Lily shrugged and carried her mug back out to the circulation desk. Louise poured a cup of coffee and jogged in place for a minute, trying to wake up.

Sylvia came in and sniffed the air. "What's that divine smell?"

"Hope's chicken and dumplings," Louise said.

"Ah, so we're finally worthy!"

"Y'all earned it," Hope said. "I'll admit, I was getting plenty bored sitting around here until you two came along. I didn't think much of y'all at first, but you done livened this place up. People want to come here now. I can't hardly go to the Piggly Wiggly without someone asking me questions about the library. Nobody done that before. And this book-burning thing really has people up in arms. Haven't seen this town so angry about something since the Gund pulled her stunt with the trailer park."

"Wait till they see what I have planned next. We're going to have a dance. Ages thirteen to eighteen," Sylvia said.

"A dance at the library?" Hope said, glancing toward Mr. Foley's empty office.

"The kids were telling me that the school isn't having one until the prom in May. And that's just for the juniors and seniors. So I thought, why not? Gets them in the library. And it'll be book-themed, of course. I'm thinking *Gone with the Wind*."

Hope shook her head. "You got guts, I'll give you that."

"I'm not letting any old fogey tell me what I can do. When's lunch?"

"No one's touching my pot till noon. Even Mr. Foley. Where is the cranky bastard?"

"Mr. Henry said he had to go out of town. I'm guessing it's goat-related," Louise said. "He won't be back until tomorrow."

"Good." Hope patted the Crock-Pot. "He said he hated my food anyways."

* * *

Later that afternoon, Louise was working the circulation desk when Brianna, Ms. Trudy, Eloise, and Eleanor came in. They all wore identical neon-green T-shirts.

"What do you think?" Ms. Trudy asked, turning around to show the back of the shirt.

" 'Improve libraries. Improve lives. Sign the petition: *Save the Alligator Bayou Parish Libraries*,' " Louise read out loud. "I like it."

"Of course we'll have to get new ones when we get this thing on the ballot. I'm thinking, 'Vote yes to literacy. Vote yes to culture.' "

"How many signatures do you have so far?" Louise said.

"I don't exactly know because I handed out sheets to just about everyone I could think of. Mr. Jude at the Piggly Wiggly, Betta at the Cut and Dye, and the pastors of all the local churches. I reckon we'll get a thousand easy," Ms. Trudy said.

"I hope so because those book burners claim they already have that many."

"Don't you believe it. They're just blowing smoke. Get it? Blowing smoke?"

Eloise and Eleanor laughed. Their T-shirts hung nearly to their knees. They must have ordered them in the sizes they wore before old age began to shrink their bodies.

A group of teenagers came in wearing the green shirts over their uniforms.

"Good, y'all wore them to school!" Brianna said, clapping her hands.

"We sure did, Ms. Brianna. They made us take them off for class, but we put them back on as soon as school was over. We're gonna wear them until y'all get a thousand signatures," a tall African American girl named Chante said. She was one of the most dedicated teen club members, participating in every event Sylvia held.

Mary was at the back of the crowd. Her green shirt fit her like a dress. She sidled around the edge of the girls, leaned over the counter, and whispered to Louise, "Smells like chicken and dumplings in here."

"Ms. Hope made it. Come on back and I'll give you what's left," Louise said.

Mary glanced back at the teenagers, but they were already headed to the young adult section. "I'd love some," she said, following Louise to the back.

"Are you hanging out with those girls now?" Louise asked.

"A little, I guess. They let me tag along," Mary said. "They don't make fun of me, at least."

"Nice shirt," Hope said when she saw Mary.

"Thanks. Ms. Trudy designed them. She said since we are too young to sign the petition, we have to be walking billboards."

"Glad to know she's found a use for teenagers. You want some of my chicken and dumplings?"

"Yes, please, ma'am," Mary said.

Hope scraped the rest of the mixture onto a plate. There was exactly enough for one serving, almost as if she'd been saving it for the girl.

Louise went back to the circulation desk. Ms. Trudy stood by the door with her clipboard, waiting for more people to arrive so that she could pester them to sign her petition. Louise shook her head. It was a good thing Mr. Foley was out of town. He would have run her off in a second.

CHAPTER 33

The next morning, Louise was rewatching the TV news broadcast about the library in her cubicle when Sylvia appeared carrying her green alligator purse. "Let's go get lunch at Anthony's."

Louise zipped up the orange interlibrary loan bag and tucked it into a post office tub with the others. The gofer from the State Library would pick it up during her afternoon run. Before Louise and Sylvia came to Alligator Bayou, they hadn't even included the library on their route. Mr. Foley didn't see the point of interlibrary loans. If Alligator Bayou Parish Library didn't have it, the locals didn't need it, he said. Louise ignored him and did it anyway.

"You look great on TV, by the way. It's not too late to switch to a glamorous career in broadcasting," she told Sylvia.

"Shut up. You sure you're not upset that Hope and I hogged the limelight?"

"Are you nuts? The last thing I want is to see all my pores blown up larger than life on the screen. Horrors, as my gram used to say."

"Ms. Trudy said the station was flooded with calls from

people who wanted to sign the petition. Some of them weren't even from Alligator Bayou."

They went out to circulation, and Louise left the interlibrary loan box next to Lily.

"We're going to Anthony's for lunch," Sylvia said.

Lily nodded and leaned forward to share another bit of juicy gossip with Ada Gautreaux, who was hunting through the wire rack of romances.

Anthony's Seafood had profited enormously from the growth of Alligator Bayou. Once a mere shack, according to Hope, it had grown to the size of a small grocery. Which, essentially, it was. Anthony's sold catfish that were killed and cleaned on premise, fresh seafood, frozen products from alligator meat to turducken, hot sauce, and prepared food such as their famous boudin balls (pork and rice sausage formed into spheres and deep fried), fried catfish, and po'boys of all descriptions. Since moving to Alligator Bayou, Louise had been experimenting with some of the more exotic offerings. Max had shown an unexpected fondness for boiled crawfish.

Louise and Sylvia stood in line in front of the fully stocked steam table.

"Oh my God. It all looks so good," Sylvia said.

"Yeah." Louise couldn't think about food. Despite the apparent success of the TV broadcast, she was worried that the library tax would fail, even if Ms. Trudy got it on the ballot. If that happened, she'd have to try to get a job in the Saint Jude Parish Library system or move again. The thought of leaving Sal was enough to give her instant heartburn. Besides, Brendan would not be happy to have come all the way to Louisiana only for her to take the kids somewhere else. He might even take her to court over it.

"All right, we're going to need some boudin balls, fried shrimp, and fried catfish. Bread. And coleslaw and two iced teas. Unsweetened," Sylvia informed the stocky black woman behind the counter.

Without saying a word, the woman assembled the food into two Styrofoam containers and passed it to the cashier.

Sylvia produced a twenty-dollar bill. "This is on me."

"Thanks." Louise tried to sound grateful, but she wasn't sure that she was capable of eating.

Once they were seated at one of the high, round tables, however, Louise's appetite returned. The catfish was crispy on the outside and creamy on the inside, and the boudin balls were spicy and delicious.

They ate most of their food in silence. "Now, you know this isn't about lunch," Sylvia said.

Louise drank the last drops of her iced tea. "Are you stuffing me full of seafood so I'll agree to some crazy scheme? I'm not toilet-papering the Gund's house."

"Exactly the opposite. We're outsiders in this town. But that doesn't mean we can't charm people—we're just going to have to work a little harder at it."

"You're the one with the great hair and TV presence. I'm just a mousy librarian type," Louise said.

"Shut up, you are not. We have to keep track of who knows who, who's related, who's had a feud with who since forever. Hope can help us. We need to start shopping at local stores, mailing stuff from the post office here, getting our hair cut by the ladies at the Cut and Dye, eating our lunch here or at Main Street Café."

"What do you think I've been doing? I moved here, you might remember." Louise ate her last boudin ball.

"I know. But you can't just walk into the Pig, get your groceries, and leave. You have to ask the cashier how her kids are, find out the name of her husband, her hairdresser, her dentist. You get the idea." Sylvia pinched the tail off a fried shrimp. "As it happens, Reverend McDonald's nephew owns this place."

"How do you know that?"

"I talk to people. And I file it away." Sylvia scraped back her chair and stood up. "Three kids, two of them in high school. I know them from my book talks."

The lunch crowd had thinned, so Sylvia approached the cashier between orders. "Y'all know if Mr. McDonald is in today?"

"Sure, honey." The woman flashed a smile, showing her gold front tooth. "He just in the back, taking a delivery. I'll call him up here."

A minute later, they were talking to a bald African American man. The only concession to his rank in the business was the knot of a tie visible above his long white apron. He regarded them with a faint air of suspicion. "How can I help you ladies?"

"Mr. McDonald, I'm Sylvia Jones and this is Louise Richardson. We work at the Alligator Bayou Parish Library. Your daughter Chante is one of my favorite Teen Club members."

The corners of McDonald's mouth lifted slightly. "Oh, yeah. She been hanging around the library a lot. I say, 'Chante, don't you want to go to the mall?' but oh, no, she'd rather go hang out with y'all. Can't say I mind that too much."

"I'm really honored to be able to provide teenagers with a safe and fun place to go," Sylvia said. "I hope they learn something too. Chante is a really hard worker. And talented. She helped me redecorate the library, and I had to ask if she was considering interior design as a career."

"Oh, not my Chante. She's way too serious. That girl wants to be an environmental engineer. Sometimes, I think maybe she studies too much, but hey, that's how you get ahead in life. But I don't think y'all came here to talk about my daughter."

"Oh, no, sir. We wanted to let you know that the Friends of the Library group is trying to get a new library tax on the next ballot. Wouldn't cost but a hundred dollars a year to the average Alligator Bayou homeowner."

"Well, I sure do think y'all are doing a good job over there. Don't know what's going on with those book-burning signs. I fought against that over in Vietnam. What we need is knowledge. Education. Hard work. Can't be holding our young people back by telling them they can read only one book, even if it is the Bible. If you read one book, you aren't going to even understand it at all."

"I agree. We're doing the best we can, but Louise and I will lose our jobs if this tax doesn't pass. We're paid with a federal grant that's due to expire. I'll make sure Chante gets a copy of the petition for you, if you're interested."

"That would be fine." McDonald turned and disappeared into the back of the store.

"That's what you have to do," Sylvia said, gathering up the extra food.

Louise called Hope from the SUV while Sylvia drove back to the library.

"You talked to Mr. McDonald? I hear he'd take candy from a baby if it suited his interest," Hope said.

"Seemed like a nice enough man. Sylvia talked to him about his daughter," Louise said.

"Huh." Hope paused, probably to sip from her ever-present coffee cup. "I know a couple other people who might could help get more signatures."

"We're bringing you fried shrimp and boudin balls."

"I'm all over this thing." Hope hung up.

CHAPTER 34

Someone had set the thermostat in the police jury room to extra frigid again. Louise pulled her sweater closed and folded her arms, trying to get warm. Mr. Henry sat in the front row. He slouched down in his chair even more than usual and coughed into a handkerchief. Mr. Foley apparently had not bothered to come.

Sylvia tapped Mr. Henry on the shoulder before taking a seat behind him. He turned and nodded in greeting. He'd taken sick leave the whole previous week. His cheekbones looked sharp enough to poke through his skin.

Louise squeezed past Sylvia and sat down next to Breaux.

"Time for the show," he said.

The police jurors filed in and took their places at the table. Mrs. Gunderson made everyone wait while she rearranged the chairs until she had the one she wanted. Delilah covered her mouth with her hand to stifle her laughter. She wore a puffy, shiny green dress that looked like something a nerdy girl would pick out for the prom. Pratt nudged her and gave her a warning look. Foster pretended to read the agenda as he tapped his foot, waiting.

When the chairs were finally the way Mrs. Gunderson

wanted them, she dropped into her seat and leaned her elbows on the table. Reverend McDonald had been lagging a few paces behind the others, and he sat on the end without making eye contact with anyone.

"You see how they all came in together?" Breaux whispered to Louise. "They had a little powwow before the meeting."

"That's not good," Louise said.

Foster banged his gavel. "I call this meeting to order. Reverend McDonald will lead us in prayer, and then Mrs. Gunderson will lead the Pledge of Allegiance."

Louise bowed her head, but she didn't hear anything McDonald said. By the time they started the pledge, she was sweating in the chilly room.

Foster read the agenda in his ponderous way. The library would be discussed first, which was good because Louise didn't think she could take the suspense much longer. Foster finished his recitation. "First item: Mrs. Gunderson has proposed that, since the parish currently lacks the funds to support the library system, we simply shut down our system and enter into an agreement with Saint Jude Parish whereby bookmobiles and other services will be made available to our parish citizens."

"Wait, that's not on the agenda," Pratt said. "No one said anything about shutting down the system."

Delilah nodded. "You can't just add it like that. Besides, I'm sure ending library service would be something the voters would have to approve."

"All right, then," Mrs. Gunderson said. "Let's go back to what we talked about, passing a resolution against any expansion of the library system."

Louise glanced around, confused. Where were the book burners? They should be supporting Mrs. Gunderson. If they had a petition, this would be the time to bring it before the jury.

"Wait!" Sylvia stood up.

"Anyone wishing to speak has to fill out a request-to-speak card," Foster said.

"Give me a card, then," Sylvia said. "Please."

The police jury secretary approached Sylvia, whispering something in her ear before giving her the card. Sylvia nodded and squeezed her shoulder. Regina Lewis had come to the library twice during the previous week—for books, but also to show her support.

Foster took a full minute to read the card. When he was finished, he motioned Sylvia forward. "Stand in front of the microphone and state your name and address for the record."

Just as Sylvia pulled the microphone up to its full height, Mr. Henry began to cough. Louise got out her phone, ready to call 911, but he stopped and gestured for them to continue.

Sylvia adjusted the microphone again. "I just want to say that we have done everything we can to make this library a vital part of the community. Without it, the local schoolchildren will be deprived of a place to get their books for school projects and for extra reading. And it's a safe hangout after school and on Saturdays. We have been adding computer classes, book clubs, and other programs for all ages. People are coming in droves. You can ask Ms. Regina over there; she is one of our regulars along with Ms. Trudy, Cheryl from the post office, Michelle who runs the dry cleaning shop on Route One, Ms. Stephanie from Main Street Café, and a whole bunch of teachers and students. The people will support this tax. I know it."

Mrs. Gunderson snorted. "No one likes taxes. And libraries are dying. Maybe you don't realize that there is something called the Internet."

"This library is not dying." Ms. Trudy stood up. "Over one thousand Alligator Bayou residents signed a petition to put the tax on the ballot." She dropped a thick folder in front of Mrs. Gunderson and went back to her seat.

Mrs. Gunderson made a show of counting the pages.

"Mrs. Gunderson," Foster said.

Grumbling under her breath, she handed him the folder.

"We are required by our own parish charter to sign these papers and submit them to the secretary of state in a timely matter. I will see that it is done," Foster said. "Assuming that everything is in order, the tax ordinance will appear on the ballot in September."

Sylvia slapped Louise's hand. "We did it, girl!"

"We will give you all a moment to leave if you wish before continuing the meeting," Mrs. Gunderson said.

"A small victory," Breaux said as they walked to the parking lot. "But the tax still has to pass."

Sylvia grabbed his shoulder and shook him. "Come on, you pessimist. The Gund can't bully the whole parish."

"Don't be so sure. That old bat has a lot of influence around here. You best watch out for her."

"What about the book burners?" Louise said. "They didn't show."

"No, but I don't think you've seen the last of them." Breaux walked quickly to his car and got in.

"Something's funny about Citizens Against Hedonism, but I don't know what it is," Sylvia said.

Chapter 35

Brendan's new house was a white mini-mansion that looked like something made out of frosting rather than wood and paint.

"Princess castle!" Zoe said.

Zoe didn't want to be lifted from her seat anymore, so Louise opened the van door, unstrapped her, and stood back. The girl climbed down by herself and jumped onto the Astroturf-like lawn.

Max got out and stared. "Is this Daddy's house?"

"Yes. He and Ms. Julia moved in last week," Louise said. The opulence of the place was a stark contrast to her own modest three-bedroom. She didn't want a big, fancy house, but seeing it still made her feel inferior. She fought the urge to flee as she guided the children up the paving stones that served as the front walkway. "Do you want to ring the doorbell?"

Max raced up the steps and stood on tiptoe. "I can't reach it."

"Zoe ring!" Zoe stumbled up behind him, crying.

Louise lifted Max and let him push the bell. "It will be your turn next time."

Tears ran down Zoe's face. Her cheeks turned an angry shade of red whenever she cried, and now the blotches appeared like magic. The taking-turns lesson wasn't worth Brendan seeing Zoe looking like she'd lost her best friend. Louise hoisted her up, and Zoe poked at the bell just as the door opened.

Julia raised her eyebrows at the sight of Louise awkwardly holding the red-faced girl. Brendan's new wife wore a tank top, white capri pants, and lace-up Roman-style sandals. The outfit appeared to be freshly ironed.

"She wanted to ring the doorbell," Louise explained.

"Brendan went to get lunch, but he'll be back soon." Julia led the way into the kitchen. It rivaled even Sylvia's for modern sleekness. Everything was new: the white cabinets without a smudge, speckled granite countertops, matching stainless appliances, and professional-size cooktop with separate wall-mounted double oven. Boxes took up almost every inch of floor space, and Julia began unpacking one, lifting out a flame-colored Le Creuset cast-iron Dutch oven.

Louise eyed the expensive new pan wistfully. Though Brendan could barely boil water, he loved to eat and had encouraged Louise's culinary experiments. She sometimes missed the days of coq au vin and haricots verts.

"I don't even know what to do with this thing," Julia said. "And it's so heavy."

Max and Zoe found some wadded-up newspaper from one of the boxes and tore it to shreds, throwing the confetti in the air and laughing. At least they weren't destroying their father's kitchenware.

Louise opened another carton. More pots and pans in pristine condition. "Did Brendan buy this stuff for you?"

Julia shoved the Le Creuset pot into one of the low cabinets. "Yeah, he thinks I'm going to learn to cook. What a joke."

"I could teach you," Louise said, immediately regretting it. She didn't really want to give cooking lessons to her replacement.

"Thanks, but I don't have time. Plus, I don't really care." Julia dug farther into the box. "What is this?"

"A potato ricer. I wish I had one of those."

"Here. Take it. I'll tell him it got lost in the move."

"Are you sure? I mean, this wasn't cheap."

"Consider it a gift." Julia opened a drawer and started shoving in spatulas, garlic presses, and serving spoons.

"Thanks." Louise crammed the ricer into her oversize purse.

"He claims he's going to learn to cook if I don't," Julia said. "I can guess how long that will last."

"He'll buy a bunch of fancy gadgets and give up after a couple of weeks." Louise helped unload a brand-new food processor and a shiny black KitchenAid mixer.

They worked in silence for a while. Louise was grateful that she recognized none of the bowls, plates, pots, or even silverware. Brendan had left her all the kitchen things and bought everything new. Still, it was very strange to be helping him set up a household with someone else.

Julia gave Max and Zoe new boxes of crayons and coloring books after they got tired of the newspaper. A child-size table with two chairs had been hidden behind a box in the corner, and Julia put drinks on it for them. She even had the kind of sippy cup that Zoe liked. Brendan had never bothered to ask about Zoe's cup preferences. Julia must have seen her use one during the last visit. Or she got lucky.

There were so many little things about Max and Zoe that only Louise knew—their favorite foods and TV shows, the idiomatic expressions they used, the way Zoe squinted when she laughed, Max's insistence on having two straws in his juice. She didn't mind that the teachers at the day care knew some of it. But the thought of this other woman finding out all about their lives made her queasy.

The front door creaked, and both kids looked up.

"Mommy, what's that?" Zoe asked.

"I think it's your dad." Louise unwrapped another dinner plate. Surely, she wouldn't be expected to joyfully greet her ex.

"Hey," Brendan said, setting two paper bags on the kitchen island. "I got sushi for the adults and pizza for the kids."

"Pizza!" Max said. "I love pizza!"

Brendan opened the pizza boxes for the kids and cleared off the center island. He began to arrange plastic sushi boxes on the counter.

Max picked the pepperoni slices off his pizza and tossed them into his sister's box. "Here you go."

"Okay." Zoe ate the pepperoni and then pinched bits of cheese off her pizza with her fingers.

Julia stopped putting glasses away long enough to dip a spring roll in peanut sauce. "Louise, why don't you leave the kids here for a while and go shopping or something?"

Louise froze, chopsticks hovering over a slice of tiger roll. The plan was to take a look at Brendan's new place and then head to the park. The idea of dropping the kids off hadn't even occurred to her. "Do you guys want to stay here?"

"Yeah, okay," Max said through a mouthful of pizza.

"Are you sure that's a good idea? I mean, we have a lot of unpacking to do," Brendan said.

"They'll be fine." Julia winked at Louise before taking a pair of chopsticks and deftly picking up a piece of salmon nigiri.

* * *

Back in the van, Louise sat for a moment, trying to collect herself. She'd eaten just two pieces of sushi before leaving. She'd wanted out of Brendan and Julia's new house as quickly as possible, and now she felt lost. There was only one thing to do: drive to Sal's farm. She was afraid to call him and find out that he wasn't there. Instead, she headed out of University Heights and got on the interstate.

No one answered the door of Sal's mobile home. What had he told her on the phone the previous night? Something about fixing a fence? Or helping his sister?

She fought her way down the overgrown path to the greenhouse, two of the larger Chihuahuas on her heels. She shooed them away before opening the door. When she saw Sal squatting next to a row of pots, she was worried. Had the new batch of strawberry plants died? She approached and put a hand on his shoulder. "How are the strawberries?"

"They're doing okay so far," he said. "Francis—that's the farmer who sold them to me—said that they were a cross between a variety that tastes really good with one that's resistant to fungus. He thinks they still need some babying, though. Bugs like 'em, and the fungus will still creep in if you're not careful. I'm trying some nonchemical sprays and elevating them so they don't get too wet. We'll see. Where are the kids?"

"Brendan wanted us to go see their new house, and he and Julia—well, Julia at least—wanted them to stay for a while."

"You could have called me. I would have driven into Saint Jude and taken you out to dinner."

"I wanted to come here. Get away, you know?"

Sal nodded. "I'm sorry we didn't plan to get together this weekend. I've just been really busy with the end of the season. Summer will be better. There's blueberries, but no strawberry patch tours or anything like that. I'm supposed to shut everything down later today—we have a big barn where we store the strawberry patch stuff during the off-season. You want some lunch? I got ham and some nice pickles Betta made."

"That sounds great."

As they walked back to the mobile home, Louise told him about the sushi and the house and the coloring books and the sippy cup. By the time they got inside, she was trying not to cry.

"Hey, look, those kids are going to be fine." Sal went into the kitchen and got out two beers. "My dad was an airline mechanic, did I ever tell you that?"

"You mentioned it, I think," Louise said.

"He had another apartment in Florida because he had to be there so much. On weekends when he was home, he slept till noon and then I'd have to help him with chores. Mowing the lawn, raking leaves. I didn't want to. I wanted to go with my friends. But I guess it was his way of being with me." Sal opened a beer and handed it to Louise before sitting at the kitchen table. "Kids need to be around their dad. It gives them a sense of who they are, if nothing else. Plus, if the dad doesn't want to see them, the kids assume it's something they did wrong. Max and Zoe aren't old enough to think that now, but they will be soon."

Louise drank some beer and nodded, trying to keep her emotions under control. Sal wasn't telling her anything new, but he made it sound simple and reasonable. Brendan wasn't the enemy; he was the father of her children.

Sal took an unlabeled jar of pickles, a container of ham, sliced processed cheese, mustard, and mayonnaise out of the fridge.

"Blue Plate," Louise said.

"Huh?" Sal half turned, a bag of Bunny Bread in his hand.

"Blue Plate mayonnaise is much better than Kraft."

Sal grinned, undoing the twist tie on the bread bag. "I'll remember that." He got out two plates and began spreading mustard on the bread. "I usually eat two sandwiches. How many do you want?"

"One is plenty, thanks." Watching him layer the bread with ham and cheese, Louise began to feel calmer. He was right. The kids would be fine. She took another sip of beer.

Brendan was ready with a list when she arrived to pick up the kids. He didn't have his Moleskine notebook, but he'd clearly made bullet points in his head.

"Apple juice," he said. "The kids keep asking for it. Do you know that stuff has arsenic in it?"

Louise didn't.

"Zoe has no interest in using the toilet. How long do you intend to wait? And she doesn't know any of her letters or numbers. You should be teaching her this stuff. She gets most of her colors wrong too. The only one she recognizes is pink."

Louise waited. There was no point in arguing with him. She had to ride it out and not break down. Thinking about Sal helped.

"Max doesn't know simple math or his sight words."

Sight words? Louise had no idea what he was talking about, but she put on a serious expression.

"He can count, but he doesn't get the concept of adding. Also, his hair is still too long. With those shorts and that big shirt, it looks like he has no pants on. And when he went to the bathroom, I noticed that his underwear was on backward. His socks don't match either."

Julia appeared behind her husband. "Hi. The kids had a great time. Thanks for letting them stay."

Louise forced a smile. She decided to assume that Julia had not contributed to the list. "I hope they were good."

"Oh, yes. Why are you guys standing in the doorway? Come in," Julia said, starting down the hallway.

Brendan looked like he wanted to say something else. Probably he had noticed more infractions: Zoe wore too much pink. Max had dirt behind his ears.

Zoe ran straight into Louise's legs. "Mommy!" Louise bent down and folded the girl into her arms. "Did you have fun?"

"I watching TV," Zoe said.

Louise smiled, for real this time. Brendan could pick on her all he wanted, but he'd let them sit in front of the boob tube absorbing noneducational programming. Behind Zoe she could see Max sitting on a puffy leather couch, glued to *SpongeBob SquarePants*.

"Hey, Mommy, I'm watching *SpongeBob*," Max said.

"I can see that," Louise said. "But it's time to go now. Say good-bye to Daddy and Ms. Julia."

"I want to watch the rest of the show."

"There's only a couple of minutes left," Julia said. "Would you like something to drink?"

"No, thanks." Louise leaned against the couch, her back to the TV.

Brendan opened a bottle of wine and poured a glass. "I think we're going to eat out somewhere. Any recommendations?"

"Um, I haven't been to any nice restaurants in town. Sylvia says that Bistro Maison is good."

"Where is that?"

"Just go up Garden Street and turn right on Commerce." Louise wished she could go there with Sal. But she'd had fun with him just eating ham sandwiches and helping put away the play tractors, bouncy horses, and picnic tables he and his sister used for their strawberry patch tours. She and Brendan had often run out of things to say to each other when they were married. But with Sal, somehow that never happened.

Brendan was staring at her. "Are you okay?"

"Yeah, just thinking, why?"

"I was talking to you."

"Oh, sorry. What were you saying?"

"Never mind."

The credits started to run on the show and Julia turned off the TV. "Time to go, guys. See you next time!"

Louise felt a stab of panic. They hadn't worked out visitation or custody or whatever. Technically, she had sole custody, something that Brendan had allowed since he didn't particularly like changing diapers. But now that he was in town, things would be different.

"How about next Saturday?" Brendan said.

"Yeah, okay."

"We'll be in touch," Julia said.

CHAPTER 36

When Louise pulled into the library lot Monday morning, Lily ran up to the van waving a stapled packet.

"They closed the library," she said. "I can't believe it."

Sylvia drove in and parked next to Louise. "What's going on?"

"Beats me," Louise said, getting out of the van.

Sylvia took the papers from Lily. "The Gund got the EPA to declare this property a hazardous waste site. The library has to be shut and torn down so the land can be decontaminated."

"Mr. Foley signed this letter. After the train accident, he was one of the people who agreed not to reveal how bad the spill was, in exchange for this piece of land. I don't know why he's talking now," Lily said, wringing her thin hands together.

"What train accident?" Sylvia took off her sunglasses.

"There was some kind of toxic chemical spill here back in the 1980s," Louise said.

"So we've been working on a hazardous waste site? Lovely."

"I thought you knew."

Hope arrived in her pickup, rolled down the window, and rested her meaty arm on the driver's side door frame. "I don't like the sight of y'all standing out here."

Sylvia gave her the packet, and Hope read in silence for a moment before climbing out of her truck. "I wouldn't put it past that boss of ours to dump a bunch of chemicals back behind the library and call the EPA. We best take a look."

"Not me," Sylvia said. "My Jimmy Choos are not stomping around in whatever nasty stuff is behind this library."

"I'm going inside to get my things," Lily said.

Louise and Hope followed the sidewalk around the back of the building. After a few feet of overgrown grass, the lot disappeared into a dense forest.

"You ain't going in there with your fancy shoes neither," Hope said. "Let me take a look." She walked through the weeds and into the woods.

Louise sniffed the air and imagined that she detected a chemical tang. Spring was coming, though, and a few of the flowers that were blooming had an odd smell. Besides, some of the foulest chemicals didn't have any odor. Why hadn't she taken Hope seriously when she'd originally told her about the toxic spill? Sometimes, she felt like her brain was a sieve. Small details disappeared through the holes.

Sylvia rounded the corner and stopped next to Louise. "Think there's anything back there?"

"I don't know. I'm sorry I didn't tell you about the train accident. Hope brought it up the first time she met me, when I was doing my research. So I guess I assumed that she told you too."

"It's okay. I probably would have taken the job anyway. I mean, how bad can it be? They built a library here."

After a few minutes, Hope returned, her sneakers caked with mud. "It don't look any different than usual to me, but I ain't made it a practice to go back there much. They coulda dumped something back there, but I'd think there would be tire tracks or empty barrels or something."

Sylvia shook her head. "Mr. Foley hates us. This is his revenge."

"Shut down his own library rather than let us run it our way? I guess it makes a loony kind of sense," Louise said. "He couldn't see an easy way to stop us. If he fired us, he'd have to hire someone else. He tried to block our ideas, but the patrons liked what we were doing, so fighting us would have made him look bad to the police jury. So he closed us down."

"I don't know what to tell y'all. Lord knows they shoulda done a better job cleaning this up. So it's maybe a good thing. But they'll have to tear down the library," Hope said.

"And the Gund will argue against building a new one," Louise said.

"For now, we need to move to the Hungarian Springs branch," Sylvia said. "Let's break in with Lily and haul out what we can."

Without Hope and Lily, Louise and Sylvia would never have found the Hungarian Springs branch of the Alligator Bayou Parish Library. It was located in a strip mall that also housed a storefront church and a computer repair shop. A burger joint that looked like an ice-fishing shack occupied the middle of the parking lot, effectively blocking the street view of the library sign. But at least the smell was divine.

"Best burgers in Alligator Bayou Parish," Hope said.

"Well, at least we have lunch figured out." Sylvia parked haphazardly near the blue-painted wooden shed. "I can't believe we've never been here before."

"Mr. Henry kept offering to take me, but I was busy. I almost tagged along with Matt once, but I think he's trying to qualify for NASCAR," Louise said.

"He does drive fast." Sylvia grabbed her tote-size sequined purse from between the seats and opened her door. "And the souped-up engine on that little car of his is louder than a motorcycle."

Louise stepped out onto the sidewalk. Now that she was standing in front of the building, she could actually see the library's sign. The large display window and wooden sign above the door made the space look more like a five-and-dime than a library. The adjacent business was the Holy Miracle Church. Louise tried to see inside, but the windows were blocked by yellowing curtains.

A bell rang when Sylvia opened the library door. The woman who greeted them wore a shapeless flowered dress accented with a rhinestone Jesus pin.

"I'm Sylvia and this is Louise. We're from the main branch," Sylvia said.

"Hi, y'all. I'm Glenda," the woman said, coming out from behind the circulation desk.

Louise guessed Glenda was in her midfifties. She remembered Hope's comments about her horrifying medical condition and lack of cooking skills. She decided not to ask about the former and to assume that the latter was exaggeration.

Glenda rolled her eyes up to the ceiling as though she was praying when Sylvia told her the main library had been shut down. "Mr. Foley said there was hardly anything spilled back then. Though, I'll tell you what, I did not like the smell coming out of those woods. Next thing you know, they built a library there and Mr. Foley was promoted to director. Folks 'round here aren't stupid. They knowed something was going on. Excuse me a moment." She held the door open for four men in green-and-white-striped Alligator Bayou Parish Jail uniforms hauling long, unpainted boards. Two guards trailed behind, stopped, and folded their arms, watching. The prisoners leaned the boards against the wall and trooped outside for another load.

"We're gettin' some new shelves for the children's room. A donation from someone." Glenda looked at the ceiling again.

"What do you think that's about?" Sylvia asked.

"Favors. Mr. Foley done something for someone."

Inside, the library looked even more like a knickknack store. The computer at the front could have been a cash register, and the few books in the room were displayed like trinkets. But maybe the new shelves would help the place seem more library-like.

"I guess we'll be operating out of here for a while," Sylvia said. "If I can use your phone, I'll go ahead and call Matt and Henry and let them know. Lily, you and Hope can start bringing our stuff inside."

"Phone's right here. I'm afraid we don't have a whole lot of space. This was a Christian bookstore for a time. Before that it was the town drugstore. The soda fountain used to be right over there," Glenda said. "Hello, Gertrude. You got you some more of those inspirational romances, I see."

A white-haired woman shuffled up to the desk. Glenda scanned the books, her flower-printed hip just a few inches from where Sylvia sat, phone to her ear.

While Glenda chatted with the old lady and Sylvia made her calls, the prisoners fashioned the boards into shelves. They worked without speaking, as though performing a dance they'd all rehearsed before. None of them so much as glanced away from their task. The deputies observed with blank expressions, motionless as statues.

Sylvia hung up the phone. "That's weird. Mr. Henry says that Mr. Foley has taken an extended leave of absence. Mr. Henry will work out of the Oak Lake branch. We are basically now running the show."

Hope and Lily came back with a computer and a box of files. "Reckon we could get these trusties to help us?" Hope asked.

One of the deputies shook his head.

"Worth a try." Hope set the monitor down on the floor. "Let me get that phone. I'm gonna call my cousin's husband who owns the U Store It off Route One. We're gonna need someplace to put all them books. He got a truck to haul them in too." She took Sylvia's chair and dialed from memory.

"Let me show the rest of y'all around. We'll figure out somewhere for y'all to set up." Glenda led the way through a narrow hallway. The floor sloped upward as they headed into the rear of the library. Clearly, the front room had once been the store, while the back part was the stockroom. In between the high shelves of books in the windowless rear area there was just enough space for a table with four computers for patron use.

"The employee break room is through this door, and the restroom is here," Glenda said, gesturing to two white-painted doors.

"Y'all don't have any more work area, I'm guessing," Sylvia said.

"No, we just have the computer up front to check out books and that little desk. Usually, there's only one employee here at a time."

"Let's take a look at the break room." Sylvia opened the door on the right.

A table and refrigerator took up most of the closet-like space. The addition of another table would have made it impossible to access the employees' lunches. In one stroke, Mr. Foley and Mrs. Gunderson had dismantled all of Louise and Sylvia's hard work from the past few months. They would barely have room to set up their computers, let alone hold Sylvia's Zumba classes or book clubs or dances. Shutting down the library against the will of the voters demonstrated the level of power Mrs. Gunderson wielded. Even if the tax passed, there wouldn't be enough money to build another library. That would require the parish to borrow money—which would take another vote of the people.

Sylvia didn't give any indication that she shared Louise's despair. She paced the length of the building with the other four librarians following. "We'll put Hope's computer in the break room. There's enough space for Matt to set up his laptop there too. Louise and I can share my computer for now, but we'll need to put it somewhere else in the library, maybe in a corner near the back."

When they returned to the front of the library, Louise stared at the rough wood shelves. The prisoners had completed their work and left without ever saying a word.

CHAPTER 37

As she packed the children into the van for another Saturday with Brendan and Julia, Louise understood a little of how her boss felt. Losing control was terrifying. Unlike the library director, however, she tried to do a good job. Sure, Max's socks didn't match again and Zoe's hair was already falling out of its pigtails, but they were happy and well adjusted.

Louise began to doubt the last part as she stood outside the van, waiting for Zoe to stop playing in the front seat. The girl screamed and cried if Louise lifted her into her car seat, but if she didn't, Zoe crept into the driver's side to tug at the rearview mirror and push buttons on the radio. This was a stage Max had mostly grown out of, but Louise had never found an effective way to deal with it. "Zoe, the radio won't play without the car turned on. Pushing the button ten million times isn't going to make it work. Please get in your seat," she said.

"Zoe, stop messing around," Max said from the backseat.

"Okay, okay." Zoe slowly climbed into her seat. Louise had to grit her teeth to stop herself from just lifting the girl up. Sometimes, waiting for the children to do things themselves required Zen-like patience.

Julia greeted them from the flower beds when they arrived. She'd been pulling weeds, and her jeans were flecked with dirt. Brendan would never have tolerated Louise's overgrown lawn and the flower beds taken over by crabgrass. In fact, she was surprised that he hadn't made a snide comment about her lack of gardening skills the last time he visited. Perhaps there were too many other things to criticize—most importantly, her parenting skills.

"We were thinking we'd take them to a movie," Julia said, brushing off her skinny jeans. "There's a new animated thing—I forget what."

"They're not really good about sitting still in theaters," Louise said. She freed Zoe from her car seat, and the girl jumped behind the wheel and turned on the hazard lights.

Julia shrugged. "Brendan wants to. Let me just wash my hands and get him and we'll go." She went inside the house.

Louise wished she could erase all her memories that involved Brendan. Many of their dates had involved dinner and a movie. Sitting in a dark theater together was a way to avoid the fact that they didn't have much to talk about, especially later in their relationship. After their initial courtship, he'd slowly lost interest in her, spending more and more time with his professor colleagues, drinking in bars and going to see live music without her. She'd convinced herself that his neglect was normal, something he had to do to get tenure, but even then she knew that most academic spouses didn't act that way.

"Can I ride in this car?" Max asked, touching the tire of Brendan's SUV.

"Yes," Louise said. "You, Zoe, Daddy, and Ms. Julia are going to a movie."

"In this car?"

"Yup."

The new black SUV was equipped with a built-in entertainment system. The kids could watch a movie on the way to the movie. It also had leather seats and enough cup holders for all the passengers to drink lattes and bottled water simultaneously.

Julia came back a minute later with Brendan. He wore shorts and dark-brown flip-flops. Louise hated sandals on men, something she'd never had the courage to tell him. Now, his bad taste in footwear was Julia's problem. It was a nice thought. Freeing.

Zoe stood outside the SUV, lower lip sticking out.

"Come on, Zoe, get in," Max called from his seat.

She pushed the lip out farther and shook her head.

"Do you have any DVDs for that thing?" Louise asked Julia.

"Yeah. I have Elmo and *Dora the Explorer*."

"Put on Elmo. She'll get in."

Julia started the engine and slid the Elmo disc into the player. Zoe immediately got up in her seat. Even though she knew it was irrational, Louise felt like she was losing her children. She strapped Zoe in, kissed her, and turned away quickly. "Love you both."

As she got in the van alone, she tried to console herself with the thought that Sal would be waiting when she got home.

Brendan and Julia had agreed to drop off the kids at home in the morning, so Louise was surprised when her phone rang at eight o'clock. She'd just drifted awake, enjoying the sensation of lying next to Sal's warm body. She wasn't prepared to deal with her ex just yet. But in a typical Brendan move, he'd made Julia call.

"Can you please come and pick them up?" Julia said. "I

don't know what's going on, but they won't do anything we say."

As though that didn't happen every day. Brendan and Julia were getting lessons in what Louise's life was like. Of course, Brendan wouldn't see it that way. "Okay. I'm sorry they're giving you a hard time," Louise said.

"Yeah, well, they're kids."

"I'll be there in a half hour." Louise hung up and pulled on her clothes from the day before.

Sal sat up in bed, looking attractively rumpled with his stubble-covered chin and bare chest. "What's up?"

"Some crisis with the kids. I don't know. Nothing serious. I think Brendan's just sick of them, really."

Sal put his jeans on and looked around for a shirt. "I'll go make coffee."

When Louise finished getting ready, she came into the kitchen to find Sal pouring coffee into a travel mug. He added exactly the right amount of half-and-half and handed it to her.

"Thanks. I really hope Brendan and Julia don't hate the kids now," Louise said.

"He can't. They're his."

"Oh, yes, he can and he can hate me for raising them badly. Or giving them bad genes. Or something. I'm sure this is going to be my fault somehow."

"If he acts that way, he is a jerk. But I don't think he will." Sal got a mug for himself. "For one thing, he married you, so he can't be a complete idiot."

"Yeah, well, I hope you're right."

Louise had never gotten a speeding ticket, but she pushed seventy on the way to Brendan and Julia's. Despite Sal's reassurances, she was worried. Brendan might decide that the kids were so badly behaved that he never wanted to see them again or that Louise was raising them wrong and he had to try to get custody.

Brendan answered the door. He hadn't changed out of his pajama pants and faded T-shirt, and his face was unshaven. "I don't know what's wrong with those kids, but they wouldn't sit still for the movie, they refused to go to bed until midnight, and now Max won't use the bathroom even though he just woke up. Will he pee on the floor?"

"He might. And I can tell you what's wrong with them. They're kids. This is what kids are like. This is what it's like to be a parent," Louise said.

"Max said that he wasn't my friend anymore and that Santa Claus wasn't going to bring me any presents."

"He tells me that almost every day." Louise edged past Brendan. Max and Zoe were sitting on the couch watching cartoons, still in their pajamas. "Max, go to the bathroom, please."

"No! Never!"

"Fine. Then, I am turning off the TV."

"I'm not your friend anymore!"

"Okay, just go to the bathroom." Louise reached for the TV remote.

"Okay, okay." Max got up and went down the hall.

Brendan sat down in a leather armchair. "I tried to take him to the bathroom at the movie theater, and he wouldn't go. He just played with the toilet paper. And he kept kicking the seat in front of him during the movie and asking when it would be over."

"Welcome to my world," Louise said.

"Zoe wouldn't sit still for more than five minutes. She wanted to walk up and down the stairs and get in the other seats. Finally, Julia had to take her to the mall instead."

"I warned you guys that a movie was a bad idea. You have to remember how old they are."

"Yeah." Brendan suddenly took interest in a spot on the rug. "Um, I know they're my kids, but I don't think I could do . . . what you do. I mean, it's really hard."

"Yes. Yes, it is."

"So I appreciate it. And I'm sorry that I criticize everything. I know I'm a jackass."

"Kids can be incredibly frustrating," Louise said. Maybe, just maybe, he was starting to get it.

Brendan looked up again. "No, it's good. We want to try again next weekend."

"Good. They'll get better as they get used to you. And you'll figure out how to handle them."

Max came out of the bathroom and stood in front of Louise. "Can we go home now?"

"Yes," she said. "Right now."

CHAPTER 38

By August the summer heat was almost unbearable. Even though Louise blasted the air conditioner in the van, she was still covered in sticky sweat by the time she got home every day. She made the kids go in the backyard every morning, knowing that was the only time the weather would be cool enough for them to be outside.

Despite losing their building, Louise and Sylvia continued to add programs and improve library services as much as they could. The owner of the strip mall turned out to be Mr. McDonald's brother. Sylvia convinced him to let the library use the defunct Holy Miracle Church building for office space, Zumba classes, and book clubs for nominal rent. Louise, Sylvia, and Sal spend an entire day ripping down the "Prayers $1" signs and tossing out leaflets advertising the preacher's inspirational cassette tapes and self-published books. The man himself had left town abruptly a year earlier, owing six months' rent. He was a former drug dealer who'd spent months hiding from authorities in the woods surrounding Alligator Bayou before a persistent sheriff's deputy finally discovered him. While serving his two-year sentence, he claimed to have found Jesus and, upon his release, started the Holy Miracle Church especially for former criminals. The landlord was of the opinion that not all of the lawbreakers had actually found the Lord.

After they'd cleaned up the interior of the church, Hope's cousin Hank arrived with a truckload of books. He also arranged for the prisoners to come back and build more shelves with lumber donated by Mr. McDonald. By the time they were finished, the space almost looked like a library.

Mr. Foley was still "out of pocket," as Hope put it. On his infrequent visits to the branch, Mr. Henry avoided questions about their boss, except to say that he was resting at home. The assistant director seemed to become frailer every time they saw him. He praised their efforts to improve the library, but there was little enthusiasm in his voice.

For a while after the main library closed, patronage was poor. But gradually, people started to come to the new location. Sylvia started scheduling two librarians to work on Saturdays because the new hours were so popular. Louise put one of the church's plush chairs near the periodical rack especially for Ms. Trudy. The B sisters made regular appearances to find new books as well as to use the computers, and Mary came for her summer reading materials. After Louise hired her as a babysitter, she'd gained enough confidence to advertise her services and regularly watched other children in town. Louise slipped her food whenever she could, but as she grew taller, the girl seemed to get thinner. She smiled more, though, and even came to Sylvia's *Gone with the Wind* dance. She wore a dress that Louise bought for her on eBay; Louise had pretended she'd found it in the back of her closet.

On one of the hottest days of the summer, Louise drove by Anthony's Seafood. As a library employee, she couldn't help with any of the Friends of the Library fund-raisers, but there was nothing stopping her from taking a look on the way to her Saturday shift. The minute she turned onto Live Oak Road, she regretted her decision. Lily would have to open the library herself because there was no way Louise would be able to maneuver through the traffic in time. Teenagers in Ms. Trudy's new orange T-shirts waved signs advertising car washes, dog washes, and jambalaya. The line of vehicles to be cleaned stretched around the block. The parking lot was overrun with at least twenty dogs sniffing one another while jambalaya cooked in giant cast-iron pots. Ms. Trudy and her group of old ladies filled Styrofoam boxes from one of the pots, selling them just as quickly as they hit the folding table. The dog washers were similarly busy. Sal coaxed a furry standard poodle into a tub of soapy water while Betta rubbed shampoo into the coat of a mud-brown mutt.

Louise inched the van forward and signaled to turn down the next side street. A car behind her honked, and then someone leaned out the window with a megaphone. "Libraries suck! Suck taxes from hardworking families! Vote NO!"

Louise twisted around in her seat to see who it was, but the car made a screeching U-turn and headed the other way, the person with the megaphone still shouting. The maroon Oldsmobile had been parked across the street from her house long enough to be unmistakable, however. It belonged to her neighbors, the Pettigrews.

CHAPTER 39

Louise's desk was one of the tables the church had used to display promotional materials. Since they hadn't found anything to use for cubicle walls, she'd set up her makeshift office in a corner of the former church sanctuary. Sylvia had decorated the rest of the space with library posters and stacked up most of the chairs to allow room for her Zumba classes.

Louise picked up a copy of *A Tale of Two Cities*, Brianna's selection for the book club. Since the first meeting, it had leveled out at ten steady members, including Sal. Sometimes, Louise caught him shaking his head at the older women, but she thought he enjoyed the meetings, even though he kept quiet most of the time. They talked on the phone almost every night, and he had a lot more to say then. Louise was grateful to Brendan and Julia for making their Saturday dates possible. Even if they just did farm chores together, the time was special, a chance to be an adult.

She stacked the cataloged book on the finished pile and took another one.

Hope walked in from the former preacher's office where she'd set up her desk. "I done got some bad news."

Louise straightened her pile of books. "What?"

"Mr. Henry. He's in the hospital over to Saint Jude. Heart attack. Marsha says we best get on over there."

"So he was at the Oak Lake branch when it happened?"

Hope nodded. "Marsha said he come to help them plan the summer reading. Was sitting there drinking a cup of coffee, stood up, and fell right down again. Glenda will watch the library while we go."

Riding in the library van with the entire staff, Louise felt like she was on a school field trip. Sylvia was in the driver's seat, Lily and Matt occupied the far backseat, Hope was in the middle, and Louise rode shotgun. Sylvia adjusted the mirrors before pulling out onto the street. "Do you think we should get some flowers or something?"

"We can do that later," Hope said.

Louise turned all the way around to look at her. "Wait a minute. What's going on?"

"He ain't awake."

"You mean he's not conscious?" Lily asked, sounding even more timid than usual.

Hope folded her arms across her chest and refused to say anything more.

The Saint Jude General Hospital was a dark-brown building with gray-tinted windows. The sunlight was blocked so effectively that inside was a constant twilight. Hope led the way to the intensive care unit. There, they had to state their business to an appropriately dour nurse in green scrubs before being allowed to proceed.

Hope strode down the hallway with the rest of the employees trailing behind. Sylvia hadn't said a word since they left the library. For the first time since Louise had known her, she looked afraid.

Hope stopped in front of room thirty-one. She hesitated, and her shoulders slumped uncharacteristically. Louise stepped up next to her and looked inside. Mr. Henry was lying on the bed, his face barely visible behind the respirator mask. His arm was hooked up to an IV filled with clear fluid. Mr. Foley sat next to the bed, holding his other hand. The library director looked vulnerable, like a sad old man rather than a tyrant.

Hope pulled herself up straight again and marched forward. "Hello, Mr. Foley."

Their boss raised his head. He seemed to have no color in his face at all except for the faint black rings under his eyes. He had lost weight, and his skin hung on him like a too-large shirt.

The library staff ventured in after Hope, stepping lightly on the tiled floor as though they were worried about waking the comatose man.

"Hey, y'all," Mr. Foley said, his tone as lifeless as his skin.

"What you been doing?" Hope asked. "You done took off on us."

Mr. Foley shrugged. "I sold the ranch."

"What'd you do that for?"

"I'm done with it. The goats, the library, everything."

"Well, what the heck you gonna do?"

Sylvia put her hand on Hope's shoulder, a hint that she should lower her voice. Hope shook it off.

"I got enough money to retire now. That's what I'm gonna do."

"What you mean 'retire'?" Hope put her hands on her hips. "Ride off into the sunset? Check yourself into the old folks' home?"

"I don't rightly know."

"What's wrong with you?"

"You want to know what it is?" Mr. Foley sat up straight

and pointed at Louise and Sylvia with his free hand. "It's them two. Me and Henry had a good thing. We ran this library system together. It was ours. And when y'all came, you took it away. Now this."

"Bull," Hope said. "Y'all didn't do nothing before these two came. Just farted around like a couple of store clerks. I remember whenever anyone had an idea to make things better, you shot it down. Mr. Henry, he might have been willing to give it a try, but you said no. And I didn't never figure out why, but he respected you. You held him back. Held the whole library back because you're so darn scared of everything. Don't fix what ain't broke, you said. It might not have been broke, but it didn't run real good neither. Louise and Sylvia pushed Mr. Henry, and they done got that spark going in him again. He tried to hide it from you some, but he was letting them do stuff."

"Y'all ruined it! You ruined him and me and everything." Mr. Foley let go of the assistant director's hand. "This is all y'all's fault."

"It made Mr. Henry happy," Lily said. She clapped a hand over her mouth. "*Makes* him happy, I mean."

"Fine. Have it your way. I quit." Mr. Foley collapsed in on himself, his head falling to his chest. His breath came out in labored gasps as he sobbed with complete abandon. Lily held out a box of tissues, and he knocked it away with a limp hand.

After a few minutes, he stood up, staggering briefly before regaining his balance. Hope stepped forward, arms out to embrace him. He shook his head and sidestepped her, covering his face with his hands. The library employees parted to give him a clear path out the door.

After Mr. Foley was gone, Hope took the chair next to the bed and held Mr. Henry's hand, tears standing in her eyes. Matt set the assistant director's American Library

Association coffee cup on the end table. "Like, just in case he needs it," he said.

Lily and Sylvia sat on the two remaining chairs and stared at the old man's shrouded body. To Louise, he looked cold with only the thin sheet and hospital blanket covering him, but she was afraid to touch anything. When the nurse came in to tell them it was time to leave, she noticed a rosary near Mr. Henry's hand. Hope saw her looking.

"Did you put that there?" Louise asked.

"Nope. Reckon Mr. Foley left it."

CHAPTER 40

Louise was ambivalent about Max's fourth birthday party being held at Brendan and Julia's house. She had pictured a day on Sal's farm with the kids running around outside. But since the temperature hovered around ninety-five degrees, it was better to have a larger indoor space.

Brendan had set up a rented bouncy castle in the shaded backyard. Max and his friends from school bounced and pretended to shoot one another, oblivious to the sweat running down their faces. Zoe refused to go in the castle, playing with Madeleine and her baby toys on the lawn instead.

Louise was glad that she and Brendan could tolerate each other well enough to share this experience. He'd mostly kept his promise about not criticizing her parenting. Things he really didn't like, he simply changed himself, like Max's haircut. He and Julia also bought him some new clothes. Louise couldn't complain, since taking Max shopping and getting his hair cut were chores she was only too glad to delegate. To her own surprise, she found herself willing to give up this bit of control for some welcome assistance.

Sylvia walked over, holding two bottles of beer. "Hey, girl. This one's for you. You deserve it. This is a great party."

"I had nothing to do with it," Louise said.

"You let Brendan take charge, which was smart and also kind of nice." Sylvia sounded just a little bit drunk.

"He let me invite Sal," Louise said, accepting the beer. She watched as Sal and Jake pretended to be upset that they were too big for the bouncy house and settled for standing outside, making faces at the boys. Whenever Sal played with the kids, Louise fantasized about him being their father. The shadow of her disastrous marriage to Brendan was slowly receding.

"I think y'all are going to be okay," Sylvia said, echoing her thoughts. "Hey, when are you going to marry this guy? Summer is no good, but fall weddings are nice. Or even Christmas. You could have red bridesmaids' dresses."

"Come on. Anyway, I thought red made you look blotchy or something."

Sylvia waved her beer bottle. "Yes, but I'm stunning in green. The point is, we're not getting any younger. You need to get this guy to propose to you already."

"I'm not in a big hurry. It didn't work out too well for either of us last time, as you know."

"Shut up. That means nothing."

"It means that I'm going to be more careful this time."

"So you'll turn him down if he asks you?"

"I didn't say that."

Sal waved to the kids, took a beer from the cooler, and joined them. "Y'all talking about me?"

Louise answered before Sylvia could say anything about rings. "Nope. We were talking about Jimmy's birthday party."

Sal opened the beer with his keychain bottle opener. "When is it?"

"Um, I forget."

"January. A good month for weddings," Sylvia said.

"Oh, really? And why is that?" Sal stared at the label on his beer bottle.

Sylvia tossed her hair. "Christmas rush is over. It's nice and cool so you can actually wear stockings with your dress. And you beat the spring wedding season. I'll bet even the wedding dresses are cheaper in winter."

"Good to know. I'm going to see how the boys are doing." Sal tipped back his beer bottle as he headed back toward the bouncy castle.

"Now you did it," Louise said.

"Yeah, I planted the idea in his head." Sylvia shrugged.

"Mommy!" Zoe appeared at Louise's feet holding a stuffed giraffe that belonged to Madeleine. "Horsey!"

"That's a giraffe, honey," Louise said.

"Horsey!" Zoe insisted, dashing off across the lawn.

"I have to get inside before I die of heatstroke." Sylvia finished her beer and scooped up the baby.

After Brendan and Julia coaxed the kids out of the bouncy castle, everyone went inside and Max blew out the candles on Louise's cherry-chocolate chip cake. The sight of him accomplishing this task by himself brought tears to her eyes. Julia cut and served the cake, which the kids ignored in favor of playing with the party hats and noisemakers.

"Time for presents!" Julia announced.

Max sat in the midst of the gifts and began tearing them open. Louise wondered whether Brendan had stuck to his idea of buying Max an educational board game or if he'd listened to her suggestion about action figures. Max ripped the paper off the suspiciously board game–shaped box and triumphantly held up a set of plastic dolls. "Yay! Superman! And Batman! And Green Lantern!"

Julia took a picture with a professional-looking camera, and Brendan actually smiled at Louise, a little sheepishly.

They were finally beginning to act like co-parents. And, amazingly, Louise wasn't jealous, just glad. As they stood watching, Sal slipped his arm around her waist, improving her mood even more.

"I hope next season is better for my heirloom strawberry experiment," Sal said, stacking up bags of potting soil.

"Me too," Louise said. One of the chores she'd agreed to help with after the party was cleaning out the greenhouse. It wasn't used much in the summer, Sal had told her, and he normally liked to put things in order before the scorching heat started. This year, the time had gotten away from him. Part of what had put him behind his schedule was helping Louise with yard work and fixing things in her new house. They also hung out and talked for hours whenever the kids were with Brendan and Julia, engaging in time-wasting activities like watching TV and spending whole afternoons in bed. It was heaven.

They had just gotten the clutter reduced enough to begin sweeping the concrete floor when Louise's phone rang. She ran to her purse, terrified that something had happened with the children. But the number was Sylvia's.

"Mr. Henry's passed on."

"I'm sorry to hear it." Louise wasn't surprised. Since their hospital visit, she'd had periodic updates from Hope, who had insisted that they didn't need to go again. He didn't realize that anyone was there anyway, she explained. But Hope felt an obligation since she knew his family. Mr. Henry's sister, who had died a few years previously, had been a good friend of Hope's mother.

"The visitation will be Monday. We'll take turns dropping by so someone will always be in the library." Sylvia sniffed. "He was a sweet man."

"Yes, he was," Louise said. "We have to keep fighting for this library. He wanted that."

When Mr. Foley's resignation letter arrived with the library mail, Glenda gave it to Hope. Louise thought she would open it immediately and hang it next to the picture of the blond-haired Jesus that the preacher had left in his, now her, office. Instead, Hope turned the yellowed envelope over and over in her hands. "I don't like the way this went," she said.

Sylvia walked over from her makeshift young adult section in the corner. "He resigned. That's what we wanted, right? Now we can actually do something with this library if the tax passes."

Hope slid a fingernail under the seal and the envelope popped open. "This here envelope's old as the hills. Glue don't even work anymore." She took out a typewritten letter and scanned it. Wordlessly, she handed the tissue-thin paper to Sylvia.

" 'Dear library staff and police jury members, by this letter, I officially resign effective immediately,' " Sylvia read. " 'I feel that the library has gone in a direction that is counter to everything I have worked for in my twenty years as director. Since I am powerless to stop this degeneration, I prefer to retire and spend more time on my hobbies and other interests. Sincerely, Foley Hatfield.' " Sylvia refolded the letter. "Good riddance. Begone, demon!"

"He weren't no demon, just an old man," Hope said.

"You said you didn't like him either," Louise said.

"I could hardly abide the man, but that don't mean it ain't sad, what's happening to him."

Sylvia stuffed the letter back into the envelope. "What's that?"

"He done lost everything he loved: the farm, the library, Mr. Henry."

"You have to tell me something," Louise said. She glanced around the front room of the library. There were no patrons in evidence. She kept her voice low just in case. "I've been wondering this for a long time, but I never wanted to ask. Were he and Mr. Henry—"

Hope cut her off. "I reckon so. They didn't never live in the same house, but everyone knew they were together."

"I feel terrible."

"Don't. He is a mean old bastard. Mr. Henry deserved better."

"Yeah, but being gay had to be tough," Sylvia said. "Especially around here."

Hope took the letter from Sylvia and shoved it into her back pocket. "Didn't nobody mind. Didn't talk about it much neither, though. 'Cept for that time Mr. Foley got caught trying to pick up dates in that park in Saint Jude."

"Shut up," Sylvia said. "He did not."

"Yes, indeed. I was the one got to run out to the parish jail in the middle of the night to bail him out. Improved his attitude toward me considerably, at least for a while. Mr. Henry was a saint to put up with that man and all those goats."

CHAPTER 41

At the beginning of September, the librarians held a meeting in Hope's office. Sylvia sat in one of the plastic chairs and balanced a legal pad on her lap. Louise took the other chair and crossed her legs, trying to get comfortable.

"Now the real work begins," Hope said.

Louise raised her eyes to Jesus hanging above the desk. A miracle was what they needed.

"How are the Friends of the Library doing?" Sylvia asked.

"They made up some flyers, but the Gund is bullying most of the places to hang hers instead. We have ours in the Piggly Wiggly, the Cut and Dye, and the gym. Betta's working on getting more buttons and T-shirts made," Louise said. "I wish we could afford a mailing, but they haven't raised enough money yet."

"The book-burning crazies are back," Hope said. "I seen some signs around. Facebook page is back too."

"What can we do?" Sylvia asked. "Not much, I'm sure."

"As public employees, we can't campaign, but we can give out information," Louise said.

"We need to make us an informational brochure. If y'all

do something up, I'll help hand them out," Hope said. "We can give 'em to people when they check out books too. We done that with the last try to get this tax passed. For all the good it done in the end."

"I'm going to make it pink. Pink makes people happy." Sylvia doodled something with a pen.

"Okay, so what's going on with the library director position?" Louise asked.

"That's why I called this meeting. I heard from Marty Pratt this morning. They are starting the search," Sylvia said.

"Are we going to be involved?"

"Apparently not. They don't have to let us participate in the process."

"We could end up with another Mr. Foley. Or worse," Louise said.

Hope turned and eyed the Jesus picture. "Don't you worry about that none. There ain't no other Mr. Foleys around."

"This is serious! If we end up with a bad director, we'll be right back where we started."

"Simmer down and listen, city girl. First, y'all need to apply for the job. Update your résumés and whatnot. Second, this here process is gonna take a while. What we need to worry about right now is getting that tax passed. 'Cause if that don't happen, we won't get no library director of any stripe."

"She's right," Sylvia said. "We have to keep our heads with this thing."

Louise sat down on the edge of her chair. "Why don't you apply, Hope?"

Hope snorted. "I ain't no library director material. 'Sides, I didn't even finish college. You think they're gonna hire my redneck behind? I'll be lucky if the new boss don't fire me."

"They can't do that!" Sylvia said.

"Reckon I'm supposed to have a college degree for this job. But I'm too old for that stuff now."

"You are not. I've had students a lot older than you."

Hope waved her hand dismissively. "Can't teach an old dog new tricks."

For some obscure reason, elections in Louisiana were held on Saturdays. Louise had to work, so she dropped the kids off at Brendan's and drove to the library. She still didn't love being trapped behind the circulation desk, but Lily seemed content to sit there and read her historical newsletters. She parked herself obligingly with her cup of coffee.

Louise paced nervously, trying to act casual when she asked patrons if they'd voted. The weather was good—sunny and cool—which should boost turnout. That should be a good thing since there had to be more reasonable people than tax- and library-hating cranks on the rolls. Louise checked the book-burning Facebook page and Twitter feed constantly. Most of the comments were from outraged citizens who had seen the previous night's news broadcast. The reporter from Channel 6 had interviewed Sylvia in front of one of the yard signs that said, "A NO Vote to the Library is a YES vote to Jesus." Sylvia had made great TV yet again. The Facebook comments were split evenly between fans of the library and fans of her.

At four o'clock, Louise allowed herself to check the election returns online. The tax was losing by two percentage points. She waited until a high school teacher with a stack of DVDs finished checking out before telling Lily.

"The returns from the Oak Lake area and Alligator Bayou proper haven't come in yet," Lily said. "All they have is Hungarian Springs. And there's a lot of people around this area who work in Saint Jude. They're not invested in the parish at all. I'd be surprised if it doesn't turn around in a couple of hours."

Louise hoped she was right. But Lily would be fine in any case. She'd be just as happy working for the local historical society or as a secretary for one of the town officials. The library was just a place of employment for her, interchangeable with any other desk job.

When Ms. Trudy came in to give her promised update, Louise met her at the door. "What have you heard? Do we have a chance?"

"I don't know, hon. Hollis Murphy is declaring that it failed."

Murphy hosted a local radio program. He usually knew everything that was going on in the parish. Could he be wrong this one time?

"That doesn't sound good," Louise said.

"Seems early to me to be making predictions. It's only five forty-five. I have a lot more work to do—driving people to the polls, making sure our teens are waving their signs on Main Street, talking to people. A lot of folks have been running errands or working all day. We need to catch them on their way home. I just want you to know that we're doing everything we can." Ms. Trudy patted Louise's arm before hurrying back out the door.

Even though Sylvia couldn't vote in Alligator Bayou Parish, she insisted on accompanying Louise and Sal to the high school. They joined the line in the gymnasium.

"Make sure you push the right button," Sylvia said.

"Shh. No campaigning. They'll kick you out," Sal said.

"Sorry, I'm just nervous. Oh my God, is that the Gund?"

Louise groaned. Seeing her archenemy casting her vote, no doubt against the library, seemed like a bad sign. Good thing she didn't believe in omens of any kind. She inched behind Sal, hoping that his broad back would obscure her just enough to escape Mrs. Gunderson's notice.

It didn't work. Mrs. Gunderson came out of the booth and immediately headed for the librarians like a heat-seeking missile. There was no escape from her purposeful stride. She halted in front of Louise, frowning as usual. She cut her eyes to Sylvia. "Ms. Jones. I hope you know you can't vote in this parish."

"Yes, ma'am." Sylvia crossed her arms and fixed the police juror with a hard stare.

Mrs. Gunderson turned back to Louise. "I trust you have heard the returns so far. Your votes will certainly not be enough to turn the election."

"Yes, ma'am." Louise couldn't think of anything else to say. She focused on her own tiny, distorted reflection in the shiny buttons on the police juror's shirt-jacket.

Mrs. Gunderson leaned in closer and whispered, "After I win this, I will find a way to shut the library system down. I don't care if it has to go to an election, I'll make it happen." She walked away, hips swaying under her too-tight skirt.

Sylvia made a rude gesture at her back.

"Now, now," Sal said. "I think it's past due time I make a little confession. It might even make y'all feel a little better."

"I'll take what I can get," Louise said.

"Me and Matt did the book-burning stuff."

Louise stared at him. Sylvia began to laugh so hard that the entire line of voters turned around and looked at her.

"I'm sorry I didn't tell you, but it wouldn't have worked if people knew about it," Sal said. "He did the Facebook page and designed the signs. I had the Twitter account. The Pettigrews helped me find people who would put the signs in their yards. That was the hardest part."

Sylvia recovered enough to give him a high five. "Awesome idea. Let's hope it did work."

"I can't believe you hid this from me," Louise said. She was happy that he'd done so much work for her and the library. On the other hand, she'd thought they were telling each other everything. Secret keeping was very Brendan-like. He'd claimed to be "protecting" her when he kept things from her. Like the time he'd passed out on a female graduate student's couch after a party. She'd found out about that one when the young woman called the next day, wanting her to pick him up.

Sal took both of her hands in his. "I'm not hiding anything else from you. I promise."

Louise looked into his blue eyes. He was not Brendan. He'd been scheming to help the library, not to hurt her. "I know," she said.

"Listen, I have to tell y'all something too. I know you're going to be mad at me and I don't blame you," Sylvia said. "But I guess it's confession time."

"What? You knew about this?" Louise asked. The election line was starting to feel like a teenager's game of truth or dare.

"No! I was as surprised as you."

"So . . ." Louise said, prompting her to get to the point already.

"Jake is taking a position in Houston. He'll be working for one of Bayou Oil's biggest competitors. Even if I made enough money to support my family—and I don't—Jake is a lousy househusband. He can't cook unless it's outside on the grill, he doesn't have any clue how to clean the bathroom, and every time I'm out late, the kids eat sugar cereal and watch TV all evening. He hates being home. He feels like less of a man, and it's making him sick. Stupid, I know."

"I understand. You don't have to explain."

Sylvia sighed. "I guess I'll be baking cookies after all."

"I can give you a recipe."

"Shut up. I'm gonna cry already."

"Me too." Louise shuffled forward as the line advanced.

When they came out, Breaux was leaning against the brick wall, flipping through his notebook. "I'd ask y'all how you voted, but I guess I don't have to."

"What's the news?" Louise asked.

"It's close. I figure most of the people who won't tell me how they voted are against the library, but even with that, it's darn near fifty-fifty." He squinted at Louise. "Listen, go home and relax. I'll call you when I got a definite idea."

Louise and Sal got in Sal's truck while Sylvia left in her SUV. Louise couldn't remember a longer day since the one she spent in labor with Max. She just wanted it to be over. Once again, she was grateful for the agreement that Brendan and Julia would watch the children on Saturdays. She just didn't have the energy to deal with them.

"That Mrs. Gunderson is one nasty woman. Sometimes bullies get far in life," Sal offered.

"Yeah," Louise said. After living in Alligator Bayou for six months, she still didn't have a clear picture of the residents of the town. She'd followed Sylvia's advice and tried to pay attention to everyone she met—making a note of their jobs, likes and dislikes, who they were related to. She'd done a pretty good job with the library regulars and the people who worked in the places where she shopped. But there were a lot of people in the parish who were outside of their circle. Some couldn't read at all and probably only had a vague idea of what the library had to offer.

"Louise? We're here," Sal said.

They were parked in front of his mobile home. She started to get out of the truck, fighting against the inertia enveloping her whole being. But before she could push the door open, her phone rang. Julia. She collapsed back onto the seat.

"I just wanted to let you know that we're taking Max to the emergency room," Julia said.

"What?" Louise's inertia was gone, replaced by a rush of adrenaline.

"It's nothing serious. I mean, well, he just stuck a peanut up his nose and it won't come out."

Louise held the phone at arm's length for a moment. She had to stop herself from screaming into it, asking who had the brilliant idea to give her son nuts and didn't they know that he did things like that when he was bored? She pressed the phone against her ear again. "Okay, which hospital? Okay, I'll be there."

Sal put his seat belt back on. "What happened?"

"Max stuck a peanut up his nose."

Sal laughed. "I'm sorry, it's not funny. He'll be fine. I did that once with a pea. Everyone panicked, but after a while, I snorted it out on my own."

"Yeah." Louise slumped down in her seat.

"Call Betta while I drive. She can start making dinner because I'm sure we'll be back soon."

The hospital was the same one where Mr. Henry died. Louise fought down panic while Sal parked the car near the emergency room entrance. Max couldn't be seriously hurt by a peanut in his nose, could he? Maybe it would somehow travel to his lungs and get stuck there. She debated asking

Sal if such a thing was possible, but she didn't want to know the answer.

Inside the emergency room, the TV was tuned to a cable news station. No one was watching the anchor drone on about the dangers of inflatable pools. A few people sat in the gray chairs, flipping through dog-eared magazines. Louise didn't see Brendan or Max. She scanned the room again, her anxiety mounting.

"They're in the corner there," Sal said.

Julia waved when she saw Louise and Sal. She started to put down her magazine and greet them, but Louise motioned her to wait. Brendan and Max were facing away from the entrance, bent over something. As they got closer, Louise could see that it was an activity book with mazes and other exercises.

"You're supposed to match the car with the close-up. Is that the Batmobile's fender?" Brendan said.

"Yeah, I think so." Max's fat pencil was poised over the book. His voice sounded slightly nasal, no doubt as a result of the peanut.

"Okay, so draw a line between them. What about that one?"

"I don't know."

"I think that's the Penguin's car. Look, it has a picture of a penguin on it."

"Yeah! That's right!" Max drew a line. "What about that one?"

Louise emphatically did not love Brendan anymore. She didn't really even like him. Still, for Max's sake, she was happy to see them doing something together. Even if it was in an emergency room with a peanut up Max's nose.

Louise walked around the chairs and into their line of sight with Sal following.

"Hey, Mommy," Max said.

"Mommy!" Zoe jumped off her chair and hugged Louise's legs. She bent down and wrapped her arms around her.

"Hey, Max. Do this." Sal took a handkerchief from his pocket and blew his nose hard.

"Okay." Max copied him, his face scrunched up in an exaggerated grimace. The peanut flew out of his nose and hit the floor by Louise's feet. "Hey, it came out!"

"Yup. Guess you guys can go home now."

"Cool." Max jumped up. "Let's go play some computer games, Dad."

"Thanks, Sal. I'm sorry you guys had to drive all the way out here," Brendan said, managing to look genuinely humble.

"It was worth it," Sal said. "Saved the little guy from the forceps."

On the way back to Alligator Bayou, Sal turned on the local radio station. Hollis Murphy was talking about the election. Sal could barely stand the guy's voice sometimes. He managed to sound superior to everything and everyone. But aside from the *Alligator Bayou Gazette*, he was the only source of news about the parish.

"It would seem that I called the results on the library tax too soon," Hollis said. "I'm not going to say the tax passed. I am going to say that we need to wait and see what the final results are. Let's take some calls."

"God." Sal gripped the steering wheel and fought the urge to pound on it. "This is driving me crazy."

"I guess as a book burner, you have a stake in it, pun intended," Louise said.

Sal glanced at her. He could tell that his deception had upset her. But she seemed to realize that his intentions were good. "I'm really sorry I did that without telling you. But, yeah, I really want this thing to pass. For you and me, but also for this parish. We're never going to get out of the dark ages if we don't have a decent library."

On the radio, Paul from Second Avenue expressed the view that the tax would hurt poor people.

"Not sure about that," Murphy said. "After all, it's a property tax. I guess it could indirectly affect renters if landlords raise the rents because of it. Let's go to another caller."

Sal turned off the radio. "We'll check back later. Is that okay?"

"Yeah. I can't take much Hollis Murphy. Though it sounds like he might support the library."

"Hard to tell," Sal said, parking the truck in front of the mobile home.

Inside, Betta was watching the TV news. She turned it off. "Is Max okay?"

"Honked it right out," Sal said, taking off his work boots.

"Good." Betta poured wine and set the table with meatloaf, green beans, and mashed potatoes.

Sal fed the dogs and took his usual seat next to Louise. Betta seemed to be adjusting to their relationship. They were taking it slow—not for his sister's sake but for the children's. Still, the pace seemed to help Betta as well. Sal didn't spend all his time at Louise's house. Mostly, they kept their visits to the Saturdays when her ex watched the kids. Betta was able to keep her routine of cooking dinner for Sal. He didn't mind. It made her happy. But he looked forward to the day when he went home every day to Louise and her kids. Not rushing was hard, excruciating really. But he had to be grateful for the time they had together.

During dinner, they all tried not to discuss the election. It weighed on Sal's mind, though, mostly because he didn't know what Louise would do if it didn't pass. Now that Mr.

Foley and Mr. Henry were gone, would she lose her job if the tax failed? He didn't know, and she didn't seem to either. She'd applied for the director job, of course. But if there wasn't any money, the position would be worthless—if it even continued to exist.

Despite his worries, he managed to finish two helpings of meatloaf and a slice of cake. After the meal, Betta stood up. "I best be going as soon as I finish these dishes."

"Don't you worry about those, Betta. We'll handle it," Sal said.

Betta's whole body drooped, just like when she was a little kid and he told her he didn't want to play with her dolls. "Okay, sure."

"Hey, come on. I'm not trying to get rid of you. I just thought we ought to do the dishes since you cooked." Sal couldn't believe that his sister was being so sensitive. Maybe he was wrong about her coming to terms with his relationship with Louise.

"We loved the food and the company," Louise said, carrying a stack of plates to the sink. "You're welcome to sit and watch the news with us. I want to see if they mention the library."

Sal found the remote on the coffee table and turned the TV back on. "Sit down, Betta."

"No, thanks. I got sewing to do."

"Okay, see you tomorrow, then. Thanks again, sis." Sal gave her a kiss on the cheek as she was leaving. He'd done all he could. Losing him was going to be tough for her. But he couldn't put his life on hold for his sister. Maybe she'd eventually meet someone. It would be difficult, though. Alligator Bayou was not normally the place to find new people. He'd been really lucky that Louise showed up.

He went to the sink and began to rinse the dishes.

Louise's phone rang and Sal deliberately kept the sink on

so that he couldn't hear what she said. He was afraid it would be bad news. He risked a glance at her. A slow smile crossed her face as she hung up.

"We won," she said.

Sal ran to her and lifted her off the ground, swinging her around in his arms. He set her down carefully and hugged her hard.

CHAPTER 42

Sylvia and Jake hired professional movers, so there was nothing for Louise to do except babysit the kids while they loaded suitcases into their two SUVs. She stood helplessly by the cleaned-out house, thinking she really might break down for the first time since Brendan announced that he'd been seeing Julia.

"Girl, if you cry, then I will," Sylvia said, carrying the last shopping bags of toys out to her SUV.

The children seemed unaffected by what was about to happen. Max, Jimmy, and Zoe played with sticks in the yard. Zoe used hers to draw circles in a patch of dirt. Max and Jimmy pretended that theirs were swords. Baby Madeleine was already strapped into her car seat, asleep.

"We'll talk on the phone every day." Sylvia embraced Louise, enveloping her in citrus-scented perfume.

Louise doubted it. Sylvia would be busy with her kids and her new life, whatever it turned out to be. They wouldn't be able to walk a few steps in the library and find each other. They'd still be friends, but it wouldn't be the same. "I owe you for finding me a new career."

"God, girl, I hope I can handle being a mommy all day," Sylvia said, pulling away and dabbing at her eyes with her sleeve.

"You'll figure it out. You'll probably get some great idea and start your own business."

"Nope, I am dedicating my life to my children. PTA, homework help, sewing their clothes from scratch. No more chicken nuggets for dinner."

"Supermom is a hard job."

"I know. I'm going to miss this. A lot."

"Come on, babe. We should be driving while Maddy's asleep." Jake emerged from the back of the second SUV, where he'd been rearranging the load.

"I'm coming," Sylvia said. "You're going to be fine. We'll both be fine. Hey, I'll come back for your wedding."

Louise glanced down at her ring—an heirloom from Sal's grandmother. He'd told her that Betta cried when she gave it to him. "We haven't set a date yet."

"Well, get on it. I'm counting on being matron of honor. Ew, that term is so yuck! But I'll still do it if you pick out a nice pink dress for me." Sylvia adjusted the strap of her oversize purse. "Come on, Jimmy. Say good-bye to Max and get in the car."

Jimmy jumped up. "Bye, Max!"

"Bye." Max watched his friend leave. He actually seemed a little sad. He was slowly becoming more aware of the fact that some things were permanent and others temporary. The broken chalk couldn't be fixed. The ripped book could be taped back together, but it would never be the same. Louise had tried to explain that Jimmy was leaving for good, but she couldn't tell whether Max really grasped what was going to happen.

As the doors slammed and the SUVs pulled away, Max

put down his stick. Zoe didn't seem to notice that anything had changed. She continued scratching in the dust.

Max stared at the driveway. Only Louise's mom mobile was left. "Jimmy is going to Texas."

"Yes," Louise said.

"I'm hungry and thirsty," Max said.

Chapter 43

For her interview before the police jury, Louise got out the navy-blue suit she'd worn for her first day of work in Alligator Bayou. While she was combing her hair, Zoe came in and touched her skirt. "Princess."

"Do I look like a princess? I hope so."

Zoe reached into the closet and got out a pair of polka-dot high heels. "Shoes."

"I don't know, Zoe." Louise eyed the peep-toed pumps. "I wasn't going to wear those."

"Shoes!" Zoe insisted.

Louise gave in. The girl was quickly developing a sense of fashion and refused to wear any of Max's hand-me-downs. Luckily, one of the regular library patrons had given Louise a diaper box full of mostly pink clothes in Zoe's size.

In the polka-dot shoes, Louise felt taller, which was good. She would need any advantage, real or imagined, in dealing with Mrs. Gunderson.

Mrs. Gunderson was late, forcing the rest of the jurors and Louise to stare at one another over the library folding table in the former church sanctuary, waiting. After a few minutes, Marty Pratt left her seat and approached Louise. "I just want you to know that you should have this thing. Mrs. Gunderson's preferred candidate isn't even remotely qualified for the job."

Louise stiffened. The Gund had a favorite candidate?

"Don't worry." Marty patted Louise's shoulder and returned to her chair just as Mrs. Gunderson arrived.

"We will have to make this quick," she said, situating her ample rear end in a chair. "I have an appointment in thirty minutes."

"Well, I'm afraid the interview might continue without you, then," Marty said.

Delilah, who was dressed head to toe in polka dots, leaned over to admire Louise's shoes. "I love those."

Mrs. Gunderson gave her the patented glare.

Reverend McDonald had just begun asking the first question when Breaux walked in, carrying his reporter's notebook. "The interviews for these positions are supposed to be public," he said.

Marty turned to Mrs. Gunderson. "You said you were going to send him an e-mail."

"I must have forgotten." Mrs. Gunderson pretended to search through her folder of papers. She positioned her chair to face the window and looked outside at the parking lot.

Breaux took a seat and waved his hand. "Please proceed."

Reverend McDonald glanced down at the paper in front of him. "We all know the improvements that you and Sylvia have made to the library over the past year or so. What I guess we all want to know is how you plan to continue that legacy, especially without her."

Mrs. Gunderson snorted but didn't look away from the window.

Louise folded her hands on the table, told herself not to look at them, glanced up at Mrs. Gunderson, who was staring at the parking lot, and focused on Marty instead. "I have a high level of commitment to this library and this community. I will do my best to hire someone just as good as Sylvia, and I have every intention of continuing our vision for the library. I won't be teaching Zumba classes, though."

Marty and her friend laughed. Mrs. Gunderson let out another dismissive grunt.

After that, Louise relaxed. She tried to pretend that Mrs. Gunderson wasn't in the room as she answered the jurors' questions. None of them were too difficult, and by the end they were talking about whether the new library building could have a kitchen for cooking classes.

As Mrs. Gunderson got up to leave, she rapped her folder against the table. "Just one more thing, Ms. Richardson. It has come to my attention that you applied for some jobs at universities outside Louisiana. So perhaps your level of commitment isn't what you claim."

"I did apply for a few positions. But that was months ago, before the tax passed. I didn't know whether I would be laid off, so of course I looked for something else."

"Well, the University of Iowa called Mr. Foley. It appears that they are preparing to offer you a job."

Louise sat down on the couch and put her head in her hands. Brendan and Julia had taken the kids to *Sesame Street Live*. Louise wasn't sure that Max and Zoe were old enough to sit through the production, but she'd let them go anyway. Now, she was glad for the silence of the house. She needed to think, or maybe wallow.

Sal brought her a glass of wine and set it on the table. "I'm not convinced that you messed up the interview."

"I hesitated. I didn't come out right away and say, 'I want to stay here, tell the University of Iowa to shove their job.' That's what I should have done and I didn't."

"It's tough. It would be a really good opportunity."

"Yeah, but I bought this house, we're going to get married, Brendan and Julia are here, and I have a job in Alligator Bayou, even if I don't get the director position."

Sal put his arm around her shoulders. "Still, it would be tempting. And I would move with you anywhere."

"No, I don't want to go. I want to stay here with you. Whether I get the director job or not."

"Good. Because I want you to stay. Let's go out to eat. We're going to celebrate that the interview is over. Even if you didn't get the job, you tried your best."

"I was fine until the end."

Sal took her hand and helped her up. "Come on. How does Main Street Café sound?"

CHAPTER 44

Sal sat at the kitchen table, helping Max assemble a scale model of the Batmobile with Legos while Louise sliced sausage for jambalaya. Zoe stood on a chair in front of the sink, pouring water from one cup to another. The dogs lounged on the couch, fought over toys, and patrolled the kitchen, searching for food scraps. The two pineapple cakes in the oven perfumed the house with the scent of brown sugar and butter. Louise almost never baked, but it was time to meet the Pettigrews and she didn't want to go there empty-handed.

She scraped the andouille into a frying pan and turned on the burner. This was the scene she had pictured before she had children. It had taken a long time to get to this place, and it wasn't perfect, but she was happy. Brendan might think that academia had more prestige than working in a public library, but he was wrong. The people in Alligator Bayou had shown her that what she and Sylvia did mattered more than an obscure academic paper that only a few people would ever read. Together, they had saved the library, but they had also gained something for themselves. Louise had discovered that she was strong—she could stand up to people and get things accomplished. And now, because of the library, she had Sal too. It was a new beginning.

Her phone rang, and she got it out of her purse.

"Louise? This is Marty Pratt. I just wanted to tell you that you got the job. We interviewed Mrs. Gunderson's candidate today, and she basically admitted that she didn't even want it. It was sort of funny, really. Anyway, congratulations."

Louise stirred the sausage, inhaling the warm, spicy scent. "Thanks! I'm really excited about it."

"Me too. You deserve it. Have a good evening."

Louise hung up and immediately dialed a number. "Sylvia, I hear there's a job opening at the University of Iowa. Some crazy person just turned it down to be the director of a crappy little library in rural Louisiana."

Over at the kitchen table, Sal grinned and gave her a thumbs-up.

Sylvia shrieked so loud that Louise had to hold the phone away from her ear. "Good job, girl!"

Louise balanced the cake on one hand and rang the Pettigrews' doorbell. As a joke, they'd left the book-burner sign in their yard and added three others that had been on public right-of-ways.

Ima Pettigrew opened the door, and a grin spread across her wide face. She wore a flower-patterned housedress and fraying slippers. Her gray hair was styled in a stiff-looking pageboy. "Come in, come in. Hunter!"

Max and Zoe hid behind Louise's legs, one child grabbing each thigh. "You all have to let go. I can't walk," she said.

"Don't be shy, children. I have candy," Ima said.

Louise shuffled forward and handed her the cake. Ima

shut the front door and gestured to the chairs and couch. "Please, sit down."

The vintage sofa was green plaid with matching pillows, and it faced a TV encased in a wooden console. Two dark-brown armchairs at either side were covered in brown-and-orange afghans. Hope was right—the room looked like a throwback to the 1950s, down to the wood-paneled walls.

Louise couldn't sit down with the children attached to her legs. "I mean it, you guys have to let go."

Hunter Pettigrew walked in from the kitchen. He was slight, a contrast to his stocky wife, and wore creased slacks and a polo shirt. He leaned down and held out his hand. Max stepped forward and shook it, like a miniature businessman making a deal.

"Come sit on the couch, boy," Hunter said. Max tiptoed forward and perched on the edge of the sofa.

Hunter sat in the chair next to Max and handed him a metal race car. "Be careful with it. This belonged to my son when he was young."

Max nodded and held the car nervously.

Ima took the cake to the kitchen and returned with a glass jar of gumdrops. "I have quite the sweet tooth. Always have to have my candy. Why not, right? I've lived long enough to be entitled to a few vices."

Zoe let go of Louise's leg and put her hand out for a gumdrop.

Ima gave her four. "Share with your brother," she instructed.

"I'm sorry I didn't come over earlier. I kept meaning to, but it seemed like I was always too busy," Louise said, sitting on one of the armchairs.

"Don't you feel bad. We should have brought you something when you first moved in. We neglected our neighborly duty. But I'd just had surgery on my hip, and after that Hunter had to have his cataracts done. Well, I guess time got away from us too. Truth is, we were fixing to go see you when Sal came to our house to ask us to help with his book-burning scheme." Ima laughed and sat on the couch next to Max and Zoe, giving them more gumdrops.

"We haven't had that much fun in years," Hunter said. "It was such a hoot, driving around with that megaphone and putting up all those signs."

Ima smiled at her husband. "Sure did wake up the old man. Put a little spring in his step."

"You all should come down to the library sometime, now that you don't have to avoid me anymore," Louise said. "Max, do not touch that."

Max didn't stop his tactile examination of the table lamp. He yanked up the shade and looked underneath.

"I'll show you how to turn it on," Hunter said, pulling the string. "Maybe we can find us some cartoons on the TV."

"Our eyes aren't so good for reading anymore," Ima said.

Hunter turned the knob on the television, and Bugs Bunny appeared in surprisingly vivid color. Both children stared at the screen, gumdrops and cars forgotten.

"But now we have DVDs, CDs, and books on tape," Louise said. "Plus, there are cooking classes, a quilting circle, knitting classes, all sorts of things to do. I'll bring you our calendar of events."

"I guess it wouldn't hurt us to get out more, now that my hip is healed up," Ima said.

"I hear you have a canasta group," Hunter said.

"You know if they do, Unser might be part of it." Ima ate a gumdrop.

"I can handle your brother. It's time, especially since he

CHAPTER 45

Louise studied the young woman sitting across the table from her. Even though Justine had just graduated from library school and had virtually no experience, Louise had a good feeling about her. She was almost doll-like, with absurdly tiny wrists and a miniature hourglass figure, but she regarded her surroundings fearlessly. And fear, as Louise herself had learned, was the enemy of success, especially in a small town.

As she pretended to study Justine's résumé, Louise tried to imagine the young woman embarking on a journey like her own. She'd begun as an outsider in this insular town, and now she had more friends than she'd ever had in her life.

She had a real office in the new library building, which had been built on the tract of land that had once supported Mr. Foley and his goats. Ms. Trudy had bought the land from Mr. Foley and donated it to the parish. No one knew what had happened to the library director. He'd sold almost everything he owned and left in his pickup truck for places unknown.

After the library tax passed, the parish was able to bor-

has the cancer. I'll tell him I'm sorry I said that the Vietnam War was a waste of American lives and we'll be all good again. It's been five years, Ima."

Ima dabbed at her eyes with a tissue from the box on the end table. "You're right, it's time."

row the money to build the library, and it was finished within a year. While it was being constructed, Louise continued Sylvia's classes and programs with the help of the other librarians. She also married Sal in a small ceremony on his farm with catering by Anthony's. It was a happy year, watching the library and the children grow, building a new and wonderful relationship.

Louise thought about warning Justine about what she was getting into. She might find that she didn't fit into Alligator Bayou at all. On the other hand, she could fall in love with the place. Louise thought about telling her the story of the deer in the old library. Or how, after so many months of suspicion, Hope had finally allowed the Yankee to taste her chicken and dumplings. Or about the B sisters, Ms. Trudy, Mary, and all the other residents who had fought so hard to keep the library open.

There was no way to explain it all to Justine, so she just said, "What do you like to read?"

Justine folded her delicate hands together on the table. "This is sort of embarrassing, but what I really love is young adult novels. Especially with vampires and stuff like that. I know I'm supposed to read deep literature and all, but . . ."

"Perfect. You're hired." Louise glanced over Justine's shoulder. With the new building, they'd gotten twelve new computers for patrons. The B sisters were huddled over theirs in the corner, and a few other young people near them seemed to be actually doing homework. Mary sat in a beanbag chair, reading *Mind Games*. Next to her was her new best friend, Chante McDonald.

"This the new girl?" Hope had snuck up behind Louise and now stood, hands on hips, studying Justine.

Justine held Hope's gaze. "Pleased to meet you."

"You another Yankee? 'Cause the last one we had . . . Well, I reckon she turned out okay once we broke her in."

"I'm from Michigan," Justine said.

"Hey, ain't that where you're from, Louise?"

"No, Minnesota."

Hope waved her hand as if to say that all Northern states were essentially the same. "Well, good luck. You'll do fine."

"I hope so." Justine stood and picked up her tiny purse.

"Let me introduce you to the rest of the staff," Louise said.

"Nah, I'll do it." Hope put her arm around Justine and led her to the back work area. "This here's our new library. Ain't it great?"

ACKNOWLEDGMENTS

Thanks to my writer friends Sam Irwin, Mark Silcox, James Minton, Greg Langley, and Gene Mearns, who have taught me more about writing than I could ever learn in a classroom.

I am immensely grateful to my agent, Steven Chudney, for all he did to save this book from slush pile obscurity. I am also thankful for my editor, Martin Biro, and the rest of the staff at Kensington.

This book would never have been written without the support, editorial help, and endless patience of my husband, Jon. I also need to thank our kids, Thomas and Audrey, for providing inspiration and an excuse to quit my full-time job.